DARA

DARA

by
Patrick Besson

Translated from the French by Nicole Irving

Hamish Hamilton . London

To Isabelle

First published 1985
by Éditions du Seuil
27 rue Jacob Paris VIᵉ

This edition first published in Great Britain 1987
by Hamish Hamilton Ltd
27 Wrights Lane London W8 5TZ

British Library Cataloguing in Publication Data

Besson, Patrick
Dara
I. Title
843'.914[F]   PQ2662.E8618
ISBN 0-241-12025-X

Typeset in Sabon by Wyvern Typesetting Ltd, Bristol
Printed and bound in Great Britain by
Butler and Tanner Frome, Somerset

1

I dropped you both off outside the block of flats on rue de Tocqueville. The sky was very bright. Cold sunlight bit into people's faces and for a moment I felt sorry for you, frozen in your little navy-blue coat, your hair wound into one of those awful buns that only Dara could produce, one that had come straight from the Balkans.

Whenever you went out together, your mother was determined that you should look well-off and distinguished. But your white ankle socks were either too short or too long, your lizard-skin handbag made you look like an old lady, and your improbable bun would always end up collapsing. When you got home, it was plain just how hard these outings were for you. You didn't even wait to get into your room to begin undressing. Patent-leather shoes flew off in the hallway. You would hang up your coat on the hook and race into the bathroom, undoing the buttons of your dress as you went. Before getting into the shower, you would switch off the light. Occasionally you'd turn on the battery-operated cassette-recorder, too, on which you'd taped the sound-track from an episode of *Belle et Sébastien* that was showing on television at the time.

It was about two in the afternoon when I left you outside 'Aunt Nathalie's' flat that day. The police often asked me whether, at that moment, I had noticed anything unusual in Dara's behaviour, or yours or that of any passer-by. I recall only that your mother was carrying a shopping basket which contained various delicacies for the old Russian woman. And you were clutching a bunch of roses and very obviously trying to avoid pricking your fingers on the thorns.

By virtue of the dreadful event which ensued, Dara has recounted to me over and over again that final visit to rue de

Tocqueville. And through the years, you yourself have filled in a number of details that remained unclear in your mother's account.

The back staircase had no lift. On the fourth-floor landing, Dara came to a standstill and set the basket down. With hands on hips, she threw back her shoulders: a habitual gesture whenever she had performed any unaccustomed physical effort. Her back gave her trouble. Everything had been tried: planks under the mattress, corsets, cures in the Auvergne. And all without result. Oh, your mother's back! God knows we heard enough about it between 1960 and 1970! Then it was overshadowed, by the rheumatism in the joints and the eye ulcers from which she suffered almost without respite until her death.

Nathalie Mikhaïlovna Balouïev, or Aunt Nathalie, lived on the seventh floor. She had been looking out for you and was waiting on her doorstep. You were surprised, as you've told me, at how small and hunched up she seemed. You imagined at the time that an empire such as Russia could only give birth to gigantic individuals. She disappeared in your mother's large embrace, then reappeared quite flushed. Once again you admired the ease with which Dara communicated her warmth to others.

Through the window of the room, one could see the roof of the building opposite and, further away, the hill of Montmartre. You settled down around a small, square table covered with an oilcloth whose design your mother greatly admired. She found everything wonderful: the small built-in kitchen at one end of the room, the photographs of Tsarist officers on the walls, the view of the Sacré Coeur. There seemed to be no other place in the world where she would rather have lived than this maid's room. Living in an attic room was so 'romantic'! Did Aunt Nathalie feed the pigeons? Of course she did. She even had her favourite, a fat, taciturn pigeon which, when it wasn't flying, got about on a single leg, for the other had been severed. Nathalie gave him seeds each morning. Occasionally, towards mid-afternoon, he would post himself on the window ledge. He didn't ask for food. He barely bothered to glance into the room. He was happy just to stay there. And when he'd had enough, he'd fly off. So then you began to look out through the window with an intensity which, after about fifteen minutes, intrigued Dara. She asked you what you were staring at. She hadn't understood that you were waiting for the pigeon to arrive. In fact, she didn't understand much, did she?

You got a large helping of biscuits and several cups of hot chocolate. Replete on all this sugar and lulled by the two women's Russian and Yugoslav accents, you were half-asleep when you saw Nathalie take some playing cards out of a sewing-box, shuffle them with a deft hand, and set them down on the table in some mysterious order. Dara hesitated for a long while before turning one of them over. She wanted to know straight away what happy or unhappy events the card announced in her life. Would her back be cured? Would I become less ill-tempered? Was Tito to die within the year? Aunt Nathalie said that to find out all of that, one card wouldn't do, she had to draw at least two more.

Later you found yourself sitting opposite Aunt Nathalie. Here, your version differs from Dara's. Your mother couldn't recall that the Russian woman told your fortune. But you are quite sure that she predicted a prosperous future for you.

Your mother said you both had to get back to Bagnolet. Nathalie protested that it was still early, you had a great many things left to talk about, and parting from friends is such a sad thing, one should do it gently, with care and consideration, in stages. Far too much of a Slav to be insensitive to this argument, Dara sat down again and, following I don't know what association of ideas, asked Nathalie if she was coping financially. She may have felt that if the Russian woman was holding her up like this, it was because she wanted to be lent a little money to see her to the end of the month. But the old lady said that money was the least of her

3

worries. She had far more than she needed. She could have eaten two steaks at every meal if she'd wanted to. The French state provided her with a comfortable pension, and it was only to make sure she got out and about that she had a few cleaning jobs. As Dara didn't look convinced, she opened one of the kitchen drawers and brandished a number of rolls of fifty-franc notes. Dara told her she shouldn't keep so much money at home. 'Who would dream of robbing a poor old woman like me?' retorted Nathalie. And she in turn asked Dara if she lacked for anything, and was I behaving decently towards her? Your mother virtually had to fight her off as she tried to slip a note into your coat pocket.

Lengthy embraces were exchanged at the door. Nathalie clasped you to her bosom. She told you that you had the best mummy in the world and that you should do your best to be nice to her at all times. So many little girls in the world, and especially behind the Iron Curtain, had no mummy at all, so that when you had one as wonderful as yours, it was a serious sin to upset her.

It was snowing when you and your mother stepped out of the building. The snow was soft and slow, and it was melting on the asphalt. But it was enough for Dara to exclaim: 'Snow! Snow!' She couldn't bring herself to go down into the *métro*. She held you by the hand and swept you along at an exhilarating pace towards a destination that seemed vague to you, one that undoubtedly lay only in her own memories. Then, noticing that you were shivering and your hair was falling away in rat's tails, she hailed a taxi. The driver asked her about her accent. At first he had thought she was German. 'Me, German?' she'd answered. 'That's a good one!' He rose to the occasion. He went through each and every nationality, apart, of course, from the right one.

Your mother was in the habit of saying: 'My charm is in my accent.' It was as pronounced in 1954, the year we met, as the day she died. I suspect her of carefully cultivating it over the years. You confided to me one day that your resistance to a man who speaks with an accent is far less than to one who has none. It's probably because your childhood was suffused with your mother's accent, a hurried cooing which called to mind the galloping of horses on Tomislav Square in Zagreb and the funfairs in Maksimir Park, as well as squabbling school children on the Strossmayer Promenade, all things that Dara would yet again describe for us at least once a week.

At eight o'clock the following morning, your mother rushed into your little room. When we'd moved to Bagnolet ten years earlier, Dara was so used to flats having only one bedroom that she'd immediately christened yours 'the studio', as if it were a separate dwelling. I remember that in the mid-seventies, when you decided to leave home, she kept repeating to me: 'But why does she want to go? Doesn't she have her own *studio*?'

She pushed you into the kitchen. You stationed yourself at the window. Dara said to you: 'Look!' Neither the Bagnolet intersection nor the Hotel Sofitel that rises above it had yet been built, and from the fifth floor we looked out over a large part of the neighbourhood. You saw chocolate-coloured streets, buildings that looked as if they'd been replastered overnight, and parked cars that were covered with snow. 'Isn't it wonderful?' said Dara. She kissed you on both cheeks and started getting your breakfast ready.

That first snowy morning of 1966 she telephoned me at work at about eleven o'clock to announce that Aunt Nathalie had been murdered. I'd gone to work earlier than usual. We were expecting a representative from the Algerian Bureau of Tourism with whom we were about to sign a contract for the next five years. There still remained a few details to check through, estimates to finalise, and I was in no position to go back to Bagnolet. Your mother never forgave me for that. You know how she could bear a grudge. She never forgot a snub and never forgave any carelessness. She was a *Croat*, and *Croats* do not accept that one should 'fail them', as she put it. She attached so much importance to her sense of dignity that in matters of love, she could never be affected. When a man failed to turn up to a date, it was her pride that was most hurt. Could she love someone who showed her no respect? Certainly not. And so she didn't suffer.

A police inspector presented himself in my office in the late afternoon. He wore a brown raincoat over a houndstooth-checked suit. I had never met a police inspector. Did one shake hands with them? I vaguely held out my arm. The man sat down, thinking no doubt that I was waving him to a chair. His eyes had a calm, grey look, and his brown hair was growing thin on his forehead, showing signs that he would soon go bald. He took out a notebook. I confirmed that I had dropped you off at rue de Tocqueville the previous day around two o'clock and that, yes, you had got back to Bagnolet around eight-thirty. He then asked me if I had been acquainted with Mrs Balouïev. I said I hadn't. That in fact I'd never even met her. For me, Aunt Nathalie was a near-mythical figure. 'Aunt Nathalie?' the inspector queried. I answered that that was what your mother called the Russian woman. He jotted down this detail. I was beginning to feel anxious. I asked the inspector if Dara was a suspect. He replied that the crime had been committed between twenty-two hundred hours and midnight, which ruled her out. So why was he here then? It was a routine check. Your mother didn't have French nationality. She was a political refugee. She wasn't married to me. Did I know all her friends? Were there any gaps in her timetable? Was she still involved in politics? I had difficulty in answering all these questions, which made me realise just how little interest I took in her life.

My secretary seemed surprised when, after the inspector had left, I announced to her that I was going home. This was unusual for me. I was more the sort to hang around at the office. Whenever we organised a drink after work, I was never in a hurry to empty my glass unless it was to help myself to another. I had all the time in the world. My aim was to reach home only just in time for supper. It was always you, in your

6

pyjamas and with a towel around your neck, who opened the door for me. You led me into the living room where we'd taken to eating all our meals since we'd acquired a television set. There was always a serial I wanted to carry on watching, a film I'd missed the first Paris showing of, or a variety show featuring one of my favourite singers. Dara didn't share my passion for the small screen, and complained we no longer had any social life or any family life. While the programmes were on, she spent her time drifting about the rooms of the flat as you and I sat in front of the set like a couple of mosquitoes drawn to a lamplight.

In the course of my conversation with the police inspector, I had slowly become aware of the mistake I'd made that morning in not going to lend my support to your mother in what was gradually revealing itself to me as one of the greatest trials of her life. Thanks to a monstrous blunder for which Algerian tourism was partly responsible, I'd forgotten that Dara's administrative position was precarious. Your mother had retained her Yugoslav nationality. I was the only person she envisaged getting married to, but my divorce from my first wife hadn't yet come through, even though we'd been separated for over ten years. Hence, at regular intervals, your mother had to renew her resident's permit. I imagined that the moment she committed any offence, however trivial, the French state would expel her. Of course, in 1962, Marshal Tito had declared an amnesty for all political refugees. But Dara said she would rather throw herself off the top of the Arc de Triomphe than return to Yugoslavia. I now understood how much the inspector's visit must have worried her, all the more since she'd undoubtedly been working on one of those dresses that she made on the quiet for a select set of customers in order to, as she said, 'put butter in spinach'. Now I urgently wanted to reassure her. In my mind, she was reverting back to the little émigrée I'd met one Sunday afternoon in July 1954 in a dance-hall near the Olympia. In her handbag, she had a swimsuit. She'd planned to spend the

7

afternoon at the Deligny swimming-pool. As for me, I had wavered between dropping in there and going to the Longchamp race-course. That's fate for you!

Dara opened the door, which was contrary to all our customs. I asked if you were unwell. She answered that she hadn't a clue. What did she mean, she hadn't a clue? I promptly went to your room, forgetting it was Dara I'd come to comfort, not you. I knocked gently on the door. No answer. It was impossible that you hadn't heard me come into the flat. Might you have been forbidding me to come into your room? I knocked once again. Without success. Dara said: 'Leave her. She's working.' I pushed the door ajar. You were sitting at your desk with one leg tucked under your bottom. How often had we told you it was bad for your spine? And in our house, that was something we certainly knew all about!

I came into the room, despite your mother's mute indignation. I leant over and kissed you on the nape of the neck, on your blonde hair. You carried on writing. I stood up, pulled a pen out of your bulging pencil-case and corrected a spelling mistake in the homework you were writing out. 'Not too difficult?' I asked. You shook your head. Your cheeks were flushed and your eyes shone strangely. I wondered if you weren't running up a temperature. All of a sudden, you turned towards me. For the first time in my life, I read hatred in your eyes. A muddled, bubbling, wild hatred. You held your lips so tightly sealed that you looked as if you could barely restrain yourself from uttering a particular word, a particular sentence. With your dead-straight nose, your little Tartar's cheekbones and your pointed chin, you couldn't quite stop your face expressing its customary mischievousness and gentleness, but even so, I could sense that I had been momentarily banished from your universe. What was going on? What nasty things had you been told about me? It was Dara, wasn't it? And then, in that little voice of yours — you had so much trouble in making yourself sound cross — you said I should have come home as soon as I'd heard the news of

Aunt Nathalie's death. How could I, at such a time, have abandoned Mummy to herself? It was unbelievable!

So, rather than commiserate with you on the poor woman's death, Dara had found nothing better to do than complain to you about my absence. She knew you were impulsive, easily upset by misfortune or unfairness. She had guessed my carelessness would appear monstrous to you and that you'd find a way to punish me for it.

All my pity for Dara vanished. How soothing it would have been to me then to charge into the kitchen and have a furious row with her! But she'd have been only too pleased if I'd given you yet another reason to be angry with me.

I asked you to let me put my case. At the time, one only had to humbly beg your forgiveness and you would melt. Actually, you haven't changed much. You've kept that side of you, the judge with a soft heart. I don't recall what tale I made up, but when I'd finished, you said it was to Mummy I should be telling all this. But I had done that already! It hadn't changed a thing. You knew what she was like. What was the point in going over it again? You shrugged your shoulders. Watching your eyes, the way your lips were moving, the rhythm of your breathing, I realised that little by little, I was winning you back. I didn't doubt that in a minute you would bitterly regret having got angry with me. And then you would burst into tears, you would put your arms around my neck and beg me to forgive you. For you could stand unfairness even less when you were responsible for it than when it was aimed at you. You hadn't really been unfair in reproaching me for my carelessness towards Dara, and by convincing you that you had, I was playing on your emotions just as Dara had done a few hours earlier. Children are never wary enough of their parents, are they?

The investigation into Aunt Nathalie's death was inconclusive. Your mother was many times summoned to the police station and to the examining magistrate. I took her in the car. Throughout those journeys she smoked one cigarette after another, Gauloises Disque Bleu. She talked of emigrating to the United States. But all the same, Paris was the most beautiful city in the world!

The months went by. We decided to send you to a children's holiday camp in the Mont-Dore for the Easter holiday. You would learn to ski. I could guess that you would neither like the sport nor show any aptitude for it. But I was worried by your pale little face and the way you'd begun to look more and more frequently dejected. As for your mother, she held that you spent too much time cooped up in your studio. Anyway, you needed 'chums'! Dara would have so liked to have tea parties for you, and even to join in the games. Sadly, you never brought friends home. It was Sylviane Brazet who, in 1969, was the first friend who came to our flat. Dara produced huge sandwiches filled with butter and eating chocolate that she brought you with two large glasses of milk. You felt very embarrassed. After Sylviane had gone, you had a long row with your mother. You accused her of having made a fool of herself and of having exasperated your friend with all her questions. You wished she wouldn't put herself out like that for the first person to come along. It was up to your friends to make her like them, and not up to her to make them like her. In humbling herself she was humbling you. 'My girl,' she retorted, 'you're becoming quite mad!' It was the rules of hospitality alone which had dictated her behaviour. No doubt you were unfamiliar with them? Only in Croatia had they remained sacred. 'We are in France!' you had yelled before going back to shut yourself up in your studio.

So in March 1967, you went off to the Mont-Dore. We left you on the station platform in front of a boisterous swarm of boys and girls of your age. It seemed a rather self-contained group for a peculiar little girl like you to join. One tear, one word, one gesture from you would have been enough for me to disregard Dara's predictable objections and bring you home again. But you had resigned yourself to your fate. You kissed us absent-mindedly. You walked away without turning

10

around. I can see you now, dressed in a brand new anorak and those ski slacks with elasticated feet. You stood apart from the group, paying careful attention to what the instructors were telling you all to do. You adopted that serious look your face had when you were about to have a test at school. Then, as you were all making your way towards the carriage reserved for the holiday camp, a little girl with plaits and glasses said something to you. You answered straight back, and a few seconds later you both burst out laughing, shrill laughter that revealed to me how, despite your apparent reserve and your slightly gruff manners, you had after all inherited from your mother that ability to befriend the first person to come along.

When you came home and told us all your adventures, I was astonished to see how much you also resembled your mother in your determination to shield yourself from the world while at the same time subjecting it to your rule. On the first day of skiing, the entire holiday camp waited at the bottom of the stairs while you finished lacing up your boots. Later, on the ski trail, one of the women instructors discovered you'd put on a pair of thin nylon socks instead of the regulation thick woollen ones. You were immediately taken back to town. The following day, you tore a muscle racing down the stairs four by four. You were let off skiing for three days. It was then that you received a set of photographs of French and foreign actors from my sister Yvonne, who worked for a printer. You spent your convalescence selling them for fifty centimes a piece. You reduced or increased the price according to whether you found the customer, usually a girl, attractive or not. There was also a particular clique, three jolly and quarrelsome girls, who got the snapshots for free. They were much sought after. People were virtually queuing up outside your dormitory to acquire them. You even ended up running out of stock. So you phoned us, reverse-charge. Your mother took the call. She couldn't make head or tail of this story of your 'Auntie Yvonne's' photos. She handed me the receiver. I, who'd imagined you were phoning to ask us to come and get you straight away, was astonished when you explained your little racket and asked me to contact my sister as soon as possible to get her to send you some 'goods'. To my questions about what kind of weather you were having and what the place was like where you were staying, you answered abruptly. Were you at least doing some skiing? A little. You'd tell me all that when you got back. Now you had to go and have supper. As soon as you'd hung up, I called Yvonne. She put the photos in the post the following morning. Unfortunately, because of Easter Monday and a strike in the Post Office, the letter only reached the Mont-Dore after the end of the holiday. The envelope was returned to Yvonne who sent it on to you in Bagnolet. The photos arrived at home amid general unconcern. They hung about on the sideboard in the dining room for three or four days, and then Dara threw them in the bin. You'd already forgotten your feverish transactions with your holiday-camp friends. Besides, as the days passed, you spoke less and less about those two weeks at the Mont-Dore. Soon, not a single memory of them would be left for you. Not even in the shape of your first star for skiing, which you'd failed to get.

One Saturday the following year, at about the same season, we got up far earlier than we usually did at the weekend. Dara made breakfast while I toasted some bread on one of the hot-plates. The sky was open and blue, slightly disturbing. Your mother got the *saucisson* and two eggs out of the refrigerator. I put my arms around her waist. She asked: 'What's up with you?' I said that now we had the right to do whatever we liked, since we were about to be married! 'Go and wake up your daughter,' she said as she broke an egg into the frying-pan. I then had a ludicrous thought, one that came back to badger me during the ceremony. Why in fact was I getting married? In order to legitimise you. It was a way of marrying *you too*. That afternoon, just like your mother, you would have another name. You would have attended the ceremony,

12

shared in the meal. It wouldn't be you whose garter was stolen, but then it wouldn't be your mother either since she wouldn't be wearing any. Of course you would spend your wedding night alone. But Dara and I had twin beds, and it was more and more seldom that either of us crossed the thirty centimetres that separated them. In any case tonight it was out of the question! We'd be far too tired.

I remember that at the registry office, an attendant asked you if you were the bridesmaid. 'No,' you answered, 'I am the *legitimised* daughter.' There was a general burst of laughter. You looked around you, proud of the effect you'd made. You were wearing a green dress and your ears were red, as always when you found yourself in company.

The lunch took place in a restaurant in the Bois de Vincennes. There were about ten of us. You'd been sat at the end of the table, far from me. Most impressed by the white tablecloths and the very 'classy' service, as Dara soon labelled it, you watched your manners. You said 'thank you' each time you were brought something, a plate, a fork or the salt. When I saw you looking helpless in front of your *sole meunière*, I signalled to the head waiter. He took your plate from you, and this earned him a 'thank you' that one could feel had come, unlike the others, straight from the heart. The man prepared your sole before your incredulous eyes. However, your admiration seemed to me a little put on. I think you wanted to convey to our guests that nowhere in the world would anyone have been so kind to a young person who didn't know how to handle a fish knife and fork. These people had to be made wholly aware that your daddy wasn't taking them to lunch just anywhere!

Your mother took it upon herself to prepare my sole for me. She wasn't keen to see me spit out the bones one after the other and assemble them into a little pile on the edge of my plate, as I usually did. People joked that she seemed to have become my maid. She retorted by saying 'that was hardly new'.

13

I wonder what that little Croat proletarian, brought up in a family for whom engagements and weddings were unquestionably the most important events in life, could have felt in marrying at forty a man who was fifty-six, and in the presence of the daughter he had given her ten years earlier. A peculiar wedding indeed! Conversations began but didn't develop. The luxury of the restaurant had a very detrimental effect on the atmosphere — something Dara in fact remarked on the same evening as we were getting ready to go to bed. The waiters were like so many watchdogs in front of whom we lowered our voices as if we'd wished the entire business to remain a close secret. We avoided drinking too much. The groom it was who settled up, for the groom's father had been dead for about forty years. And as we got up we knew very well, your mother and I, that I did not have two plane tickets to Venice in my pocket. Not even two train tickets to Bruges!

Dara, who always wanted everything done according to form, and whom you subsequently hurt a lot by not introducing her to a single one of your successive 'fiancés', showed herself strangely satisfied with that day which had swung between the burlesque and the boring. Her only regret was that the meal should have cost such a lot. She had insisted on seeing the bill. This was still at the time when we got confused over the old and the new francs. She asked me to give her the price in centimes. When I mentioned the figure, I saw in her eyes that she was working out the number of dresses she'd have had to make at home to pay for such a meal. I felt I was going up in her esteem. But I got the painful impression that my revelation was spoiling her pleasure, as it transformed in her mind all the delicate dishes that had been set before us into as many lengths of fabric, needles and reels of cotton.

There was also the 'Douglas–Mitchum' incident. As we were beginning to eat our asparagus, two men and a woman settled down at a table next to ours. The woman had sharp features framed by short grey hair. The two men paid her no attention. Turning one towards the other, slightly bent forward, they exchanged impassioned words. They didn't even take the trouble to decide what they'd have to eat. The woman took charge of that. Suddenly your mother nudged me in the ribs. 'That's Kirk Douglas,' she said in my ear. I looked at the younger of the two men. He had light-coloured eyes and a dimple in his chin. It wasn't Kirk Douglas, it was Robert Mitchum! 'No it isn't,' Dara protested, 'I tell you that's Kirk Douglas!' She quickly put Yvonne in the picture about our argument. You know your aunt. Always eager to find a compromise. From the time of our difficult childhood with a half-mad stepfather, she's inherited an absolute terror of family conflicts. She said it could be Kirk Douglas just as well as Robert Mitchum. And, she added, why shouldn't it be someone else? This way she had of hedging her bets annoyed Dara, so she resorted to her friend Peggy. She summed up the situation for her. Peggy then turned around so abruptly that the men looked up and seemed to weigh her up with a kind of chilly puzzlement. Peggy decided it would be clever to stare him out. After a few seconds, the actor shrugged his shoulders and resumed his conversation with his companion. Mortified by this snub from 'Douglas–Mitchum', Peggy turned as red as the spots of wine that now speckled the fine white tablecloth. In our family, we have never had very good table manners. And I must say that despite your breathtaking ascent in society, you haven't broken the tradition. You've told me yourself that during business lunches in restaurants, it's always your place that's the most messy. 'So?' Dara asked her friend. Peggy, bristling, declared: 'I've no idea whether that's Kirk Douglas or Robert Mitchum, but whoever he is, he's certainly not very nice!' Your mother was fast reaching the end of her tether. For goodness sake, it was, it could only be Kirk Douglas! I didn't want to admit I might be wrong, and more important still, I derived a pleasure from her exasperation that would soon surpass any I knew with her, so in that mawkish and slightly plaintive voice that murderers adopt when they know their false alibi is rock-solid, I said: 'You're

15

mistaken, my dear, the man you see there is Robert Mitchum and no other. I accept he does look a lot like Kirk Douglas. Any neophyte would confuse them.' She protested. She didn't know the meaning of the word neophyte, but she did know what Kirk Douglas's face was like! The entire table was put to work. Everyone discreetly examined the actor. Opinions were pooled. From this joint investigation, the conclusion was reached that it was 'perfectly possible that it was Kirk Douglas'; Mitchum didn't have such a pointed nose, nor such high cheekbones. 'You see!' Dara said, with a look of triumph. What should I have seen? All this proved nothing. She bit her lip. I was definitely getting on her nerves. She addressed not a single word to me until the head waiter, whom Peggy called, confirmed that our neighbour in the restaurant really and truly had been the famous American actor, Kirk Douglas. He had left a few minutes earlier. I said to myself that we'd annoyed him into cutting short his lunch. Or had he simply felt the food he'd been served wasn't good?

The wedding party broke up shortly before five. As soon as your mother was in the Peugeot, she opened her window and lit up a Disque Bleu. That frenetic and truly sensual way the Slavs have of smoking! According to you, it's due to their fascination with all that isn't real, tangible. They like only what burns, what scatters and vanishes.

The day was cold and grey. There was hardly anyone on the streets. People were staying in watching television. Occasionally, you could read on the walls: 'Victory to the OAS!' Or the initials OAS were crossed out and replaced by FNL. Out-of-date inscriptions that made me think of the Dubonnet advertisements you'd see flaking off the walls of old houses in small provincial towns.

You were sprawled out on the back seat. Your cheeks and ears were bright red. Occasionally, our eyes met in the rearview mirror. In yours, I could see something like the beginnings of sickness. I asked if you were feeling ill, which often happened to you in the car, especially when we went to

16

a family lunch. You said you weren't. Even so, I sensed you were in a hurry to get home, to get back to your studio.

Basically, you'd hated that day, and you would hate it more and more as the years went by. At the time, you had loved being in a way the star of the occasion, playing your part of the *legitimised* daughter, and in the weeks that followed, you had a great time explaining to your friends why your name had changed. But the comic side of the situation would soon wear off to reveal a great sadness, one that you still carry in your heart and that no one has ever had sufficient strength or courage, or a great enough capacity for self-denial, to free you from. Perhaps it's impossible. I sometimes think of you as a travelling salesman forced to go from town to town to flog a batch of useless articles — cumbersome, outdated articles that are very heavy and that no one will want to lumber themselves with.

I describe you as a taciturn little girl, but there were also moments when you changed into a fidgety chatterbox of a clown. The various features of the scenery, our idiosyncrasies, our way of speaking, became so many props for the pantomime you would begin to enact in front of us. You've told me that these same fits of jollity also occurred with boys and girls of your own age, especially when you'd only just met them. Overwhelmed by the joy of having found new friends, you threaded together the barmiest jokes and sketches, at the risk of being taken for a lunatic. As for Dara, she said that you could see at such moments what a malevolent and destructive spirit you kept hidden away in your well-behaved grey eyes and behind that perfect schoolgirl's high forehead of yours. I could feel her wavering inwardly when you let fly at her with 'the charm of my personality is in my accent,' mimicking her with *le* and *la* in the wrong place. She couldn't stand being made fun of. Indeed, she couldn't see what was so amusing about making fun of someone. She couldn't understand what pleasure we took in it. And, as you know, when your mother didn't understand something, there really wasn't very much

17

point in explaining it to her.

Our honeymoon, that was something we did two years later. We went to Yugoslavia. What a strange destiny ours was! A wedding after ten years living together, and a honeymoon two years after our wedding, all under the slightly distraught gaze of our daughter. And on top of everything, your mother had suggested to Peggy that she come with us. The latter eagerly accepted, although not without having tactfully phoned me at work to check whether her presence would bother me. Goodness, I answered, Dara and I were no longer what you might call newly-weds, and I'd genuinely appreciate her company.

Peggy was a year or two older than your mother. She was small and plump. She was very keen on wearing flimsy dresses that showed off her legs and shoulders. Much as she found her friend splendid, Dara deplored that side of her, and whenever she was making her a suit or a skirt, she did her utmost to make them longer than Peggy wanted them — with the result that Peggy hardly ever wore them. This clash, which had become legendary among our friends, went back to the two women's first encounter. Peggy had come to our flat on the recommendation of one of her neighbours who'd praised Dara's know-how and low prices. It was mid-afternoon. Your mother served tea and biscuits to her new customer. She always had to get people to eat! Peggy immediately fell under the spell of this tall, spontaneous and expansive Yugoslav. She ordered a cocktail dress. They discussed its shape and colour. Peggy had no specific wishes. In fact, she was overcome by the unexpected pleasure of drinking tea, eating biscuits and leafing through fashion magazines in this modest flat whose smell and furnishings she'd initially hated. She couldn't bring herself to leave! It had got to the stage where your mother had wondered whether the 'little lady' from rue de Courcelles didn't have 'particular inclinations'. Your return from school put a stop to this situation. Peggy got up, smoothed down her skirt and said she was longing for the

18

first fitting, which your mother arranged for the following Monday. She asked Peggy if she wanted her to call a taxi. The answer was: 'I've kept the one I came in. He's waiting for me downstairs.' You can guess how much these two sentences threw your mother! That evening, she could speak of nothing other than this eccentric woman who'd allowed the meter of her taxi to tick over for more than two hours. Peggy went through the same rigmarole at the first and second fittings. Through the window, Dara could see the car parked along the avenue. The driver read a newspaper or thoughtfully smoked a cigarette. Your mother told me she was worried about making a mess of the dress, because the thought of that meter ticking over for nothing while Peggy gazed at herself in the big hall mirror stopped her concentrating. At the third fitting, making the most of the fact that her customer now seemed to see her as a respectable acquaintance rather than a suburban dressmaker, she owned up to all the embarrassment being caused her by that stationary taxi into which vast sums of money were pouring that she couldn't help thinking would be better spent on Unicef or the Red Cross. There was so much poverty in the world! Peggy defended herself with effective unconcern. It was such a handy arrangement. And anyway, it didn't cost as much as all that. She negotiated a set price. This argument disarmed Dara. She told me that she'd suddenly felt herself stop hearing the dreadful click-click of the meter, and her mind had been completely at ease as she'd launched into a lively discussion with Peggy, the first of a long series, on the appropriateness of shortening the dress.

The two women were soon very close. They telephoned one another at least once a day. They went to the theatre together or shared a plate of sea food in a *brasserie* on the Grands Boulevards. Their greatest pleasure was to go around the shops together. They swapped comments about the clothes in the windows. They'd walk in, determined not to buy anything. Each would try on two or three things, while asking the assistant what Dara called 'trick questions'. Then they left,

19

saying they might call back, a promise which I imagine left the assistant quite cold. Towards the end of the afternoon, they'd have a cup of tea in the Café de la Paix. Their feet hurt. Their discussions were always in some way related to fashion. This seemed to Dara incompatible with dress-making. The dresses *she* created were unique! You weren't afraid when you went out in the street or arrived at someone's house that you'd see someone else dressed the same. To be fashionable, didn't that mean more than anything to look like no one else? For Peggy, knowing how to dress was like knowing how to undress: it had no purpose other than to seduce men. This entirely sensual approach to the matter shocked Dara. But she had her very own way of being shocked. She tipped her head back, gave a low laugh, and said that Peggy was priceless. What on earth was it that she found in men? They were either louts or pimps or, and it seems to me that Dara classed me in this last category, complete pains in the neck! Who might have imagined that it wasn't out of offhandedness that this beautiful, loose-limbed and elegant woman talked about men in this way, but out of pure fear of sex? At the age of forty your mother hadn't resolved any of the sexual problems that teenagers face — which, as you can imagine, could hardly be said of Peggy.

At eighteen Peggy had married a greengrocer, a handsome young man with a romantic face. Rapidly, and to the astonishment of all those who knew him, he had made a fortune. In 1955 he bought the Cours des Halles on avenue de Courcelles where, throughout the sixties and seventies, we shopped for our supplies of melons and avocado pears. It was there that, one morning in July 1964, he died of a heart attack. Peggy found herself alone. She had not a single woman friend. For many months, she lived in a state of indecision. She didn't dare have the good time she was desperate for. She never managed to warm to any of the women customers sufficiently to share a few moments of relaxation. As for the other women traders in the neighbourhood, she found them vulgar and untrustworthy. So she stayed at home on her own. She listened to the radio, drinking small glasses of Suze, her favourite apéritif. You can understand why she was instantly seduced by Dara, whose best friend she did her best to become within weeks. Your mother was neither one of those snotty-sounding *bourgeoises* whose reserve Peggy found so tedious and fearsome, nor a sly and boastful haberdashery or café owner. She was modest, but knew how to hold herself. Admittedly, she was no intellectual. But then nor was Peggy. And she envied Dara her singing accent and her relaxed, good-natured manner that saved her ever appearing ridiculous in company. Finally, Dara always agreed to any suggestion to go out: the cinema, theatre, music-hall, or a Chinese restaurant. The ideal companion for a widow who aspired with all her will to being happy! In addition, Peggy soon noticed that your mother had the knack of attracting men while simultaneously and magically banishing their shyness. The pair of them were accosted at least ten times a day! Of course, out of the total, there were many rejects; but each time an appetising prey presented himself, Peggy expended a great wealth of ingenuity to fix a meeting without Dara noticing. The business would be concluded a few days later in an hotel in the XVIIth arrondissement, on the place Clichy side. Two *métro* stations away from the Cours des Halles. You're wondering how I know all this? Well, Peggy herself told me.

I seem to be saying that the relationship between Peggy and Dara was the same as that between a shark and its pilot-fish. But that would be to overlook your mother's puritanism. She was never the willing acomplice to Peggy's escapades, and the latter had to listen patiently to the lectures on morals that your mother gave her whenever Peggy ventured to tell her about one of her adventures. Dara didn't blame her for having a good time. Far from it. What seemed sinful to her wasn't the fact of having pleasure, but of having it with someone you weren't *in love* with. Ah, your mother and love! She placed it so high up that I get the feeling she was never able to grasp it.

Had you asked Dara to tell you about her friendship with Peggy, she would have begun by saying that it had been one of the great fortunes of her life. The thought that so rich a woman should feel so much affection for her both astonished her and elevated her to heights of happiness and self-satisfaction of a sort she'd probably never reached before. But what surprised her wasn't that she'd been chosen, but that such a well-off woman should show good taste. There'd been so many others who'd been stupid enough to treat her like a maidservant and to give her the attention they'd give a fly. This had been all the more wounding to her because, since her adolescence — the time of her first customers, refined Zagreb women whose accounts of their travels entranced the young dressmaker — she had harboured a passion for people who were her social superiors. Given the same intensity, the friendship shown her by a poor woman had as much value as that of a rich one. But so much did she appreciate fine language and fine manners that she was as it were magnetically drawn towards better-class people. So long as they weren't snobbish, of course. Yes, Dara loved above all else to be liked by these delightful, magical creatures, and I don't think Peggy ever suspected the degree to which she gratified your mother by putting her on an equal footing, and that's discounting all the times she placed her on a pedestal, praising her beauty, her kindness, and even her intelligence!

The day of our departure, we met up with Peggy at the station buffet in the Gare de Lyon. Yugoslavia began on the platform. Cardboard suitcases held together with bits of string. Enormous *casse-croûte*, as your mother called them, wrapped up in tablecloths. People bought their last cartons of American cigarettes. They shouted out to each other from one carriage to the next. In the second-class compartments passengers piled suitcases up dangerously on the luggage racks.

It was a gloomy December evening. You had turned up your anorak collar. You hadn't wanted to trust the porters with your sports bag in which you were carrying magazines, a torch and half a baguette, something I was only to find out the following morning. As she always did when we were going away, Dara had given you a few francs to buy sweets to help you through the boredom of the journey. You'd chosen to buy bread. Less pricey, and better for filling you up. As if we were going into exile! As if this were the exodus!

Dara had taken charge of the operation. Peggy and I, dazed by the bustle in the station, faintly dreading the idea of soon finding ourselves in a socialist country, watched her with admiration. The porters obeyed her hand and foot. It was with obvious pleasure that she stopped them outside a first-class sleeper. It was decided that I'd get into the compartment and the suitcases would be handed to me through the window. Peggy came with me. Dara oversaw things from outside. You stayed to one side, motionless. You looked a bit offended, as if our excitement were disturbing some important daydream.

Dara was delighted because we'd be just the four of us in the compartment. 'It's a bit as if we were travelling in a proper sleeping-car,' she said. She settled down in one of the upper berths, the one facing the front of the train. Unfortunately, the front of the train was to become the back of the train during the night, and she woke up feeling very ill. Like your mother, you loved fresh air and heights. Thus, without having really intended it, Peggy and I found ourselves together at floor level. 'You're not going to keep your clothes on!' protested Dara, just as we were lying down as discreetly as possible on our SNCF blankets. Since there were no outsiders among us, it would have been silly not to make ourselves comfortable. Your mother got a pair of pyjamas out of my suitcase. Peggy, a little embarrassed, took from hers a négligé and a dressing-gown. She went off to change in the carriage toilet, while I, grumbling and bumping into every corner of the compartment, took off my shirt and trousers. Dara made my bed. When she was climbing back up the ladder, I drew her to me and kissed her on the mouth. One of those cold, wet little kisses that I'd christened 'Return of the wage-slave' and that Dara, who was never able to pronounce the French 'u' of *bureau* correctly, turned into 'Return of the executioner'.

When Peggy got into bed, Dara wished us all sweet dreams and put the light out. Soon, my eyes having grown accustomed to the darkness, I saw you crouching on your berth with your nose glued to the window.

After about ten minutes, being unable to sleep, I turned on my night-light and opened the *France-Soir* that I'd bought on the platform along with a couple of bottles of mineral water. I read the sports page and the entertainments page. I wasn't interested in politics. I was just starting on the home news page when I got the feeling that Peggy was watching me. Your mother has often told you about the tendency I supposedly have of thinking that all women are mad about me. Fine! All the same, let me tell you that she was misreading my thoughts as usual. One day, I'd simply said to her that any man, if he can take the trouble, is capable of seducing any woman. And vice-versa. You see how she stretched the truth. So I looked up from my paper and turned my head. I then got a shock that took me way back into my past, a shock similar to the one I'd had when, at thirteen, I had first caressed a woman's breast. Peggy had pushed back her blankets and shaken her thighs free from their cocoon of sheets. Her well-rounded breasts and the triangle of black hair showed through the négligé which was as transparent as cellophane. But the most extra-ordinary thing was the prurient, sparkling look, at that moment, in the eyes of your mother's best friend. It promised me much pleasure, and I realised I really had set off on a lovers' journey. So in the same way as I'd felt it was you I was marrying rather than Dara, I felt it was with Peggy rather than your mother that I'd be spending this honeymoon. Peggy held out her hand to me. With my spectacles on the end of my nose and *France-Soir* on my knees, I grasped hold of it, and we remained like that for a few minutes, delicately stroking

24

each other's fingers or, in fact, playfully attempting to break each other's bones.

We reached Zagreb the following day, in the late afternoon. The entire evening was spent going from one flat to another. Whether we were in the Upper Town or the new developments of Zaprude, awaiting us were the same expansive cousins, the same slices of that *saucisson* Dara called Hungarian salami, the same walnut biscuits, the same small glasses of plum brandy. The undoubted queen of the feast, Dara drank, ate, laughed, talked, sang, while Peggy and I sat in our corner and simply nodded our heads each time de Gaulle was called a great man and Paris named the capital of the world. And as we had to speak to each other, a vague intellectual complicity added itself to the physical attraction we'd been feeling for one another for a few months already, and which had expressed itself the previous night on the Paris–Zagreb express. And, towards one o'clock in the morning, as we were going back to your grandfather's in one of your cousins' car, it suddenly became evident to me that not only would Peggy soon become my mistress, she would also remain so after we had come back to Paris.

Your grandfather would have been exceedingly offended had we stayed in a hotel, as had been our original intention, and that was how we all found ourselves in the Sevnicas' small flat, halfway between Kvaternik Square and Maksimir Park. During the two weeks our stay in Yugoslavia was to last, Peggy and you were to sleep in the same room as us, with the grandfather and his wife occupying the tiny room adjoining the living room where we had installed ourselves. I can see you again, in your pink pyjamas, shyly lying down alongside Peggy. Your mother stood at the open window, smoking a last cigarette. I was leafing through a Croat–French pocket-dictionary, while keeping an eye on the movements of Peggy's legs under your eiderdown. Dara finally turned out the light and got into bed. A few seconds later, she snuggled up against me, which she hadn't done for at least a year or two. She was crying. Although she was very sensitive, she rarely cried, and never in my arms. In a hushed voice, she told me that during the latter part of that day, she had undergone more than she could bear. She had been totally depressed by the combination of the tiring journey, memories of her youth, her father's spectacular ageing, the sadness of the town and the poverty of its inhabitants. I tapped her shoulder gently. Did she want us to make love? No! No! She wasn't in the mood for that! Besides, was I forgetting that Peggy and Brigitte were in the nearby bed?

During the days that followed, we visited without much enthusiasm the city's historic sights. Neither your mother, nor Peggy nor I were museum addicts. We weren't interested in history, and I'm sorry to say, art left us cold. In front of a painting, a sculpture or a monument which were not contemporary, the only thought Dara was able to express could be summed up as: 'And to think all that dates from so many centuries ago!' But she had misgivings where Peggy, for example, simply could not have cared less. We had to get to wherever it was and spend a certain length of time there, however little we all cared about what was to be seen. I remember in particular the irritated tribute we paid to King Tomislav when, on Dara's orders, we contemplated his statue for long minutes as the temperature nudged five degrees below zero. On top of this, misled by a blanket of sunshine that had spread over Maksimirska soon after we'd woken up, Peggy had dressed less warmly than on other days, favouring a jersey skirt instead of her usual trousers and neglecting her fur-lined boots for delightful little patent-leather shoes. She stamped her feet on the frozen ground and gave her shoulders a vigorous rub as she puffed on a cheap Yugoslav cigarette given her by your Uncle Vladimir, and she showed signs of an impatience bordering on anger, smacking her tongue continually and muttering incomprehensible words while Dara calmly carried on translating into French the sentences inscribed on the plinth of the statue. At the time your mother didn't comment on this, but that night, in bed, while Peggy had already been monopolising the bathroom for a good three-quarters of an hour, a habit which incidentally nearly drove your grandfather mad, she confided to me in a slightly sad tone of voice that her friend was adorable, but wasn't sufficiently interested in improving her mind.

My memory of Zagreb is of an old-fashioned provincial town with trams and a great many paved roads. The few cars on the streets seemed in a bad state. Bumpers attached to car bodies with bits of string. Broken windows replaced with cardboard. People in the streets were poorly dressed. As early as our third day there, your mother gave up walking about in her astrakhan coat. She had had enough of the hostile looks she got, and also of turning down the overtures of those who wanted to buy the coat from her.

What did I enjoy about our stay in the Croatian capital? The cups of hot chocolate I drank at eleven in the morning, alone in a café on Kvaternik Square, reading a three- or four-day-old copy of *France-Soir*. Our walks, Peggy's, yours and mine, in Maksimir Park, before those over-long suppers we ate every evening with one or other member of the Sevnica family. And then, of course, the morning when Peggy and I made love on the little bed in which we knew that Dara had slept throughout her childhood.

As the days passed, the Sevnicas' attitude to your mother changed, but so slightly that none of us apart from her noticed, and it was only many months later that she revealed to me what had happened. You recall how at the station she'd been welcomed like an empress returned from exile whose legitimacy has suddenly been restored. Amid the porters and the bunches of flowers, we'd attended a kind of coronation. Then at your grandfather's, there'd been the episode of the presents. From Paris we'd brought bottles of perfume, electric razors, silk stockings, pens, bottles of cognac, and even antibiotics! The handing-out took place with everyone in a state of euphoria. People kissed one another on the mouth. Taking me to one side, a nephew of Dara's had suggested exchanging our francs for us for half as much again as the legal rate. At the time, you got 100 dinars for 66 centimes. I would get 300 dinars for one franc. I agreed. Later that evening, another nephew, in the same quasi-English, talked to me about exchange rates. He told me that on the black market, I'd have no trouble in getting 400 dinars for a franc. I understood that I'd been taken for a ride, but this did nothing to alter my mood. I was already drunk, and besides, for what you could buy in this damned country. . . . The next day had also been one of perfect harmony between the 'exile', her family and her old friends. There was more handing out of lighters and miniature tin Eiffel towers. The first slightly pointed questions concerning Peggy hadn't come till later, and, oddly enough, after various cousins and nephews, excited by Peggy's low neck-lines and near-permanent provocative postures, had chatted her up eagerly, but to no effect. I was soon suspected of having brought my mistress on my honeymoon! A Frenchman was quite capable of such a thing! Dara said about Peggy: 'Without her, my husband would get bored. At least he has someone to talk to.' It took her several days to understand the meaning of the discreet smiles that would then be exchanged, and it was only in the middle of our second week in Zagreb that she asked me, with that forced cheerfulness she resorted to when she was at the height of embarrassment, if I found Peggy to my taste. The question gave me a jolt, because an hour earlier, while you were all at the cathedral market, Peggy and I had slept together for the first time. I told Dara that her friend was very seductive but, I added, smiling, I felt myself too old to satisfy her. Your mother nodded her approval, with the air of someone who knows more than she's letting on. Even so, she was never able to convince the Sevnicas that between Peggy and me, there was nothing save the friendly feelings that the circumstances called for; and she who'd arrived so triumphantly at Zagreb station, showing off with equal pride her French passport, her well-fed husband and her well-dressed daughter, was, on leaving, nothing more than a poor little wife whom I was unfaithful to with her best friend during our honeymoon! Yes, she'd got somewhere in life. But at what cost! Until her death, Dara suffered the pain of the fall she took at that time in the esteem of her family — a fall for which Peggy and I were in fact far more responsible than she ever thought.

You had an excellent holiday in Zagreb. Your grandfather developed a passion for you the day when, shortly after our arrival, you nearly beat him at chess. Delighted, he announced this to everyone in the room. We formed a circle around the chess-board. Then you lost your nerve and made two or three mistakes. The game ended in a stalemate. The grandfather called Dara and asked her to translate what he wanted to tell you. Then, in the oppressive warmth of the living room, between the piles of walnut biscuits and the bottles of white wine, and in the middle of five or six competing conversations, he declared that fear of winning was to fear of losing what fear of living was to fear of dying. For Dara, used to his endlessly recounting his regimental days or singing Croat folk songs, it was the first time she had heard him state such an abstract precept, which incidentally she had much trouble translating. The grandfather could not keep his eyes off you. He wore round spectacles and had a small, straight moustache reminiscent of Adolf Hitler's. Slowly, he raised over you his heavy, calloused, former carpenter's hand. I was observing the scene from afar. I had, I don't know why, a sudden absurd feeling that he was going to slap your face. I was about to rush over to you when I saw that he was stroking your cheek. He said a few words which Dara didn't translate, so obvious was their meaning. Seeing your three faces close together, as if for a group photograph, I realised how strongly you belonged to the same family, with your almond-shaped eyes, your rounded foreheads, the extreme mobility of your features and, in particular, the combination of flightiness, mischief and determination that showed in your

29

eyes. You were Sevnicas. *Croats*. From Zagreb. In fact, the only comment you made about that trip was, a few weeks after we'd got back to Bagnolet, that you missed the long evenings 'at Grandfather's', where so many people turned up, brandishing a bunch of flowers or a bottle of slivovitz, then stayed for ten minutes or three hours, drank, sang, told their life stories, read a newspaper, had a game of chess or even a little nap, and went off again amid the sound of laughter and raised voices. 'Your daughter, at least, enjoys family life!' remarked Dara. Was she forgetting that seeing your *French* family drove you to fits of exasperation that sometimes even made you physically ill?

Lastly, there was the Strossmayer Promenade episode. It was a few days before we left. We were in Gradec, looking for a few things to take back to France as presents to give to our friends. 'For me,' said Peggy, 'the problem's easily dealt with: I have no friends other than you!' However, she dutifully followed us from one shop to the next, giving her opinion on the place-mats, tea pots, dolls or shawls Dara was thinking of buying. She enjoyed asking, in pidgin or sign language, for information she was incapable of understanding. Nor did she dislike bartering. She had often told us that story of the gandoura she'd bought in Marrakesh, whose price she'd managed to knock down by at least two-thirds. From time to time, she would turn towards me and, smiling, throw a conniving little look at my flies.

We walked past Lotršćak Tower and reached the funicular railway station. The branches of the chestnut trees were weighed down with snow. You ran towards the parapet. You leant over to look at the city. I called out to you to be careful not to fall. Your mother said: 'You'll make a right little coward of your daughter!' The cathedral spires stood out against a very pale blue, nearly white sky. You got a supply of snowballs ready. Peggy turned up her fur collar and said you'd think you were in Moscow. Did she know Moscow? No, but that's what the Strossmayer Promenade reminded her of. She was one of those people one thing always reminds of other things they don't know.

A snowball hit me right on the back of my neck. I turned around. You were hopping up and down, hands clenched in your mittens, a delighted smile on your lips. Behind you, the small yellow houses of Gradec, their snowy rooftops. The soft snowball I hastily scooped up disintegrated as soon as I threw it. Your laughter, like so many dazzling crystals launched into space. I ran after you, grunting like an ill-tempered buffalo. You stumbled, you fell gently into the snow. I caught up with you. You still had a snowball saved up! By the time I'd got over my surprise, wiped my eyes and forehead, you were already off. You zigzagged between the people out walking, hung on to the trunk of a chestnut tree so as not to slip, and crouched behind a bench.

I gave up chasing after you. I walked in Dara's direction. There was a man standing next to her. Both seemed to be observing the snowy steeple of Saint Mary's Church. I went closer. In their conversation the only word I recognised, or thought I recognised, was the Christian name Nathalie, uttered by the man. I didn't try to make anything of my advantage. I warned Dara of my presence by tapping her on the shoulder. Your mother introduced the man to me as a former neighbour, from the time when the Sevnicas lived in a flat on the Vlaška Ulica. He slipped away very soon after.

For a long time, Dara insisted that she and he had never spoken together about 'Aunt Nathalie'. Was she afraid I would go and recount the incident to the police inspector who had led the investigation into the murder of the old Russian woman? Following Peggy's death, your mother even maintained that the man with the round hat on the Strossmayer Promenade had only been a figment of my imagination. I attributed this lie to the abrupt increases in blood pressure to which Dara was by then victim, and which noticeably upset her mental faculties.

The sky was grey, now. In a few minutes' time, the

windows of the houses would light up, and it would be too cold to stay outside. 'Let's go and have tea with Mrs Bartaković, my old employer,' said Dara. We still had a whole weekend to spend in Yugoslavia, but in my mind our honeymoon came to an end that day, at five o'clock in the afternoon, on the Strossmayer Promenade.

2

When Dara met the man who was to become your father, I'd known her for two years and had been living with her for eight months. It was summer. Neither of us could afford to go on holiday. Dara was working for a Yugoslav tailor. I was translating American bestsellers into French. This provided the finances for the law degree I was slowly completing. I was in no hurry to launch myself into a career, which was why Dara claimed I was a bit of a joker.

It might seem strange or even shocking to a young woman today, but we shared a bed; it was a common set-up in those days. There was an acute housing shortage in the Fifties. You're too young ever to have heard of abbé Pierre. He was a great defender of the poorly housed, and he'd be able to explain very clearly to you why, in 1954, any number of female students, office and factory workers shared hotel rooms. At the time, twin beds were in very short supply in hotels, so these young ladies nearly always found themselves lying one against the other under the same blankets, and this occasionally led to passionate embraces. Thanks simply to this chance promiscuity, serious-minded, hard-working girls who were not predisposed to sexual deviance in the least discovered that they were, at heart, true Messalinas. And perhaps the post-war housing shortage will figure in the history of lesbianism in the way that Jesuit colleges do in the history of pederasty. You're wondering whether your mother and I made love together? Naturally we did. In fact we used to quite often. In the beginning I think it was out of friendship that she gave in to my advances. She could see how strong my desire for her was and it would have upset her to hurt me. She made herself do it. I can still remember the way she caressed my breasts the first time. It was as if she was choosing melons.

What she also liked was not having to worry any more about getting pregnant.

The hotel was on rue de l'Éperon, near the place de l'Odéon. It has been pulled down since then. We had a room overlooking the street, on the third floor. The toilet and the showers were at the end of the corridor. Despite the threats of eviction the hotel owner made regularly, most of the tenants cooked in their rooms. Dara and I ate at a small, square table which served as my desk during the day and which Dara requisitioned after supper for her dressmaking — moonlighting without which she wouldn't have had much left to feed herself with, once she'd paid her hotel bill. I'd settle down on the bed with a book and some cigarettes. She'd tell me all about the little events of her day at Monsieur Dvednirović's, the tailor. She didn't understand that reading requires far more quiet than sewing. Occasionally I got angry and told her off. She would apologise feebly for having got 'carried away'. She had the greatest respect for 'culture' and 'cultivated people' (and invariably pronounced the French *culture* as '*coultoure*' and *cultivé* as '*coultivé*'), even though she didn't much like being given books as presents, and at those few parties I took her to, kept away from any man or woman who, enthralled by her beauty, would have wanted to share with her that '*coultoure*' she was supposedly so fond of. Having cast a friendly, mischievous glance at me, she'd start off again on her tale that would go on and on while I closed my book, emptied the ashtray into the bin, went to brush my teeth at the washstand, undressed, kissed Dara, went to bed, turned out the bedside lamp and went to sleep.

It's strange to think that in 1954, your mother was the age you are now, paying me this visit: thirty. She was about your height. Her hair was very dark, whereas you belong to that category of women whose hair changes colour according to where they are: it looks black on photographs, blonde on a beach, red in night clubs and auburn in town. You have the face of a French woman one vaguely suspects has a little

34

Tartar or Mongol blood, whereas your mother's Balkan roots positively shone out in her face. Throughout her adolescence in Yugoslavia, she had done gymnastics, and this had left her with solid shoulders. Yours are more frail. But you have inherited Dara's long legs. However, the biggest difference between the two of you is that Dara came across as bold, enthusiastic and self-assured, whereas you seem to advance through life taking small, carefully considered steps, even though you sometimes hurl yourself along dangerous paths — such as the one that has brought you here, for example.

Let's get on to that July Sunday when your mother made Frank Laurens' acquaintance. Paris was in the grip of a stifling heatwave. In the street, passers-by sought out the shade. You got the unpleasant feeling that you'd become an undesirable member of society and that all the radiant members of the French middle classes had abandoned Paris and rushed off to the forest at Fontainebleau or the Normandy beaches. Dara, wearing pants and a bra, with a cigarette between her lips, was cutting her toenails in front of the open window. She was going through one of those periods when what she said and what she was suddenly seemed rather off-putting to me. It was perhaps because she didn't take well to the heat and would flood the bed with sweat; her hands were always clammy and her cheeks as red as a barrow-woman's. And besides, I was beginning to feel fed up with those stories that were all in some way or other concerned with Monsieur Dvednirović. I sighed conspicuously. With her customary '*tou*' for *tu*, Dara said: 'You want make love, don't you?' In that heat? Definitely not. She got up without answering, drew the curtains, walked towards the bed and asked me to take off her pants which, naturally, I hastened to do. I'd be prepared to bet anything that with men she was never as relaxed in her desire as she was with me. For Dara, sleeping with another woman was a giggle, a game whose rules she'd immediately mastered. But she would place all her hopes in men, and that was what made her behaviour towards them feverish and

35

timorous.

At about one o'clock we had lunch, a tomato and a few slices of *saucisson*. Dara suggested I go with her to the Deligny swimming-pool. I've no idea now why I declined. Perhaps I felt it would be too crowded. Or perhaps I was simply fed up with the sight of your mother and the sound of her cooing like a turtle-dove on heat. She went off, dressed in a flimsy blue dress, her swimsuit tucked away in her handbag. From the window, I saw her come out of the hotel, walk along the pavement and turn on to the boulevard Saint-Germain. I noticed she was beginning to stoop slightly. But perhaps the image of a young and beautiful Dara, out to conquer the boulevard Saint-Germain, has been blurred in my memory by the vision of the broken, frightened and rather drab woman she would soon become under your father's influence.

She stationed herself on the platform of the bus. During the journey, she remembered having promised one of her Yugoslav friends that she'd go with her to a dance-hall where the girl had a date with one of those broad-shouldered Frenchmen with crewcuts that, at the time, all the young refugees from the East were running after. But these girls also had a very acute fear of pimps, and that was why they often brought along a girl-friend to a first or even a second date.

A promise was a promise for Dara. She got off at the first stop and found herself in the heart of the VIIth arrondisse-ment. It was an area she never went to. She had a lot of trouble finding a *métro* station in all those long, desolate streets and deserted squares. Twenty minutes later, she was climbing up the stairs at Richelieu-Drouot and walking along the boulevard Haussmann. She had a quick look inside the dance-hall: her friend was no longer there. She heard at the workshop the next day that all had gone perfectly well between Milena and her Frenchman who, far from being a pimp, worked as a technician for the Paris transport people. They were married the following year and were doubtless far happier than your mother and Frank Laurens ever were.

36

Sauntering down the place de l'Opéra feeling for her swimsuit in her bag, Dara wondered what she would do. She'd been told another dance-hall had opened behind the Olympia. She decided she would see how it looked. She made her way straight through the crowd with her energetic walk, pretending not to hear men propositioning her, which a few did. So it was in an entirely new venue — in fact half-empty that day — that the process began which would gradually transform the mischievous and fanciful young Croat, Dara Sevnica, into a soured *petite-bourgeoise* soon to be confined to the Paris suburbs.

In 1954 your father was a massive man. On first meeting him, one thought to oneself that he must dance a perfect tango. He wore dark blue or charcoal grey suits. He had a cream-coloured 4CV which he drove quite indifferently — even a touch clumsily. He'd married before the war and had a twenty-year-old daughter. Having started work in a factory at the age of fourteen, he'd by now begun to earn a good living and fully intended to make the most of the advantages it brought. He divided his spare time between dancing, women and football, of which he was a devoted fan. Another of his pleasures was stopping outside every restaurant and studying the menus when he was out walking on the Grands Boulevards or the Champs Élysées. He'd come back towards us calling out: 'The *chateaubriand au poivre* costs 300 francs here!' Or: 'A dozen *belon* oysters cost 690 francs. I'd rather open them myself and eat them at home. They cost me a third of the price and taste just as good!' And he'd assume an expression of barely controlled bliss at the thought of saving 400 francs each time he ate a dozen oysters. Then he would go off jauntily towards the next restaurant in sight. What else can I tell you? He generally expressed himself with a frivolity that I realised pretty quickly served to hide a complete lack of confidence in himself and his fellow human beings, a sort of constant fear of what might happen in life as well as in the course of a conversation.

37

The first thing your mother noticed when Frank Laurens came and invited her to dance was his height. Your father was as tall as any Yugoslav. One good mark to Frank Laurens. At the time many Frenchmen were short, no doubt due to the 39–45 war for the younger ones and to the 14–18 war for the older ones. They've grown a lot taller during the past thirty years, just when your mother was shrinking away. But in 1954 it was difficult for her to find a Frenchman of suitable height.

Laurens was an excellent dancer. He was elegant and supple; he had presence and a good sense of rhythm. Dara had immediately felt herself taken in hand. She let him lead her. Of course there was still the risk that he might be a pimp. But he didn't hold her too close and his French seemed ultimately refined to her. I used to swear a lot more!

As was invariably the case when she was about to sleep with a man, Dara fussed over me that evening while she told me all about her meeting with Frank Laurens: she gave me the precise number of waltzes and tangos they'd danced together; she described with great feeling the good quality cloth of your father's suit and was most insistent on the fact that he wasn't a pimp. He was on the managerial staff of a big Paris printer, the sort that still existed in those days. But she'd been quite incapable of recalling what they'd talked about! And for a perfectly straightforward reason: she hadn't been listening! For three hours, she'd done nothing but quiver, daydream, chatter, twitter and laugh. She didn't once bother to look at Laurens the least bit sharply. During the entire meeting she paid attention only to herself, scrutinising the rapid evolution of her feelings with avid curiosity. She pictured herself married to Laurens and both of them settled in a large flat in her beloved Latin Quarter. She also imagined your father taking her to America on the *Liberté*, which they in fact visited — in harbour — many months later. She thought she'd at last found the man who would release her from the profound weariness that had begun to weigh on her after ten years of a more than precarious way of life. But as to what Laurens thought, sought, wanted or concealed — as to that, Dara took not the slightest trouble to think.

He brought her back to rue de l'Éperon. I was lying on the bed reading. I heard a car door slam. I told myself it must be her. She thought it very distinguished to slam the door when she was getting out of a car. She always took great care to do it. Just as in the summer she liked letting the window down and having her arm dangle outside, bending her head so the wind mussed her hair.

When she reached the end of her story, it seemed to me that in her mind there were three things playing against Frank Laurens: first, he was married; next, he'd arranged a date only for the following week, one she was in fact determined not to turn up for; finally, he was sixteen years older than her and she really only felt at ease with people who were very young or who'd retained the vitality and easy-going approach to life of adolescence. But he held one decisive trump: at about five o'clock Dara, who was fatally clumsy when it came to anything closely or distantly related to crockery, had tipped her champagne all over Laurens' lap. 'It doesn't stain,' he'd said grimly. None the less, she felt guilty. She felt in some obscure way that she'd incurred a debt towards him. Through sheer force of circumstance, broken glasses, upset dishes and burnt kitchen cloths have always had an important place in your parents' life together.

Laurens called your mother the following day at M. Dved-nirović's workshop. He wanted to see her that very evening. She asked why he was suddenly in such a hurry. He answered that he'd been very happy the previous evening and felt he hadn't the strength to wait a week to be happy like that again. Dara suggested he come and pick her up from the hotel at about seven o'clock. As the very hot weather made her perspire a lot, she wanted to have a shower and a change of clothes before he saw her. 'I'm going to hang up because boss is making face,' she said.

That same day, I got back from the university in the late afternoon. I made myself a cup of tea, drank it, and then went to pay a short visit to the girl who was our neighbour on the right, a pleasant young chemistry student. I soon recognised Dara's step on the stairs. I was about to leave the girl to join Dara when I realised that Dara, who'd no doubt thrown her handbag on the bed and picked up a towel from the washstand, was striding towards the showers in the most determined way. And yet we hadn't planned to go out together that evening. Might she be going out with someone else? . . . Frank Laurens, maybe? Back from her shower, she rubbed her hair with the same energy she put into everything and declared that she wasn't simply going to spend the evening with Laurens — and looking forward to it — but he'd also be picking her up from rue de l'Éperon and she had every intention of inviting him to come up to the room so that the three of us could have a drink together. 'Like that, you'll tell me what you think,' she commented, calling me '*tou*', of course.

And what didn't I think on seeing his tall silhouette framed in the doorway! Dara offered him our only armchair. He asked: 'Do you think it's advisable?' 'Ha! Ha!' she said. But she quite clearly didn't understand what he was implying. He sat down, visibly pleased with his little witticism. Dara brought three glasses and the bottle of port. She fussed around him like a manicurist around her customer. He insisted on our clinking each other's glasses and said: 'Chin-chin!' He looked at me as if he thought he only needed to lift a finger for me to throw myself at his feet, and he treated me with the sort of deliberate friendliness you show towards a woman you instantly know will have no more than a derisory place in your life. I also guessed that, within that new social status he'd battled to achieve, he'd already cast Dara once and for all in the double role of spectator and decorative object. He stared at her with the same self-satisfied smile he must have had when he looked at himself in a mirror. You could feel that he saw her as bringing the finishing touch to a creation he'd been perfecting for a long time.

I'd be lying if I said he hadn't made her happy, at least for the first few months. He paid her a lot of attention. Once or twice a week, he went and picked her up in his car from M. Dvednirović's workshop. They'd go and have a drink at a café terrace on the Grands Boulevards. Laurens didn't like the Latin Quarter and, after some time, Dara only ever came back to the Left Bank to sleep. On Sundays they had alfresco lunches in the Bois de Boulogne or on the banks of the Marne. Because of their working-class backgrounds, they both felt as happy in any *guinguette* as in the best restaurant. Subsequently Dara found out that in fact Laurens liked only these outdoor café-cum-dance-halls: shyness, a disease that seems to worsen with age — contrary to what people think — played as much a part in this preference as his irritation at having to watch his manners. But in any case most of their time was spent on the dance floor. I once ventured out with them and got bored to death sitting alone at our table for hours on end. Tangos, cha-cha-chas, jive, waltzes, paso dobles: for them, anything would do!

Three weeks after they met, Frank gave your mother a pearl necklace, which she angrily refused to accept. He advised her to sell it and buy whatever she wanted with the money. She asked him if he took her for a tart. Mimicking her French he answered that he took her all the less for a '*poutain*' in that they hadn't yet made love together. So, was he holding that against her? No. He was in no hurry. Didn't he have a wife at home? Dara got up and left the Café de la Paix. Laurens quickly settled the bill and ran after her. He caught up with her outside the *métro* station. He asked her to forgive him. Did she want him to throw the necklace down a drain in order to prove he wasn't trying to 'buy' her? Dara shrugged her shoulders. No, of course she didn't want him to do that. That kind of behaviour was a crime against humanity, in any case, since the thing was worth about ten months' rent for us. So

Laurens took her by the arm and led her along rue de la Michodière where the 4CV was parked. I always laughed when I saw those two giants having to more or less fold themselves up to get in there! 'I've booked a table at the Auberge yougoslave,' said Laurens, putting the necklace around Dara's neck. Then he drove off. Your mother's comment, in her rolling French: 'I said to myself: Dara, old thing, you're for it. Tonight you're going to get the business.'

This pessimistic prediction turned out to be inaccurate. Dara and Laurens ate, drank and danced until dawn. To begin with they were the darlings of all the waiters, but they ended up by being a complete nuisance. When, at five-thirty in the morning, Laurens insisted on being brought blinis with pickled cucumbers, the answer came that the cook had gone to bed. 'Let's go,' said Dara who felt she'd slipped into the mantle of a Russian princess leaving a Saint Petersburg cabaret at dawn on the arm of a ruined gambler–prince. Laurens was brought the bill. He put on his spectacles and studied it carefully, which rather surprised Dara because five minutes earlier he'd seemed at the height of romantic exhilaration. He picked out an error and drew the head waiter's attention to it with obvious pleasure. While the cashier was being admonished, your father took Dara's hand, deposited a small kiss on it and said that, in life, one should never miss an opportunity to replace falsehood with truth. He left huge tips, I imagine to show that he hadn't had the bill put right out of tight-fistedness. In the 4CV, he kissed your mother at length on the mouth and then, clasping each other tightly, they fell asleep, exhausted.

They didn't make love until a week later, at Houlgate. It was a Saturday. They'd spent the afternoon on the beach. Dara swam three times. Laurens, who didn't dare admit he couldn't swim, used the excuse of four hours' driving to remain in his deck chair, reading and rereading the same home news in *France-Soir*. When Dara came back dripping wet to sit near him, he stroked her knees without looking up from his paper. She took off her swimming cap and shook her head vigorously, stretched out her legs and, with her eyes half-closed, let the sun tan her skin. Ten minutes later, as she was just as incapable of keeping quiet as of keeping still, she turned her face towards your father and suggested a game of *boules* or a walk along the water's edge. He preferred a game of *boules*. She discovered on that occasion that he was a bad loser. That made her laugh. He also got very annoyed each time he saw her picking up in her arms pretty much any child who got in their way.

At about six o'clock, they went back to the one-star hotel where, from Paris, Laurens had booked a room with bathroom for the weekend. In her lifetime Dara hadn't often had the chance to use a bath, so it was with great joy that she went about filling it and sliding into it. Laurens, leaning against the wall, watched quite impassively as she plunged her head in the water and produced great glugging sounds. She also amused herself by clapping her hands while keeping them half-submerged, which flooded a good part of the floor tiles. 'I should have bought you some little plastic boats,' commented Laurens. Before getting out of the bath, she asked him to turn around. He protested. But she wouldn't be swayed, whereas with a woman she would doubtless have had a lot of fun revealing her nakedness little by little. She would have lifted one leg out of the bath, screaming that it was slippery and she was afraid of falling over. She wouldn't have objected as the woman leant over to dry her small breasts and her muscular ex-gymnast's thighs. But she was paralysed by the fact that, like any man, Laurens represented a possible future for her.

They ate a supper of fish and shellfish sitting by the Channel. As usual, your father picked out an error in the bill, but he paid without mentioning it, telling himself that on an evening like this, it would be clumsy to make a scene for 300 francs. Even so, on the way back to the hotel, he couldn't stop himself cursing these restaurant owners who feel robbed if once in their lives they're forced to behave like honest people.

43

And that was without mentioning their totally casual attitude towards tax inspectors — the *fisc*. Your father, on the other hand, couldn't earn a single centime without the *ministère des Finances* immediately knowing about it. It impressed Dara enormously that the *ministère des Finances* should show so much interest in the money Laurens earned. Never in her life had she paid any taxes and she barely knew what it meant. As for the *fisc*, because of its resemblance with *flic*, the slang for policeman, she imagined it as some huge barracks where men in uniform sifted through the pay slips of the entire French nation — which, when it comes down to it, isn't very far from the truth.

In bed, Dara asked your father to be careful. He told her not to worry. So little did she worry that nine months later she gave birth to you in a clinic in a Paris suburb. As you know, after that birth she had recourse to back-street abortionists in France, and in Belgium and Switzerland too. Your father, who hated using sheaths, didn't 'hold himself back' as successfully as he imagined. As your mother put it: 'With age, brakes pack in.' On her side, she was quite extraordinarily fertile. She said: 'To get pregnant, only need look at flies.'

It was the following day that Laurens announced he was going to leave his wife. He no longer loved her. It was your mother he loved. So she snuggled up against him and suggested they go on an '*excoursion*'. She had a passion for '*excoursions*'. Laurens objected that they'd be spending some of that night on the road in order to reach Paris before the offices and factories opened, so it was perhaps better to spend a quiet day on Houlgate beach. Dara agreed, but she had such an urge to see Deauville. A terrific urge. 'A pregnant woman's urge,' she specified, not knowing how near the truth she was.

When they were on the *planches*, Laurens entrusted his Rolleiflex to a passer-by, asking him if he would take his and Dara's photograph. It's this photo here. A nice-looking couple, don't you think? Both in shorts. Dara is hanging on to your father's arm. It must be one of the few photos in which she is smiling quite unselfconsciously. She has the sun in her eyes, which gives her a thoughtful air. Her legs and arms are tanned. I gave her that white short-sleeved shirt. She's holding a beach bag in which there's probably a picnic. Another of her passions.

Dara turned up at our hotel reception desk at a quarter past seven on the Monday morning. She was surprised to see the key to our room hanging on the panel. It also saddened her a little. In Laurens' car she'd pictured with great pleasure her return to rue de l'Éperon, my surprise at her looking so well, and especially the heated account she would have given me of those two days in Normandy during which so many things of importance for her had occurred. As she was making her way sadly up the stairs, she wondered where I could be. She didn't immediately see the note I'd left on the table. She opened the wardrobe and realised my things had gone. Taken aback, she turned around and noticed there wasn't a single book on the bedside table. Only then did she find my letter and open it; in it I explained that to spend one more Sunday in Paris in this heat was more than I could stand, and that I'd decided to take refuge in Le Croisic where I had family. At that very moment, I was probably lolling about on the Brittany sands and I wished my dear friend much courage for the hard week of toil ahead of her. A hasty departure and a discreetly bitchy missive which I won't conceal from you were my double retaliation for her affair with Laurens and their lovers' weekend on the *côte fleurie*.

When I got back from Brittany about ten days later, Dara no longer lived at rue de l'Éperon. She was living in a furnished flat in Passy with Laurens. Their landlady was an old marchioness who inhabited a small room at the end of the corridor in which she'd assembled all her treasures: curios, paintings, family souvenirs and rare books. She shared the kitchen and bathroom with your parents. Laurens realised very quickly that while they were out, she helped herself quite brazenly to their coffee, but Dara appreciated the fact that at the beginning of each month, as soon as your father had paid the rent, she invited them to supper in her room and received them lavishly. No doubt this was a refined way she had of taking her revenge on these two rather common people who relegated her to a room that was barely the size of a linen cupboard. What I mean is that I don't believe she felt anything for your mother or Laurens. Besides, the rent she got from them was extortionate. But she'd had the good fortune to meet Laurens the day when, clutching a suitcase and 500,000 francs in cash, he'd just left his wife and needed for that very night somewhere to shelter his passion for Dara Sevnica. The one-time printer had liked the area and had guessed that Dara would like it too. And then it's very likely too that your father succumbed to the aristocratic charm of this old lady with her big feet. I only ever saw her once, but I remember her very clearly. She was at least head and shoulders taller than me. She held herself as straight as a horsewoman or a dancer. She had small blue eyes set deep down in their sockets, as if they wanted to hide and keep watch on you undisturbed. A short nose, a pinched mouth. For Laurens she was the archetypal aristocrat! And in fact she wasn't as old as all that. Fifty-five, sixty. I'm sure he wouldn't have needed much encouragement to have an affair with her. Perhaps he did have one.

I'm coming on to the so-called pea episode, that you must have already heard about from one or the other of your parents. It happened at the end of September. Dara had just realised she was pregnant. Laurens took the news very badly. He was being trapped! Nevertheless, ever chivalrous, he gave your mother the money she would have needed for an abortion — a way out which she very firmly rejected. To begin with, she was frightened. And anyway, she felt like having a baby. So that was how things stood, and if it didn't suit him, she was quite prepared to pack her case and go back to rue de l'Éperon. Laurens gave way, swearing to himself in some dark and foul recess of his mind that he would get his revenge. Of

46

course, when he held you in his arms for the first time, he understood that until the day he died you would be his only love. But late that September, he was in a very different frame of mind.

The evening of the peas, I'd got myself to bed after a stroll in the neighbourhood. As usual I was reading. There was a knock on the door. It was Dara. I asked her in. We kissed. I noticed she'd been crying. I asked her why. She told me it was 'because plate of peas tipped up'. She sat down on the bed and asked me for a cigarette. We smoked. I got out the bottle of port. We drank. That reminded Dara that as well as helping herself to their coffee, '*madame la marquise*' sipped the couple's wine on the quiet. This sent Laurens into furious rages. To begin with, he wouldn't believe it was going on, but on Dara's advice he'd discreetly drawn some marks on the bottles. There was no doubt about it. The worst thing was, there was nothing they could do about it. They didn't want to fall out with her. They enjoyed living in Passy too much. Or at least Frank did. As for her, apart from the 'all-mahogany' bedroom and the pleasure of saying to M. Dvednirović every evening, 'Right, I'm off back to *Passy*', she found the area pretty tedious. There wasn't a single nice café and the cinemas were three kilometres apart. Doing the shopping was 'a devil of a job'. 'Of course,' she said, 'people in area can't care less, they all got nice little maid!' She was talking fast, as ever. But now a bit faster even then usual. She smoked cigarette after cigarette. I asked: 'What about the garden peas?' What a business! That evening she was on her way back from near the Opéra where M. Dvednirović's workshop was. During the entire journey on the *métro*, she hadn't stopped asking herself the same question: 'What cook for Frank's supper?' Lamb chops with peas had seemed a good idea. She was already busying herself in the kitchen when Laurens appeared with the inevitable *France-Soir* tucked under his arm. He pointed out to her that the table wasn't set. Well, she retorted, it's quite simple: he only had to set it himself! What? What?

But his wife would never have talked to him like that. So your mother said that a), she wasn't his wife and b), Mme Laurens quite certainly didn't spend her days sewing in a workshop under the thumb of a degenerate Serb by the name of Dvednirović. Laurens clasped his head in both hands and shouted: 'For pity's sake, Dara, don't say another word to me about that Dvednirović!' In his place I'd probably have had the same reaction. 'If you only knew what he does to me again today!' said your mother. Rather than hear any more of this, Laurens had preferred to slip out into the dining room and set the table. Then he sat down, poured himself a glass of beer and opened his paper. 'I'm sorry,' Dara said a few seconds later as she leant over to give him his lamb chop and peas. 'I hate peas,' he said. 'Leave them then,' answered Dara, quite mortified. She settled down opposite him. He had put the paper down next to his plate and carried on reading as he was cutting up his meat. Dara asked if it was good. He didn't answer. He ate a few peas. 'They're not cooked,' he said as he unfolded his paper to turn the page. Your mother said: 'No matter, since you don't like them.' He picked at his peas once more and chewed on them sadly. And then all of a sudden he was in a terrible temper and said not only weren't they cooked, they were also absolutely disgusting. Never would his wife have dished him up such crap! What on earth had Dara cooked them in? Washing-up water? But no, she couldn't have done since she never bothered to do the washing-up. In what then? Was she going to tell him, yes or no? Dara was so upset by his hostile attitude and his crude language that she fought back her tears and, taking her courage in both hands, yelled in his face that he was 'a pain in the arse'. Leaping at the opportunity like a hyena on a dead zebra's carcass, he answered back: 'Well, sweetheart, you can cheer up: I shan't be for much longer!' As he got up, he tipped his plate over. He swore and left the room. Dara had been finding out over the past few days that he was at least as clumsy as her. Your mother heard the front door slam. At first she thought he was simply going to stretch his legs on the landing, or at worst out on the pavement. But after twenty minutes had passed and he still wasn't back, she realised he was going to spend the evening elsewhere. For a second, she wondered if she would pick the peas up from '*madame la marquise*'s' carpet. She vowed that she wouldn't, and then went out too, quite determined not to come back until Laurens had, even if it meant spending part of the night in the second-class waiting room at the gare de Lyon.

It was only some time later that Dara unravelled the whole story. It came about on one of those evenings when Laurens let his more benign side show through, and revealed to your mother, with much delight in his voice and kissing her with the eagerness and haste of a child who's been alone all day, all his little tricks and machinations. That evening in September 1954, there was a football match at Colombes. Who was playing who, I've absolutely no idea. Anyhow, this was a game your father was determined to watch. He'd already bought his ticket. He knew that even though she hated football, your mother would feel offended if he went out without her. Why wouldn't he have taken her with him? Ah, Brigitte, how little you know him! He was over-sensitive to the point of neurosis. It would have spoilt his pleasure to have Dara there by his side but not sharing his pleasure. And you know, his pleasure was quite simply sacrosanct. Before you were born, it was the only thing he lived for. So one way or another he'd had to find a way of being free at eight o'clock, and had preferred to spark off a domestic row rather than patiently embark on a conversation which I think after her exhausting day's work would in any case have resulted in Dara's unconditional surrender. You think it was cruelty that made him behave like this? I'm sure it wasn't. First, he wasn't so much afraid Dara would take advantage of him, but that while talking it over, he himself would weaken, he would fall victim to his own kind-heartedness and give up the football in order to stay near his nice little Slav that the Commies had

49

already given such a bad time to. And then, it exasperated him that he couldn't spend his time freely in whatever way he chose when there was no official document to make him account to Dara Sevnica for his comings and goings. After all, they weren't married. And so, at the age of forty-six, he'd taken the trouble to leave his wife and daughter, he'd installed his mistress in a flat that cost him an arm and a leg, he spent each day working like a black, and his sole reward was coming home in the evening to find the table wasn't set and eating what had been prepared for him by the worst cook in the whole of Western Croatia and, on top of all that, when he ventured to feel like spending two hours at a football match, he couldn't even talk about it openly! It really was enough to put you in a temper, wasn't it?

Dara was looking out into our street. She asked me, almost shyly: 'Can I open window?' The times she'd asked me that, the previous winter! Whenever she was about, whatever the outside temperature, there had to be fresh air. And if I was freezing cold? Oh what a fuss! I only had to put on a jumper! For a moment, I felt moved by the thought of those endless and sometimes slightly hysterical conversations we'd had in front of that window — a window Dara would no longer get up in the night to open surreptitiously. There were many other things she wouldn't be doing again, such as placing a chair on the table and sitting on it to sew nearer the light, or preparing enough tomato soup to last eight days and upsetting it even before we'd swallowed a single spoonful. 'Can you hear the sound of it, *my* Latin Quarter?' she asked, leaning with her elbows on the window ledge. She didn't yet know she would never be coming back to live there. After you were born, Laurens took her straight from Passy to Bagnolet and you know as well as me she never budged from there until her death.

It was nearly midnight. I told Dara I wanted to sleep because I had an early lecture the next morning. I added she could sleep here. It wouldn't bother me. We were used to it, weren't we? She smiled. When I brushed my lips against hers, she blushed but didn't turn her face away. When I drew her to me though, I felt her resisting. 'Doesn't matter,' I said, kissing her once again on the mouth. I undressed, got into bed and turned out the light while Dara, who'd pushed the armchair in front of the window and settled down in it, smoked a cigarette. I could imagine she was thinking about those ten years she'd spent in the Latin Quarter. Her Yugoslav friends had gradually scattered all over the world. They sometimes sent her postcards. She told me about them. Gavrilo, a former officer, was working as a mechanic in London. Miroslav had opened a bar in Frankfurt. Nikola had married a lot of money. 'It's only natural,' Dara commented, saying '*natourel*', 'he had the looks of a god.' But in their different parts of the world, they all remembered the generous, impetuous Dara Sevnica whom they'd seen turn up in Paris one evening in May 1946 with her swimmer's build and her long black hair, a girl who'd just as readily have gone into a swoon at the sight of the majestic façade of the Palace of Versailles as at the news-stands on the place de l'Odéon.

When your mother got into bed beside me, I understood from the slight tingling in my mouth that she'd just woken me up. She asked if I was asleep. Snuggling up against her, I said I wasn't. So she began drawing up a bewildering list of all the qualities she considered Frank Laurens was endowed with: he never hung around in bars drinking *apéritifs* with his colleagues; he'd had the courage to leave a wife he'd been living with for over twenty years in order to start from scratch with a Yugoslav political refugee about whom he knew nothing; he dressed with immaculate good taste; he was intelligent and '*coultivé*'; he took her to '*bonnes restaurants*' and above all, he made a fantastic partner on the dance floor. Aside from that of course, he did have a few sizeable shortcomings. But in the end, if you weighed it all up, he was, despite everything, an exceptional man who provided a change from the 'eternal *étoudiants*' and the men who pretended they were big-time

51

industrialists that she'd so far had to make do with. Having heard a speech like that one, it came as no surprise the next morning to find that I was alone in bed. Dara had got on the first *métro* to join Laurens in Passy. Her night-time view of the rue de l'Éperon had inspired her to reflect on her future just as much as on her past!

I didn't hear from her for a number of days. Intrigued, perhaps a bit worried too, I phoned Passy. Laurens answered. He indulged in his usual game of flirting, asking me reproachfully why it was they never saw me. 'You only have to invite me over more often,' said I. But, look here, didn't I know I had a standing invitation! He laughed emphatically when I retorted that this hadn't fallen on deaf ears and in future they could set a place for me at every meal. And then I asked to speak to Dara. 'You two are going to say nasty things about me again!' he remarked, sounding far more worried than he thought he was letting on. 'You're not our only topic of conversation,' I said. I reminded him that Dara and I had lived together for eight months before that fateful July day when she'd had the misfortune to meet him! He again laughed that little forced and slightly feeble laugh I'd found difficult to stand from the moment I first heard it. Then he said it would have delighted him to hand the phone over to Dara. But hard luck, she was having a bath. Could I call back later? Or then Dara would call me back. It was just as I liked.

I waited for half an hour, three quarters of an hour, an hour. I heard nothing. So I dialled the number once more. And again it was Laurens who answered. He said I was right on cue. Dara was just finishing dressing and was about to phone me. I didn't believe a word of all this. Whether it was in cahoots with Laurens or under his influence, or even against his wishes, Dara had decided not to call me back. I got the feeling she was about to drive me out of her life. Why? What had I done? Had I at any moment got in the way of her plans or jeopardised any chances she may have had? It seemed to me she'd never had to live through any of those neurotic fits of

jealousy that so often plague homosexual relationships. I'd
never compelled her to do anything in bed, and when we were
out I was always careful not to take advantage of the slightest
opportunity of touching her arm or putting my hand on her
shoulder — so much so, in fact, that, accustomed like all Slavs
never to go walking with a girlfriend without hanging on to
her arm, Dara would end up asking me what the matter was
with me, keeping such a distance from her. And I had been
more than obliging, too, towards her successive lovers! Once I
had even left our room to your mother and a massive Montenegrin for the whole night — a night neither of them ever
had the curiosity to ask where I'd spent! No, really, I could see
no reason to be repudiated in this way. . . . Anyhow, perhaps I
was giving in to the panic that grips you when a seductive
stranger is prowling around the person you love, and all the
more so when he's already laid a hand on her! So well had I
managed to reassure myself in those few seconds that it came
as a shock when I heard Dara's aloof tone of voice and
realised how ill at ease she sounded as she delivered a string of
curt little sentences that I could definitely sense left no space
for me. She was very pleased to speak to me 'on phone', but
unfortunately she couldn't stay long since she and Frank were
going to the races at Longchamp. She asked me to excuse her
for a minute because Frank was saying something to her. I
heard him suggest she invite me to join them. There was a
silence. 'Frank says you come with us,' she said with an
arrogance and coolness that froze me on the spot. Obviously I
refused. I hung up, stepped out of the phone booth and paid
for the coffee and bread and butter I'd consumed during that
dreadful late morning, pushed open the doors of the café and
found myself standing bewildered on the boulevard Saint-
Germain. Alone there on the pavement, wrapped up as if in
an old, worn-out scarf in the drabness of that grey September
Sunday, I experienced a moment of deep heartache.

Yes, Brigitte, it was that day that your mother left me,
rather than the day she threw her arms around your father's

53

neck and told him perhaps she was in love with him, or even the night they conceived you on an uncomfortable little Breton bed. In the years that followed and until our final falling-out which, as you know, took place in the summer of 1965, I saw her about once or twice a month. We'd have lunch or tea together. Our conversations were perfectly friendly, but if I made anything resembling a specific allusion to our past, Dara would dart me a threatening look. Quite obviously she no longer wanted to hear it mentioned. That's why I was never able to find out why after the scene over the peas, the night she spent in our old room and her return to Passy, she put up between us that impregnable barrier which changed us overnight from intimate friends into vague acquaintances. Of course the explanation that would suit me best is that, unable to see any possible social outcome to her liking for me, she preferred to put a brutal end to our relationship rather than draw out an ambiguous situation which might have jeopardised her relationship with Laurens. Aware of her own cowardice and of the hurt she was inflicting on me, she'd chosen not to see me for a while and thus to avoid exposing herself to any feelings of remorse she might come to have. Later she was to contrive to see me without really seeing me, that is, she placed between us a screen of politeness and frivolity, and this was another way for her to evade a sense of guilt.

Still, I must tell you the end of the peas episode. Even though it was very late, your mother was the first to get home. She got herself to bed. Five minutes later, Laurens arrived. She heard him go into the dining room. And then nothing. Silence! Your father was on all fours under the table picking up the peas one by one!

A few months after your birth, Laurens decided to move. The Passy flat was both too expensive and too inconvenient. On top of that, the owner's kleptomania was going from bad to worse with each day that passed. *Madame la marquise* was now raiding your nappies! 'You can only wonder what for!'

Dara remarked. Perhaps, I said, she was fed up with seeing them drying in her precious bathroom. In fact if the *marquise* didn't have much time for children, she couldn't stand babies. This feeling, that Dara found quite inexplicable, soon changed her in the couple's private mythology into some malevolent creature one had to do everything to avoid coming into contact with — a creature with which there was a pressing need to have nothing further in common.

Laurens looked for a flat to rent in Paris. He found one for sale in the suburbs. Since his wife was refusing to divorce him, he simply had to make Dara a present of this flat. After all, she was his second child's mother! In case anything happened, she at least had to have a roof under which to shelter with you. One Saturday in mid-October, he drove you both to Bagnolet and, while you bawled energetically in your cot, your parents visited the three minute rooms in which Dara was to spend the rest of her days. They seemed huge to her, compared with the succession of tiny corridors that constituted the Passy flat. She'd also very much liked the view. Of course, it wasn't very central. But then Passy wasn't either when you thought about it! The building was decent looking. There was a lift. The only thing that upset her a bit was the address. Bagnolet definitely didn't sound as good as Passy. But she immediately reproached herself for being snobbish.

Your father had quite his own way of giving presents. He would hold out the parcel carelessly as if he'd been giving someone a light. He didn't much like being kissed thank-you. He said over and over: 'It's nothing, it's nothing . . . .' Then, as the days passed, he showed more and more interest in the present he'd given. If it were a pair of gloves, he complained he could detect a spot on them, which with Dara was very often true. He also asked your mother to open her jewellery case to check that none of what he'd given to her had been lost. Eventually the moment came when he resented you for all the presents he'd given you. It was mostly during quarrels that this grudging attitude became apparent. An example:

'When I see the way you treat me, I say to myself I should have bought that camelhair coat I was so tempted by rather than treated you to those crocodile-skin shoes you never even wear!' After which, by the way, it wasn't uncommon for Dara to throw the aforementioned shoes in his face! Well, it was in pretty much the same way that he behaved over the Bagnolet flat. One evening as he was opening his newspaper, he told Dara he'd decided to buy it for her. He spelled out his reasons rather curtly. She threw herself in his arms. He gently pushed her away and asked her what she'd made for supper. The next day he took her to a solicitor. They moved in a month later. Laurens had left the task of choosing the furniture and wall-paper entirely in her hands. He didn't much like her choice. One day, when the housework hadn't been done, he muttered that it wasn't worth giving a flat to people who only enjoyed living in a pig-sty. And from one year to the next his attitude worsened, to the point where those three little rooms became a running sore in your parents' life together.

Until that afternoon in August 1965 when, in the garden of my house at Le Croisic, everything between Dara and me was finally shattered, I was able to witness the gradual change in your mother, and this I did with a curiosity that was tinged with a little sadness. But we also had some good laughs, like the time Dara told the story of how Laurens had nearly got himself done over by two motorists one day when, in the pouring rain, he'd calmly sat watching his mistress change a tyre on the 4 CV. Our conversations were far more painful when she talked about her abortions which nearly always ended up in hospital with a curettage. One of them that had gone particularly badly was, I may add, the work of a Croatian back-street doctor.

Despite everything, the great event of Dara's adult life definitely was this change from being a spinster living in a hotel to becoming the owner of a flat and mother of a French child. She got Laurens to take a photograph of her with you in the dining room and sent it to Yugoslavia. She was extremely proud to be able to announce to me in mid-May that Laurens had already booked a room in an hotel in Plestin-les-Grèves for the month of August. He also took her on a skiing holiday. He had first seen the sea at the age of thirteen and had never been anywhere near a pair of skis before he was in his forties; now he quietly stayed in the hotel playing cards or doing the crosswords in *France-Soir*, while your mother took you off on long walks around the ski-trails. She often didn't come back till late. She loved the moment when the chair-lifts stopped functioning. Silence descended on the fir trees and she let herself be carried away in a daydream that invariably took her back fifteen or twenty years to the time when she was a beautiful, romantic young girl that boys had to fight over every Sunday, for that was the only way they could settle which one of them would take her to the skating rink or to Sljeme. She hadn't once been up into the mountains since leaving Yugoslavia. To hear once again the sound of snow crunching underfoot, to sink thigh-deep in powder snow, to take in the view of a deliciously pure landscape, one that seemed scrubbed clean by the cold, all this gave rise to such emotions in her that by the time she got back to the hotel, her eyes were often filled with tears.

In the Laurens family she was thought of as a pleasant eccentric. She towered above the women, as she was ten or more centimetres taller than any of them. Of course she had immediately offered to make dresses for them for nothing. She treated the men in the exuberant and relaxed manner that, coming from her, was a sign of a kind of indifference. They could always rely on her to liven up the atmosphere at Christmas or New Year's Eve celebrations or birthdays. When a quarrel broke out between two members of the family over dinner, they nearly always had recourse to her good offices to patch things up. But in fact, when two people did quarrel at table, it was frequently Laurens and her. The women admired the way she stood up to the family's only awkward character, and she delighted everyone whenever she fired off at Laurens remarks like: 'When you don't know how to change car tyre, you don't go about playing he-man!' It was rare with her that Laurens had the last word. His favourite conclusion to scenes of this sort was: 'Ah, these Slavs, they're really too much to swallow!'

The permanently aggressive attitude they had towards one another was to worsen with time, and when I had them to Le Croisic, it had reached proportions that were difficult to stand for anyone who wasn't familiar with the innumerable conflicts through which it expressed itself. By now Dara was blonde. I've always thought the way your mother lightened her hair must have presented you with a serious psychological problem. She'd put on weight, which suited her. She'd taken to speaking loudly like people who live near an airport or work in a market. She was wearing a summer dress that was a bit too long for her.

We fell into each other's arms. Then I shook hands with Laurens and bent down to kiss you on the cheeks. I hadn't seen you for three or four years. You made a bad impression on me. You had a nice bright complexion but you looked a little sly. When you were sitting down, you didn't stop crossing and uncrossing your legs, as if you'd been constantly wondering which position made you most look like a grown-up. When the cat came and sniffed your shoes, you moved your feet away. Not in the least discouraged, he jumped up on your lap where, after a cursory wash, he fell asleep. I had to explain to you that there wasn't a chance in a million that he'd let himself go and pee on you — the fear you'd so stupidly expressed.

We set up the table in the middle of the garden. I can't remember what we ate. Melon, I expect. In summer when we eat outside, it's often melon. Laurens made various compliments to me about 'Pen Avel'. He kept glancing at the house in the gloomy way of someone who will never be a house owner. When we reached the dessert he was unable to contain himself any longer, and he asked me how much this 'little

Versailles' had cost me. 'Not a penny,' I said. I explained that I'd inherited it. He nodded his head and gulped down the last piece of the orange he was eating. Dara said I was lucky and I should 'thank Lord'. But after all, she added, the pleasant thing about staying in a hotel was that you escaped from all the chores. One month of the year spent doing absolutely nothing was hardly unwelcome!

The conversation went on like this until the middle of the afternoon. Gradually I was warming to you, mainly because of the bored and ill-at-ease expression you were wearing. How I shared your feelings! It created a bond between us!

It was, you might remember, a brilliant August day. After lunch, we went for a walk around the harbour. Your father was holding your hand. Your hair was far more blonde than now and you had on a frightful yellow nylon shirt with a pleated skirt. Despite Dara's objections, Laurens treated you to a huge ice cream. After three licks you no longer wanted it. 'Throw it away,' he said. 'I warned you!' Dara barked. 'She's not hungry any more, the little one!' Quite unruffled, Laurens took your hand again and led you off towards a trawler which was just leaving port. 'She's rotten, that kid,' Dara remarked. I asked why. 'Too spoilt,' she said. I couldn't stop myself saying that at any rate she wasn't spoilt as far as her shirts went. 'I dress my daughter badly, is that it?' retorted Dara. I thought she mut have been aware of the fact or she wouldn't have been so touchy. Sensing this, I was thinking of talking about something else, but I don't know why, perhaps because it upset me too much to see you parcelled up in that fabric that to my mind represents the worst of what we've produced in the textile industry since the creation of the first spinning-mill, rather than simply say I didn't like yellow or on such a beautiful summer's afternoon, you could have come to me in shorts and a top, I triggered the process that would, within three hours, bring about the final rift between Dara and me. The memory of that scene has remained so vivid that last week I was in two minds about attending the funeral. Yes,

I was! Are you surprised? But you know, there's nothing to show that your mother would have come to mine. I fear we were both as prone as each other to bearing endless grudges!

It happened in a number of stages. The first was the strained conversation I had with Dara about the way she dressed you. Her main argument was that I didn't know a thing about it, given that I hadn't even taken the trouble of bringing a child into the world. Things got calmer when we got back to the house. But well aware that I was far from convinced by what she was saying and because in any case she wasn't much more convinced herself, Dara carried on being jumpy and irritable. She started to take it out on Laurens. He reacted with a petulance that she probably wasn't expecting. I saw her turn a little pale as he flung a few home truths at her that he seemed to have been keeping bottled up for a good while. Your mother had launched her attack unpremeditatedly, more out of sheer exasperation with herself, and for one moment she seemed stunned, or even one might have said, overcome by an immeasurably deep sadness. Then she regained her composure and, not knowing how to react to a provocation by any means other than a greater provocation — in my view a specifically Slav trait of character — she launched herself mind and body into a row which soon turned into an orchestrated scene of frantic lunacy. You looked on with quite open distaste. I was thinking of that world of feelings that was forming in your young girl's heart and which, with their present behaviour, your parents were ransacking and trampling down. I could foresee, and I don't think I was so mistaken, that your relations with people would be if not jeopardised for ever, at least made dangerously complicated thanks to the continuous rows which Dara and Laurens forced you to witness.

A ring on the doorbell interrupted this bout of marital all-in wrestling. I wasn't expecting anyone and was as surprised as everyone else when I opened the door and Annie V. kissed me on both cheeks and walked into the living room. She was a red-haired girl of average height who was spending her holiday in La Baule-les-Pins. I'd met her a couple of weeks earlier in Le Pouliguen. It was about ten o'clock at night. She was queuing outside a confectioner's shop. So was I. As we were chatting, we discovered we shared the same irrational passion for nougat. I brought her home and after we'd set our sweets down on the bedside table, we made love. She was about twenty-five. On the skinny side. She was single, very active, belligerent even, and wondering as you might be what direction she should give to her life. For her I represented a kind of beacon. But I was afraid of directing her along the wrong path and that she might find herself stranded at my feet.

Annie's arrival provided fresh ammunition. It seemed to me Dara couldn't understand how at my age I could still have love affairs. As for Laurens, he was circling around my girl-friend as if she'd been a pot of fresh honey. We started up a conversation that soon veered towards various subjects of a political nature. Annie expressed opinions that shocked your mother. 'She doesn't know what she's talking about!' she exclaimed. Trying to be conciliatory, I told Annie that Dara had had to leave Yugoslavia clandestinely in May 1945. 'And I wasn't the only one!' your mother added. Annie retorted that nor was Pétain the only one to take the road to Sig-maringen in 1944. Dara barely knew who Pétain was and she'd have been hard pushed to say whether Sigmaringen was the name of a country, a region, a town or a type of *saucisson*, but she understood that Annie's comment was rude towards her — a feeling I shared. I made the point that the Yugoslavs who'd fled Tito's régime were not all dedicated Nazis, far from it. '*Moi, je ne veux pas qu'on me toutoie . . .*' Dara added, 'I don't want to be addressed as *tu* or called comrade by someone I don't even know!' Annie said that servants were addressed as *vous* and some dog owners called their animals '*Monsieur*', a bitchy comment that went way over Dara's head but that Laurens recognised for what it was, that's to say an insult. He got up and asked Annie who she thought she was. Things were starting to get sticky. In fact I think Annie was exasperated at not having found me alone. She was the kind of girl who always had secrets to confide. In addition she was letting me know quite clearly by means of various gestures and mimicries that she found it absolutely ludicrous that I should be spending time with two people who showed every sign of belonging to the most obtuse and killingly boring *petite bourgeoisie*!

Things then turned sour pretty fast. Laurens said he wasn't about to be taught anything by some female who was still a student at the age of twenty-five when he'd first crossed the factory gates in 1922. When I rose to Annie's defence and pointed out that it wasn't because someone didn't belong to the working class that they were intereted in Literature with a capital 'L' and nothing else, Dara turned on me with a viciousness that seemed to me to spring from far further back than the present quarrel. After eleven years of indifference towards me, was she perhaps succumbing to her first fit of jealousy? She said: 'If you're communist, why didn't you turn down inheritance?' She then went on in ironic vein about the 'rich' who 'had fun playing politics'. She invited Annie and me to go and have a look at what was going on 'behind Iron Curtain'. She got really angry when Annie said that if she hated communists so much, she should have stayed in Yugoslavia to fight them instead of coming to swell the already large ranks of French proletarians who took the side of the bosses in any workers' struggle. We had enough 'scabs' here as it was! Dara pounced out of her chair and declared in a quavering voice that she'd never have imagined that anyone in France might one day say such things to her. She had nothing further to do in this house. She told you to go and get your jacket. You replied that you had it on your lap. She took you by the hand and walked towards the door. Bewildered, unable to believe what was happening, Laurens looked at the four of us in turn. He was one of those men who, due to a very masculine mix of laziness and cowardice, easily get into arguments while rarely getting angry. I felt he was inwardly pleading with me to patch all this up. Why didn't I? Well, I think I had just become aware that I no longer liked your mother *at all*. Too blonde and too dumb. Seeing her near the door gave rise in me to a pleasure that only half an hour earlier, I couldn't have dreamt would have been so great. I could sense the kind of deep distress that Dara's aggression covered up and I thought I could more or less understand what your mother had been trying to get across to me through the maze of that afternoon, but for reasons which at bottom were no more impressive, I now wished to strike her out of my life. Between the two of us we'd managed to wreck too much. It had just hit me, and I wanted never to see it again.

As for this Aunt Nathalie you started by asking me about, I never knew her personally, although at the beginning of my affair with Dara, I heard your mother talking about her to a Serb who left a few months later to settle in Argentina. He was a Četnik officer, I believe. To some he was known as 'commandant' and to others as Milŏs. Milŏs Nikšić. I remember the name because Dara once spent an entire evening teaching me to say it properly.

3

On the tenth of April 1957, a man of sixty-eight sat eating supper on the terrace of a restaurant in Buenos Aires, a grey, indifferent city where you step on a war criminal's toes at least once a day. Having swallowed the last mouthful of his chachlik, the man let out a small belch and moved his huge ears about in a satisfied way. After this, he raised one of his shaky, parchment-like hands. The waiter came and cleared away his plate and cutlery. 'Shall I bring you a pistachio ice cream?' he asked. Because he was busy pouring himself a glass of that Croatian red wine we call *frankovka*, the man didn't hear the question, but he showed no surprise whatsoever when, a few minutes later, a rather heavy glass cup in which two greenish balls were swimming was placed under his nose. He put his head down and began eating voraciously and so noisily that one of the customers on the terrace turned around and called out: 'Hush!' The old man lifted his head. His mouth was covered in ice cream. From behind his thick grey eyebrows, he swathed his neighbour in his clouded gaze: the gaze of someone who hasn't had any real rest for a long time.

It was one of those humid and stifling evenings that are typical of the late summer here. The man finished his ice cream, paid for his meal and got on a bus which took him to Palomaro, a place in the Buenos Aires suburbs. He lived there under the name of Pablo Aranjos, at number 643 Jean Mermoz Street, with his wife and two daughters.

He walked slowly along the muddy paths of the garden city. Many windows in the surrounding blocks of flats were open and poured out waves of popular music on to Jean Mermoz Street. Aranjos took off his flannel jacket, an old one he'd bought in Milan immediately after the war and that was

64

a bit hot for the southern hemisphere. He rolled up his shirt sleeves. He could hear the reassuring sound of his two body-guards' footsteps about ten metres behind him. When the first shot rang out, he thought it was a car back-firing. This was always happening here at home at that time. We had a shortage of good mechanics. With the second shot, he became panic-stricken and started trotting along as fast as he could. He was an obtuse and slightly hysterical Zagorah, you know, a spineless little Croat totally lacking in physical courage. With the third and fourth shots, he felt as if two arrows had passed within a hair's breadth of his face. He dropped his jacket on the ground in order to run more easily. A few seconds later, he got a proper blow in the back and knew he'd been hit. Furious and humiliated, he turned around, ready to insult the two blond giants responsible for protecting him, but all he saw was a tall, slim man who was pointing the barrel of his revolver at him. '*Zašto?*' whined Aranjos. '*Nisam kriv!*' The man with the revolver wore an elegant white suit and a boater. On the third finger of his right hand he had a gold signet ring, and Aranjos, whom fear had sent into a state of virtual hallucination, was convinced that this was none other than Marshal Tito come specially to Latin America to execute him. '*Hrvat si, kao ja!*' he yelled. The man nodded his head sadly and fired a sixth shot, hitting Aranjos right in the chest. Then he disappeared into the night.

Reappearing as if by magic, the two blond giants carried the wounded man to his flat. They called a doctor whose advice was that Aranjos be taken to the Syrian–Lebanese hospital. There it was realised that the engineer Pablo Aranjos, building contractor, was in fact the Poglavnik of Croatia who, officially, had never entered Argentina.

Yes, Miss Laurens, that old slightly stooped man, as Croats often are beyond a certain age, that seemingly inoffensive devotee of chachlik and pistachio ice cream, was none other than Ante Pavelić, founder of the fascist organisation Ustaše and former leader of the Independent State of Croatia, a state so independent that it had been created by a decree of the Wehrmacht general staff on 12 April 1941. Pavelić will remain in people's memories on a number of scores and in particular as the inventor of children's concentration camps: at Sisak, 3055 little Jews and Serbs were exterminated. He was, in other respects, an exemplary Catholic. Which confirms my idea that from time immemorial more acts of horror have been perpetrated in the name of God than in the name of the Devil.

I must say, I do hold it against the UDBA agent or dissident Ustaša who fired six shots at the Poglavnik, that he only managed to lay him up in bed for eight days. It was only two and a half years later that Pavelić died, in the German hospital in Madrid. I may add that the clumsy Palomaro gunman — who had the good taste to preserve his anonymity — conforms to a long Yugoslav tradition of failed assassination attempts. A tradition started by a certain Žerajić, one of the founder members of the Bosnian Youth League. He had decided to kill Emperor Franz Joseph when the latter visited Mostar on 3 June 1910. In his pocket he carried a loaded revolver. He was very close to the emperor, but he did not pull out his revolver and shoot the little man whose face might have reminded him of a poodle if only he'd known what a poodle was. Very angry with himself, he rushed to Sarajevo and, following the opening of the Sabor, fired five shots at General Varešanin, the governor of the two provinces. He committed suicide with the sixth bullet in the belief that his assassination attempt had been successful. Sadly this was not the case. The governor didn't even have a scratch! He ordered his driver to stop the car and ran back to the bridge where Žerajić lay dying. Blood ran from the youth's mouth. This brought forth not the slightest hint of pity in Varešanin, who smothered him with insults as if the dying man were still in a fit state to answer back and kicked him in the ribs, which is never pleasant even when one is dying. Ha! Ha!

Žerajić had his followers. On 8 June 1912 in Zagreb, a

Bosnian student fired on the royal commissioner of Croatia. He missed him but hit in the neck a member of the government who was in the car. Three months later, another student climbed up a telegraph pole which stood opposite the same royal commissioner's residence, and when the latter appeared at the window, fired. He missed, of course! Following Žerajić's example, he committed suicide. It seems quite clear that to commit suicide with a firearm, one need not be an excellent shot.

As for the Sarajevo assassination attempt, it was long blamed for having caused the First World War, whereas in fact it merely served as a pawn in the hands of the various warmongers concerned, and its involuntary and unhoped-for political outcome was the dismantling of three violently oppressive empires: the Austro–Hungarian, Russian and Ottoman empires. But in fact it required all the carelessness and stupidity of the Sarajevo police for Gavrilo Princip to succeed in carrying it out at all. It is indeed a tale of complete and utter incompetence. During the Balkan wars of 1912–13, Princip hadn't managed to get into the Serbian army. Too short. His accomplice, Čabrinović, was tubercular. As for Gabrež, the third man, he was the son of an Orthodox priest and wet his bed. Well, it was these three men — the dwarf, the sickly fellow, and their incontinent comrade — these three dreamers who were more readily moved by books than by weapons, who had renounced women and alcohol through idealism and who were not yet in their twentieth year who, on the morning of 28 June 1914, in the capital of Bosnia–Herzegovina, were to assassinate Archduke Franz Ferdinand, heir apparent to the throne of Austro–Hungary, and Countess Chotek, his morganatic wife. It wouldn't be easy. When the seven cars of the official procession reached the Appel embankment, Čabrinović asked a police officer: 'In which car is His Majesty travelling?' — 'In the third one,' came the kind answer — the police officer was a fat Hungarian who was probably thinking about the chicken paprika his wife was getting ready for him. Čabrinović moved a few steps away, took out the bomb from his belt and struck the detonator against the streetlamp. He couldn't wait for twelve seconds as he had been advised in Belgrade which had supplied the requisite logistical support, because then the car would have been too far away. He threw the bomb towards the green feathers adorning the archduke's hat. It landed on the folded roof of the car, fell on the road and exploded under the next car, wounding about ten people. The archduke was unhurt. There followed the arrest of Čabrinović who had had the time to swallow a tablet of bad cyanide, jump in the river and shout out just as he was being safely fished out: 'I am a Serbian hero!' The procession returned to the town hall. Franz Ferdinand was furious. This great hunter of stag and chamois was not accustomed to being the prey. He wished to go to the military hospital to see one of his wounded officers. After what had just occurred, it was decided not to go along Franz Joseph Street for it was deemed too narrow and dangerous. They would speed along the Appel Embankment as far as the hospital. Everyone congratulated themselves on this fresh security measure. And amid the general euphoria, no one thought of informing the archduke's driver. This oversight was to prove fatal to Ferdinand. The driver would follow the first two cars which it had been agreed would keep to the original itinerary. He thus turned into Franz Joseph Street. Governor Potiorek, realising the mistake that was being made, shouted out to him to stop and reverse. The driver stopped. Right in front of Princip. Princip didn't take aim. He even turned his face aside as he fired two shots before the crowd and the police came and lynched him. In the car, Ferdinand and Countess Chotek went into a coma they would never come out of. Miss Laurens, Yugoslavia was born on that day. She was conceived in crime by three chaste youths who couldn't stop sweating with fear. Ideal conditions for producing an abnormal child, wouldn't you agree?

But I can imagine that you've not crossed the Atlantic

Ocean or passed through the Tropic of Capricorn to hear an old Serbian officer harping on about his country's history. So you want to know who Aunt Nathalie was, and perhaps for you this is another way of asking me who your mother was. Even so, let me add that for me Princip's action is a symbol of the disorderly, clumsy and savage passion we have for freedom. This passion, as you can see, brought me as far as this, to Buenos Aires, thousands of kilometres from Arandjenovac where I was born, in Serbia.

I occasionally wonder how I've managed to live for nearly forty years so far from Europe and so close to Uruguay. I could have stayed in France where, like many young middle-class Serbs, I did my secondary schooling, and whose language I speak fluently. But Europe was a drab, faltering place at the time. You lived on top of one another, three in a hotel room, and you still had to have ration cards to buy a hundred grams of meat. I had just left behind me four years of fighting, and I wanted lots of space and steaks the size of my hand. I also found it pretty disgusting that Europeans considered us Četniks as traitors whereas we'd been among the first occupied people to 'go into the forest' or, as you say in France, to take to the *maquis* and to mount terrorist actions against the Germans. In any event, I had no way of knowing where Stalin would stop, had I? I preferred to put the Equator between us. I was like your mother: I had no desire for people with whom I hadn't reared pigs — which, in case you don't know of it, is a national tradition — to call me 'comrade'.

I feel that you dislike Buenos Aires just as I felt in the past that Dara would dislike it. She wouldn't have been able to stand the acute heat that seizes you around the throat six months out of every twelve. The streets are too long, they have too many house numbers. Zagreb, as you know, is a circular and intimate city. In any case, this agglomeration built right next to a desert was the opposite of what would have suited Dara, who liked above all to have space to *turn around*.

A few weeks after the beginning of our liaison, she told me in detail the story of how she had arrived in Paris one evening in May 1946. She was wearing an English Red Cross uniform that she'd bought on the black market in Italy and that had enabled her to cross the border without showing her papers — papers she would in fact have been hard pushed to take out of her bag, since they didn't exist. She was expecting that the station in Paris — and she absolutely couldn't understand why some travellers insisted on calling it the '*gare de Lyon*' — would lead straight on to the Champs Elysées, just as Zagreb station leads on to the line formed by Tomislav, Strossmayer and Zrinsky Squares. Terrified by the huge, shapeless black mass that Paris appeared that evening, a Paris that seemed to have despatched all its night spots to the United States in exchange for some scanty supplies of food, she stepped into the first hotel she came across. She didn't want to spend a minute longer on that dark pavement with her cardboard suitcase and her high-heeled shoes that were a little too high for a lady from the Red Cross. 'Me foreign,' she said to the receptionist, and would say no more in answer to his question about whether she wanted a room with or without a bath-room. He led her up to a cramped room on the top floor which had no doubt housed some of the staff before the war. Dara found the place positively luxurious and wished she'd enquired about the price. For a moment she wondered whether she shouldn't go back to the receptionist on the ground floor to check, and if it were too expensive for her small purse, go off looking for a more modest place. But what the devil, she had just arrived in *Paris*! She could afford to treat herself!

The first thing she did when she found herself alone in her room was, as you'll have guessed, to open the window. She breathed in a great gulp of Parisian air and leant out only to see, five storeys down, a rectangular courtyard adorned by two well-filled dustbins. She remembered that the window in the passage looked out over the street and, feeling that even though it was late, she wouldn't be able to get to sleep, she took her packet of cigarettes and a box of matches and went and stood at the end of the passage for about twenty minutes, trying to make out through the play of roof and chimney outlines all the streets, squares and monuments people had told her about during her stay in Italy and also during fittings at Mrs Bartaković's when the wives of Domobrani officers and the mistresses of high-ranking Ustaše officials told the young apprentice seamstress about the holidays they'd spent in pre-war Paris. She couldn't see much: two policemen on bicycles, a window lighting up, another going dark, a couple kissing under an archway. Not a sign of the Eiffel Tower or the Arc de Triomphe. She went back to her room after having asked herself at length whether, despite her fear, she shouldn't go out and launch herself straight away onto the streets of this city she'd spent so much of her adolescence trying to imagine. She'd go wherever the streets led her, and when she was tired, she'd get a taxi to bring her back. She wasn't that hard up! But apart from the fact that the area around the station didn't seem very prepossessing and she was worried her nocturnal walk might end up in a pimp's cellar, attic or trunk, her tiring journey was beginning to tell on her. Even so, she took the trouble of washing meticulously before going to bed. Lying down, she said her 'Hail Mary'. She was Catholic, but not to the extent of going down on her knees at two in the morning. She hadn't drawn the curtains, for she wanted to be woken up by the daylight so she could set off promptly to conquer Paris, but when a ray of sunlight moved across the bed and drew her out of her sleep, she groaned, got up, lurched to the window and crossly drew the curtains before getting back to bed. She slept until midday.

She had the phone number of a hotel where a few Serbs she'd known in Italy were living. Two of them volunteered to come and fetch her. These were lads I wouldn't have chanced spending much time with. But for Dara, the fact they were Yugoslavs, exiles and opponents of Tito made up for their

71

shady existences. They'd been among the very first émigrés, spineless characters who had been so frightened by the Luftwaffe's bombing of Belgrade on 6 April 1941 they'd run as far as Cairo without once looking back, and from there they'd promptly embarked for Madrid, London, Barcelona or Milan. During the war, these chaps had wangled a living, and that's what they were still doing now. Black market cigarettes. Grocery shop break-ins. Stealing bikes. Some even had a go at pimping. I find it ironic that your mother, who never let a day go by without warning any woman she knew against the dangers of the white slave trade, had, on her arrival in Paris, put herself in the hands of men who weren't averse to being kept by young French women — and some of them ended up quite simply putting girls out on the streets.

The Yugoslavs lived in rue Tournefort, next to the place de la Contrescarpe. They went there by bus. Your mother of course insisted they stay on the open platform at the back. It was an exquisite May morning with a smooth, blue sky and a warmish breeze which billowed people's shirts. Because of the shortage of petrol it wasn't very noisy in the city. They went over the pont Henri IV. The Seine lazily twined itself around the île Saint-Louis. 'The Left Bank!' said Branko Marić, one of the two Yugoslavs, pointing out with a broad wave of his hand the Jardin des Plantes and the quai Saint-Bernard. Dara, shading her eyes with one hand, could make out the golden gates of the gardens and the elegant architecture of the conservatories. Since she'd got on to the bus, the city had begun to seem to her enormous, inexhaustible. She felt she'd already covered a distance of five or six kilometres and was surprised that there were still houses on either side of the street. She congratulated herself on having waited for her friends before dipping her toes into this urban ocean and wondered how she'd manage to get about in it once her two guides left her to attend to other business. But strongest of all was her feeling of fulfilment and exultation. She couldn't have dreamt of a more successful entry to the capital of France. She could leave to

72

others the airports, limousines, luxury hotels and Maxim's! The presence of her compatriots, the bus platform and, quite simply, the splendour of Paris were enough to make her utterly happy. Soon she was to have lunch with some fellow Yugoslavs in a hotel room. She would have goulash or lentils that might not necessarily have been cooked with sausage, but she was looking forward to that prospect far more than to, say, sitting in a first-class restaurant where she'd have had to put under wraps the sheer joy she felt at being alive, young, beautiful, free and . . . Parisian!

The bus went along rue Bouffon and then started the climb up the montagne Sainte-Geneviève. In rue du Cardinal Lemoine, Dara lavished jokey encouragements on an out-of-breath cyclist with a bright red face who returned the compliment with a friendly wave of his hand. 'We're nearly there,' said Marić. He was a tall chap with narrow shoulders and soft lips that seemed to be constantly moving even when he wasn't speaking. He looked at your mother with that friendly and amused smile that men from my country have when they're faced with more or less any woman, a smile that means: 'I'm game if you are!' His companion, Dušan Tarković, whom Dara was to set her sights on eighteen months later and with whom she lived until we met in 1951, was of average height and had a more mature, resolute face. Unlike Marić, he hadn't loosened his tie and you felt that despite the heat, he wasn't about to take off his jacket or 'tomber la veste', to borrow one of the idiomatic expressions with which Dara would soon pepper her meagre French vocabulary. You immediately felt that his sense of dignity was the only thing over which he was prepared to take a bit of trouble. Later Dara would describe to me the more preposterous guises that his laziness adopted. Years later, she still couldn't get over it! I think he was about thirty. Blond with very blue eyes, he looked like a Croat, or even a Macedonian from the time of Alexander the Great, but he wasn't at all like the idea one has of a Serb, the long-legged, fiercely dark shepherd you see in the illustrations of French works about the First World War. He was the son of a Belgrade politician whom the departing Germans had packed up in their luggage but had abandoned on the way, along with the horses and the heavy artillery, so that Tarković's father had spent a number of months in a concentration camp trying to convince his gaolers that he'd been playing a double game during the four years of Nazi occupation. 'Which isn't entirely untrue,' Dušan would comment cynically. 'He preferred collaborating with the Italians rather than the Germans.'

If Dara really liked what she saw of Paris in the course of that bus journey, she positively fell in love with the montagne Sainte-Geneviève which I would describe on this occasion as a sort of anti-Buenos Aires. It's a *quartier* as closed in on itself as a family circle. In fact, the place de la Contrescarpe is the size of a living room that's just large enough to welcome a few carefully chosen friends. The old houses that surround it are no more than two storeys high. They allow the sky the space it needs. And something else Dara appreciated enormously was being able to overlook the whole of Paris. You know her predilection for anything situated high up: couchettes, panoramic restaurants, maids' rooms or double-decker buses. Perhaps it's hereditary. Against the Turkish invasions one of the few defences the 'Southern Slavs' had was to crowd into tall towers, close the door firmly behind them and wait for it to be over. Anyhow your mother would soon be delighted to find that three-quarters of the inhabitants of the Contrescarpe were students. She loved their youth, their carelessness, their rowdiness. Rubbing shoulders with them, she felt she was joining in with their joyful march towards a great future, one that most of them ended up acceding to while Dara tirelessly went on making dresses for private customers after her day's work, sewing so late into the night that the owners of the hotels she stayed in always charged her extra for electricity.

The hotel on rue Tournefort was of a very inferior class to the one where your mother had just spent the night, and the

74

young woman was again overcome by panic at the thought of the bill which the surly receptionist in rue de Lyon would present her with in a few hours' time. Here there wasn't even a receptionist. No carpet on the stairs. You could hear the tenants calling out to one another from room to room. Dara recognised the harsh Serbian of Belgrade and the softer tones of some Dalmatians, as well as the full-throated shouts of a Northern Italian. Marić and Tarković shared a room on the third floor. It was of course Marić who went about preparing lunch, while Tarković stayed perched on the window ledge chain-smoking the American cigarettes he'd brought back on his last trip to Belgium. Behind him, the dome of the Panthéon stood out against the blue sky. Other Yugoslavs soon joined them and were greeted by Marić's enthusiastic exclamations and Tarković's placid smiles. An appetising smell of onions frying in lard was beginning to fill the room. Dara was bombarded with questions. Was she quite certain there was no organised group in Yugoslavia trying to make the different peoples rise up against Tito? She couldn't be more sure, she answered. It wasn't even possible for more than two people to meet in Yugoslavia without having the political police on your back. But what about them, what were they doing to topple the communist dictator? The Yugoslavs looked at one another and one of them said, laughing: 'Black marketeering, mostly!' But that didn't amuse your mother one little bit. Her sense of humour wasn't particularly well developed, as you no doubt had many a chance to notice. 'It's ready!' Marić cried out as if it was a miracle. Dara loved the irrepressible way in which he'd been circling around her ever since she'd seen him in her hotel lobby two hours earlier. She said to herself that if she decided to sleep with a man again one day, it would be with him. But when she did take that decision, a year and a half had passed and Marić had been lying in Gentilly cemetery for coming on five months.

After the meal, Tarković picked his teeth and then yawned discreetly but pointedly. He then started staring at the bed that Marić and Dara were sitting on, eagerly recalling their Italian adventures. After a moment, Marić leant towards your mother and said in a quiet voice: 'I think Dušan is feeling sleepy.' He smiled, got up and cleared away the crates that acted as a table. 'Forgive me,' Tarković said in Dara's direction but without looking at her. Then he took off his jacket. Your mother, who anticipated plenty of things from Tarković but definitely not this, understood she wasn't wanted. She was about to leave when Marić shouted from the washroom they'd turned into a makeshift kitchen: '*Čekaj, Dara*!' A few seconds later he was following her down the stairs with his shirtsleeves still rolled up, carrying his jacket and wearing that broad smile that rarely left his long face and that he may have presented to the two men who came to murder him one morning in July 1947. He said: 'If Dušan doesn't have his siesta, he's in a bad mood for the rest of the day.' They laughed. They got back to the place de la Contrescarpe and walked down rue Mouffetard which, exhausted by its intense morning activity, lay sleeping in the sun. Dara had to go back to rue de Lyon to pay for her room and pick up her things. 'I'll come with you,' said Marić. She worried about whether there wasn't something else he should be doing. 'I have got something else to do,' he said, 'but I'd rather stay with you.' She insisted: 'But your boss . . . .' He took her arm: 'I'm not saying this to flatter you, but you're a lot more exciting than my boss . . . .' She pulled her arm away and murmured with a reproachful look and a shake of her head: '*Srbin* . . . .' No, she seemed to be thinking, these Serbs really are not serious-minded and never will be. Nevertheless, she allowed a hint of warmth to creep into her voice to convey to Marić how pleased she was that he wasn't leaving her alone on a day like this.

To save the cost of the two bus fares and also because they weren't in a hurry, they went on foot. Whenever Dara listed all the dreadful crimes committed by Tito's agents since he'd come to power and reached the story of Branko Marić's tragic end, she always recalled the walk they'd taken together that day while Tarković was having his ritual nap. They went along rue Rollin. Going down the very steep steps that lead to rue Monge, Marić took your mother's hand. 'I've already fallen once,' he explained. 'It hurts.' Laughing, she asked him: 'Do you want me to fall with you?' They walked round behind the Jardin des Plantes. In rue Buffon, Marić suggested they sit at a terrace and have a coffee. She said she'd been advised in Italy never to have a drink on the terrace of a Paris café because, quite apart from the exorbitant prices, all the waiters were either thieves or pimps. 'Don't be silly,' Marić said. Your mother wasn't too pleased by this comment. They sat down at a table not far from a group of American soldiers. Noticing Dara's uniform, one of them said a few sentences to her in English that she of course didn't have the faintest inkling about. She laughed her loveliest laugh, that *crushing* laugh which you sometimes hear from famous singers after they've announced they're 'very happy to be here this evening', and she said in English: 'I don't speak well. I've always lived in Paris.' Marić, worried about the unfortunate turn that such an encounter could take — such as, for example, the intervention of the MPs followed by an identity check — urged your mother to drink up her coffee. They went off again towards the pont d'Austerlitz. Dara asked what those flat black boats lined up along the embankment were. 'Barges,' said Marić. She leant on the parapet and gazed at the tip of the île Saint-Louis and the towers of Notre-Dame. I'd imagine that Marić made the most of this to scrutinise her bottom. At any rate, that's what I would have done in his shoes. He probably found it slightly on the flat side, which it was.

At the hotel he succeeded in making such a nuisance of himself that Dara was given a ten percent discount. They came back to rue Tournefort on the bus. Marić helped your mother to install herself in a room on the top floor that was already lived in by a young Dalmatian woman who was waiting for her visa to the United States. In the evening, along with Tarković — looking so well rested, he was a pleasure to see — they went to a bar on the Right Bank where a few Yugoslav émigrés gathered and where for the first time Dara met Nathalie Mikhaïlovna Balouïev, also known as 'Aunt Nathalie'.

The Monte-Carle is at the intersection of rue de Provence, rue Cadet and rue du Faubourg Saint-Denis — a welcoming refuge with something approaching a family atmosphere in the otherwise quite anonymous IXth arrondissement. The Yugoslavs always congregated in the back room. Marić introduced Dara as a young and innocent victim of Titoism. There was a sticky moment when, in the midst of all these hard-bitten Serbs, Dara announced that she was a Croat. Even so, they made some space for her on the wooden bench. She ordered a coffee. She seemed upset when a former Serbian Radical deputy, a friend of Milan Stojadinović's, asked her how she'd managed to escape from Yugoslavia. It was Tarković who, many years later, told me this story. The cigarette smoke had formed into a cloud of fog that seemed thickened and condensed by the din in the bar. The French customers standing at the bar occasionally turned towards the back room to try and work out what was causing the raucous hilarity of all the Balkans gathered there. 'It's a long story . . .' said Dara. 'You must tell it,' intervened a woman who was sitting next to the deputy. She was about fifty and wore a severe black dress. Her hair was tightly pulled into a knot at the nape of her neck. She added: 'We have all the time in the world, Miss Sevnica.' This, as I'm sure you've realised was Aunt Nathalie. When she got there your mother hadn't paid the woman much attention. She could have had no idea that the highest émigré royalist authorities had entrusted to this slight individual with her awful hairstyle the task of checking on the reliability of all émigrés, a task which mainly consisted in making contact with all new arrivals and, if need be, investigating them.

When I got to know your mother, Nathalie Balouïev had already gone to settle in Spain. She felt Madrid was politically a more secure city than Paris. And compared with Paris, the Iberian capital also presented a number of advantages at the time. The supply of food was ten times better. From time to time, Nathalie hopped over to Paris, never forgetting to bring silk stockings, bottles of drink and various items of food which were still scarce on this side of the Pyrenees. All this is by way of saying that any information I can give you about Mrs Balouïev and her successive missions in Europe is second-hand. I only saw her two or three times, and we said virtually nothing to each other, except that once she pressed me or rather tried to press me in her fragile arms and murmured: 'Heroj . . .,' a word which, don't you agree? needs no translating.

I think Nathalie was born in Leningrad in about 1900. In 1917 she followed her family to Athens. Since the collapse of the Russian front, war was raging in the Balkans. As a young woman she took part as a nurse in the August 1918 offensive in which the French and Serbian armies were engaged. She conquered everyone with her courage and she received a number of decorations although, as she never wore them and never mentioned them, I couldn't tell you exactly what they were. After the armistice, and for reasons that neither Dara nor I were ever able to establish, she remained in Serbia. She spoke perfect French and after her heroic conduct at Salonica and in Southern Serbia, she would have had no trouble obtaining a sinecure in the French administration. Yet she chose to settle in Belgrade. Perhaps she wanted to stay close to her native Russia. It's not clear how she spent her time between the year 1918 and the bombing of Belgrade. She didn't marry. Dara used to tell me that Nathalie had been in love with a young French officer who fell at Salonica and that this had put an end to her love life. But your mother had such a propensity for romanticising everything that she may well have misunderstood something the Russian woman confided to her, and it's possible that something completely different came into play, some disability maybe, or simply a total lack of interest in human beings. As for Nathalie Balouïev's professional life during the twenty-three years that she spent in Belgrade, it remains a mystery. Nevertheless, judging by the nature of her actions after the war, I wonder whether she might not have played a part in the secret service set up in 1918 by Vladeta Milicević which always had as its principal aim the struggle against the Ustaše both inside and outside the country.

Nathalie was not impressive to look at. You told me a while ago how the child you were in 1966 had been amazed at how extraordinarily tiny her mother's Russian friend was. I fear there's nothing else worth mentioning. Nathalie Balouïev could lose herself in a crowd without any trouble. It goes without saying that she also lacked that Austro–Hungarian concern with her appearance that Dara prided herself on. She dressed in whatever came to hand, and the results were pretty heavy-handed!

So for your mother, that evening really and truly took on the shape of a cross-examination. But she considered she owed nothing by way of explanation to Serbs whose only merit was that they'd fled their country at the very time when it most needed them. She drank her coffee slowly in order to work out how she would react. Her first instinct would of course have been to claim Nathalie was nothing but a '*flic*' and that the rest of them were 'Balkan louts who weren't good enough to polish shoes of lowliest Croat', after which she would have taken pleasure in getting up abruptly and leaving the Monte-Carle swearing nice and loudly she'd never again set foot in a place where you had to keep such bad company, and slamming the door behind her. But she could see all the disadvantages that would result from that kind of reaction. First, you never knew the precise number of knives a Serb might be carrying, nor at what stage of his anger he'd decide to make use of them. In addition, Dara didn't have ten words of French and nor did she know a soul in Paris, so she was entirely dependent on this group, and one of its members at least had shown towards her a kindness she didn't feel inclined to do without. So she swallowed her anger and explained that she'd crossed the Italian–Yugoslav border at Divača by lying beneath the train while the passports were being checked. She could recall the sound of the partisans' boots moving up and down the platform. She heard a whistle blow. She would soon have to get back into the compartment where half a dozen ashen-faced passengers were expecting to be shot at any moment because of this young Croat who was supposedly so desperate to be reunited with her Italian fiancé. They all started when they saw a leg come in through the window. The rest of the body followed just as the train jerked into motion. It was when she saw what terror there was on her travelling companions' faces that Dara really understood she had just risked her life. When she arrived in Trieste, she suffered a kind of breakdown.

Nathalie, and the man who seemed more and more clearly to be her second-in-command, looked as though they believed in the truth of your mother's story, a story that had in fact had quite an impact on these people who, beneath a thin veneer of civilisation, were unpolished and, more importantly, secretly terrified of the modern world and the sophisticated forms of violence it came up with. Dara had then been asked to give her reasons for leaving Yugoslavia. Well my goodness, she answered, they were hardly difficult to guess. She didn't want to live under a communist régime, that was all. 'Why not?' asked Nathalie. What a question! Because Tito was a tyrant! 'And what did she call Pavelić?' Nathalie then asked. The same thing, said your mother. And then, noticing the harsh and even hostile exression every Serb in the room had adopted on merely hearing Pavelić's name, she judged it useful to get angry. This is approximately what she said at that point as she later told it to me: 'Because I am a Croat, you think I'm in league with the Ustaše or even that I myself am an Ustaša

81

perhaps! But the Ustaše numbered about a hundred when they came back from Italy and Hungary to take power in Zagreb and, at the end of the war, there were barely ten thousand of them, whereas there are many million Croats! There wasn't a single Ustaša in our block of flats, no one at my school would have agreed to go out with an Ustaša, no one in my family ever had anything to do with them. I even believe that we preferred the German soldiers to Pavelić's gangs because they didn't frighten us so much.' She looked around her with calculated intensity and, slightly indulging her liking for melodrama — something she wasn't averse to doing — concluded: 'It is as a Croat that I speak.' Nathalie declared rather shortly, aggressively even, that what ten thousand Ustaše had done during four years had been made possible by what five million Croats had been thinking for twenty-seven years, to which someone at the table retorted that there surely weren't five million Croats capable of thinking, especially not for twenty-seven years! Tarković told me that at that moment they had all burst out laughing, apart from Nathalie, Marić and of course, Dara. Indeed she'd been on the verge of bursting into tears. In truth Marić had the utmost difficulty in keeping a straight face, for by temperament he laughed from morning till night and all the more so when he had good reason. Leaning towards your mother, he said: 'Don't be angry with them, they're joking, they don't really mean to be nasty.' Nathalie on the other hand went on coldly staring at her. Her look, at once incisive and unhappy, was that of a woman who's less than one metre fifty tall. She asked: 'What happened to you and your family at the liberation?' Dara had preferred to tell the truth. Your grand-father Josip, a civil-servant in Zagreb town-hall, was imprisoned at Stara Gradiska by the partisans. As for your uncle Vladimir, a non-commissioned officer in a Domobrani regiment — the national army of Croatia — he had fled to Austria, been driven back into Slovenia by the British army and miraculously escaped the Bleiburg massacres that I'll tell you more about later. Interned in a concentration camp in Serbia for six months, he had been freed thanks to his father's contacts who, in the meantime, had had his job in the town hall restored to him along with some of his privileges. Nathalie asked Dara why she had mentioned neither her sister, her mother nor herself. She answered that in the Balkans, women's destinies and opinions always came second and that it had been for that reason, too, that she'd decided to come and live in France.

Marić was shifting about on his chair. He cast sideways glances in Nathalie's direction. The inquisitorial tone she was adopting towards your mother was annoying him. At the same time, he was secretly amused because he was sure he'd soon get a chance to play a trick of his own on Nathalie, either a heated debate into which she would sink up to her knees or an improvised *kolo* in the course of which her standoffishness would become apparent and show up like a stain against the relaxed good spirits that come so naturally to Yugoslav women. He ordered a bottle of cognac. 'With what are you going to pay for it, Mr Branko, if you don't mind my asking?' asked the *patronne*. 'She knows very well what I'll pay for it with,' he said in Serbian, and again the back room was filled with the sound of the émigrés' raucous laughter. They all drank, and they all sang patriotic songs, while many thousands of kilometres away, in a cell two metres by three, General Draža Mikhaïlović, the Četnik leader, waited for his parody of a trial to begin, at the close of which, on 17 July, he would be condemned to death and executed. When Nathalie made the most of an unexpected lull in what was looking more and more like a New Year's Eve party and asked Dara what had been her political record during the war, Marić felt that here was the opportunity he'd been watching for for nearly an hour. He said to the Russian woman: 'You mustn't forget that you and Dara don't belong exactly to the same generation. She wasn't forty-one when the war broke out, but eighteen. Beautiful as she is, she was doubtless far busier turning away her admirers than running off copies of royalist tracts in smoke-filled basements!' Nathalie assumed a regal air and held her head high as she retorted: 'Mr Marić, I believe you're trying to offend me, and offending people never does any good, in politics as in anything else.'

When the café closed, about half a dozen of them piled into Milovan Vukmanović's Citroën. He was a mechanic in a suburban garage and his boss often lent him a car for an evening or even a weekend; in return for this Milovan was more willing to work overtime. Tarković left on foot for an unknown destination. As for Aunt Nathalie, she had her bicycle outside the café. From inside the car, Marić and your mother saw her take off the lock, lift the bike down onto the street and mount it rather heavily. '*Zdravo, Nathalie!*' Vukmanović called out. Without turning around, she made a small sign with her hand and disappeared into the night.

During the next few days, Dara scoured the city in search of work. She was sorry she didn't have the time to make the pilgrimage she'd dreamt of for so long around Montmartre and all the other historic places of the capital. She found a job as a cutter in a dressmaker's workshop. She gradually started to operate the system that had worked well for her in Italy: she'd get in contact with the workshop's few private customers and suggest making the same dresses for them for cash for half the price. This was a success. So she spent her evenings and a good part of her nights 'pulling the needle' as she said. She only stopped to eat and sleep. She did take a little time off to enjoy herself two or three times a week, but it was never without inwardly panicking at the thought of all the work she was leaving behind at the hotel. She went back to rue Cadet a few times, but it was a little far from where she lived and she preferred meeting her Yugoslav friends at Dara's, a restaurant on rue Boutebrie, near the boulevard Saint-Michel. How often I heard her suggesting to me that we have supper in 'her' restaurant! To which she'd add, as if I hadn't yet got the joke after all that time: 'It has the same name as me!' She bumped into Nathalie Balouïev again, but the Russian woman showed no hostility towards her, nor indeed any interest. She very clearly had other fish to fry and the session at the Monte-Carle was now no more than a bland memory for her.

Marić spent the summer in gaol for stealing a handbag. In Fresnes he made some good contacts that he unfortunately never got the chance to make use of. It was the time when the period the French call the *épuration* was drawing to an end — and it was a mere picnic compared with the way scores got settled in the Balkans after the Germans left.

The evening Marić reappeared at the hotel, Dara was sitting with her back to the window sewing as usual; she could feel the warm breeze below her shoulders and her mind was filled with the street noises. She was aware of a commotion on the stairs, and then the door was thrown wide open revealing Marić and Tarković; they were clasping each other tightly and jumping up and down on the spot as if to dance the *kolo*. '*Hajduk je ponovo ovde*,' said Tarković, which means: 'The bandit is back.' Needless to say, a celebration was instantly organised in the two boys' room. It was Tarković who saw to everything. Judging by the unaccustomed eagerness with which he filled the glasses, cut the slices of *saucisson* and handed out the American cigarettes, it was obvious that he'd missed Marić badly. The latter went from group to group, proudly airing his prison smell as if it had been Chanel Number 5. Your mother devoted herself pretty much exclusively to lecturing him. So he could see now what dishonesty led to! He eyed her in a gentle manner. He told her she was looking pale. She explained drily that she hadn't had the time to acquire a sun tan. He placed his hand on hers. Why didn't they make the most of the last fine days and go on a few jaunts around Paris? Since both of them had been locked indoors at the same time, they could very well go out together! Dara said she had too much work. 'If you go on like that, you'll get ill,' said Marić. 'And then you won't be in a state to do any work at all.'

The following morning they took the train from the gare Montparnasse. Vukmanović had promised them the car but phoned Branko at the last minute to tell him it had fallen through. He'd been held up at the garage, so he couldn't come with them and it was quite out of the question that his boss would let a car out without being sure his employee would be there to keep an eye on it.

Dara appeared for Branko in a white dress with blue polka dots, and as always she was only very lightly made up. Two days earlier, Tarković had supplied her with a pair of silk stockings to thank her for having mended a few items of clothing for him and now, under the glass roof of the station, she wore them proudly, taking big strides along the platform and boldly raising her knees far higher than she need have done to get on the train. Her thick black hair was loose on her shoulders. Around her neck she had a small silver chain, a tiny piece of jewellery which had come from her mother. There was about her an aura of freshness and — in a word — virginity.

I think that never in her life had she seen a building as large as your Sun King's palace. When she reached the ornamental pools opposite the terrace, she caught sight of the left wing of the palace and exclaimed: 'But there's more!' Branko had his hands in his pockets and was trying hard to look relaxed and slightly disdainful like an estate agent showing some customers around a house he knows they couldn't afford to buy anyway. She asked who lived there. 'No one,' he said. She thought it was a horrible waste, and for a long time afterwards, perhaps even for the rest of her life, she enjoyed imagining that an American multi-millionaire would buy it all up and give it to her without demanding anything in return. She would turn it down in the first instance and then, touched by the magnate's disinterested generosity, let herself be persuaded to accept the gift. And in fact she would be content to inhabit a room up under the eaves because it was more '*sympa*' as she put it, nicer and cosier than the state apartments or the Hall of Mirrors. In the evenings, she would sew in front of the open window, gazing up from time to time to contemplate the moon's reflection on the surface of the *canal* . . .

They walked down towards the bassin de Latone. Your mother's usual way of walking showed a peculiar mixture of martial energy and the carefree manner characteristic of most South Slavs, but now Branko noticed that she was keeping her back quite straight and placing one foot in front of the other with infinite care; she wasn't swinging her arms about as she normally did; and finally she also seemed to be turning her head slowly to one side and then to the other as if greeting with an air of indifference some imaginary courtiers. Branko led her to the allée Royale. Every twenty metres or so, she swung around to see the palace shrinking away between the two lines of poplars. It really was far more beautiful than the blackish, squat Ban's Palace in Zagreb or the Arts Pavilion on Tomislav Square. There was simply no comparison! On that day, Miss Laurens, your mother made the discovery of three notions which she was always to associate with France: space, refinement and scale. And that discovery was in fact one of the reasons why between 1951 and 1954 I failed in my numerous attempts to take her with me to Argentina.

It was, already, a proper October sky that had unfurled itself over the end of the canal. A brittle, cold sky that seemed to have been carved out of blue marble. Branko and Dara went all the way to the end of the park, searching perhaps for a miniature Versailles built with them in mind three centuries previously, nestling unbeknown to anyone in its patch of greenery, simply awaiting them. They installed themselves on the grass in the sunshine. Dara carefully set out the picnic on a white tablecloth embroidered with her initials: a few slices of *saucisson à l'ail*, a chicken breast, hard-boiled eggs and two oranges. Branko opened a bottle of Bordeaux. Another gift from Tarković. Because they felt hungry, they ate quickly.

Then they stretched out near the remains of their meal and began to talk while chewing on stalks of grass. Branko drank his Bordeaux in patient, regular little sips. Your mother doubtless imagined that what he was looking for in the wine was the courage to confess that he'd been in love with her from the first and wished to marry her, but the way I see it, he was getting drunk more in order to heighten his pleasure at lying on a lawn that had been trodden by the feet of Marie-Antoinette, Mme du Barry and Mme de Maintenon when only one week earlier, he was answering the prison roll call. He ended up falling asleep, firmly ensconced in his ecstatic drunkenness. Dara got up and shook out the tablecloth, sending the chicken bones, egg shells and orange peel flying off in every direction. And then, feeling puzzled and confused, she waited without making a sound for her companion to wake up.

They kissed on the train back, both of them too tall to see in which station they had stopped. Branko took your mother by the waist, placed his cheek against her hair and slowly moved his lips across her face — the face of a dumbfounded, positively petrified Dara. She said, in Serbian: 'You're drunk.' 'Prove it!' he said. She laughed, and soon after pressed herself against him, dipping her head like a boxer. Then, in the midst of the tightly packed Parisians carrying home their empty baskets and sunburnt noses, he performed for her a kind of improvised spectacle of folksongs and gags in which the frenetic imagination of a one hundred per cent Slav intermingled with the banter of an adoptive Parisian, all of this in a hushed voice and embellished with quick, silent kisses. A campaign of charm to which your mother — for reasons you will understand in a moment — could not quite give in, however much she may have wanted to.

From Montparnasse they walked to the hotel. Night had fallen. Branko kept pinning Dara in archways. She put up a feeble defence. She let him kiss her and caress her, but when in a dark dead-end, he tried to slip his hand into her *Petit Bateau*

88

pants, she pushed him back with a threat of a slap across the face. After that, as they were walking towards the hotel, going more and more slowly the closer they drew to it, as if delaying the moment when they'd have to part as well as the one when they'd have to confront the other Yugoslavs, she suggested that he become her *pobratim*, which is to say her brother by oath. This old Slav custom allows us to establish a bond with people who don't belong to our family — a bond we place above friendship and beyond love in some mysterious realm that you Westerners rarely bother to explore. Branko refused. 'You must be mad!' he said. 'You want us to end up committing incest!' Underlying this little wisecrack, she could feel that he in fact found the idea of having a woman as a *pobratim* quite shocking. Three months in gaol hadn't rid him of the ancestral prejudices he owed to his race, quite the contrary. Do you know, a Serb who hasn't been to gaol at least once isn't considered a fully-fledged man by his friends, and he comes out feeling the same satisfaction as a soldier just back from the front line. He went on: 'And anyway, why do you want me to be your *pobratim*? It's a daft idea! We like each other as man and woman, not as brother and sister, don't we?' She nodded. Silence. They had settled down on a bench and were holding hands, gazing at the Panthéon. 'What's going on in your head?' Branko asked. 'It's too long to explain,' she told him.

A month passed. On her way home from the workshop, she would catch sight of Branko leaning up against the counter in one of the many bars on rue Mouffetard. She'd buy half a *baguette* and a piece of cheese and go and shut herself up in her room. He'd drop in to see her towards eight or eight thirty. He'd suggest taking her to dinner at Dara's. More often than not, she said no, pointing wearily to the pieces of fabric spread out on the table. When she did accept, they'd walk down towards the boulevard Saint-Germain. In the restaurant, she would talk to everyone rather than him. The poor man couldn't understand what was going on. Should he

89

have it out with her? He'd been thinking about it for a long while already, but didn't make up his mind until a number of weeks later — the first Monday in November to be precise. On the place de la Contrescarpe, he caught sight of his friend going back to her hotel with her half-*baguette* and her camembert. He leapt out of the bar where he was drinking his fourth or fifth cognac of the day and ran across the square. His jacket flapped behind him and a packet of cigarettes fell out of his trouser pocket. He didn't bother to retrieve it. He caught up with your mother near the bench where they'd rested for a moment after their excursion to Versailles. He took her by the shoulders and demanded an explanation. 'You're hurting me and you smell horrible,' she said. There emanated from him that smell, a mixture of stale perspiration and alcohol, which for me will always be the smell of Yugoslavia. 'That is not what I call an explanation,' he yelled. This scene takes place at a time when the inhabitants of a particular area or street know each other, talk to each other, don't hesitate to comment openly on each other's lifestyles; when someone shouts in the street, you open a window and, if there's any call for it, you have a go at the culprit yourself, if only to keep in practice with the spirited banter that is of such primordial importance to Parisians of whatever class. And so Marić saw half a dozen faces, each more unsmiling than the next, appear at the windows of the first few buildings on the street. He heard a student call out from up in his maid's room: 'Do you need help, Miss Dara?' She said she needed nothing. Then she looked steadily, almost harshly at Branko and, just as he was about to set her free and escape as far as possible from the Contrescarpe she, ashamed at having behaved so grossly, put her arms around his neck and covered his face with little kisses oddly lacking in sensuality. It was a little as though she'd been in a competition whose rules demanded that she cover a male face with kisses in a minimum amount of time and without leaving a single space untouched. Branko was dumbfounded and kept repeating: 'You must explain,

90

you must explain. . . .' Dara lifted a distraught, tearful face towards him. She looked beautiful in a desperate, useless way, a way that made you think of someone left standing with their arms dangling, helpless. 'Explain yourself!' insisted Branko. 'No!' she said firmly before fleeing towards the hotel. First he felt relieved as if he'd rid himself of something. He took a few steps. On the place de la Contrescarpe, he began to miss your mother. And when he walked into the café where Tarković would join him about ten minutes later, he was in a state of near stupor and could feel one of those moods coming on when he could no longer talk to people, he could only talk nonsense and systematically say the opposite of what seemed true — one of the ways he'd devised of spitting on life.

Dara was never to find out that the attempted rape of which he was going to make himself guilty that evening had been heartily encouraged and perhaps even decided upon by Tarković in that café where the two men sat for many hours drinking a vast number of cognacs. Dušan told me that at the time he found the way your mother was behaving towards Branko disgraceful, and that he'd simply thought up with him a means of teaching the young woman a small lesson, which is a perfectly acceptable version of the events. But I rather suspect that he was busy furthering the secret aim of separating Dara from his friend. You see, he felt he was in every way superior to Marić and even though he had no special feelings for your mother, he found it faintly appalling that she hadn't leapt on him the moment she'd seen him and that, on top of that, she'd landed herself with a wet rag like Branko.

An almost wintry north wind was blowing over the montagne Sainte-Geneviève. The two men staggered about between the streetlamps. With their jacket collars turned up and their hands thrust deep into their pockets, they attempted to make their way back to the hotel. Because they couldn't walk straight, they frequently bumped into each other, carried on shoulder to shoulder for a few seconds, then parted like two billiard balls and went on chewing over their private thoughts on separate sides of the street. There was no one at the reception desk, a carelessness which for the hotel owner was quite customary, and which one can easily see as responsible for costing Marić his life on the morning of 11 July 1947. Tarković left his friend outside Dara's door. 'It's your move,' he said. And he was right: it was a sort of game they were playing. But Branko had no inkling he might be the plaything. He knocked on the door. 'Who is it?' asked your mother. Branko said he'd torn his trouser leg and asked if she could do something for him, if it were only to open the door. She opened it.

It was she who told me about the precise moment that evening when Marić walked into her room and she realised there was nothing the matter with his trousers. She was about to make him leave, but soon understood that this time things wouldn't go as easily as on other occasions. He smelt of alcohol as strongly as if he'd been put to soak in a barrel of cognac. He locked the door and put the key in his pocket. Your mother asked him what he wanted. In a slurred voice he demanded that she take her clothes off. She told him he was mad. From the pocket into which, only a moment earlier, he'd stuffed the key to the room, he pulled out a flick-knife. Until then his gestures had been unsteady; he avoided meeting Dara's eyes, but once he held the knife in his hand, it was as if he were secretly delighted at having stepped beyond the point of no return and could now wallow in violence. He became rude, restless. Your mother was very frightened. She threatened to scream if he came close to her. 'If you scream I'll cut your throat,' he said. She couldn't believe her ears. She forced herself to think that deep down he didn't believe in what he was doing, that ultimately he didn't even feel any desire for her, and finally that one carefully chosen word, one smile, or even one shrug of her shoulders would be enough to bring this ridiculous farce to an end. She said, 'Stop, Branko!' But he was coming towards her, and she was astounded to see that as he was walking he was starting to undo the buttons of his flies.

It's from Tarković, to whom during the months that followed Branko never tired of describing the scene, that I learnt what Marić had felt as he advanced, his prick out of his trousers, upon a frantic and imploring Dara. He took great satisfaction from displaying himself to the young seamstress in his natural state, and felt at the same time stunned and slightly embarrassed at finding himself in such a situation, he who'd always treated his mother and sisters with the greatest respect and who had only raised his hand to two or three women in his entire life — which some might consider a breach of Balkan traditions. Not forgetting, either, that like many Slavs he worshipped the Blessed Virgin. And so it was with a certain relief that he saw Dara suddenly snuggle up against him. He mentally congratulated his friend Dušan for having encouraged him to use violence to get this Minerva to yield to him, for she was now melting in his arms like an ice cube on a radiator. He felt a slight twinge in his right hand, glanced down and wondered how your mother's scissors could manage to stay upright on their own. It took him a fraction of a second to understand that the brownish liquid spurting out around the scissors was his, for the good reason that it was in his hand that your mother had planted her scissors. He yelled out and an ashtray hit him square in the face. Once he was on the floor, she kicked him in the ribs a good few times, after which she opened the door and called out for help — help that, one has to admit, she didn't really need.

Following this painful scene, your mother and Branko went for many days without seeing each other. One morning they passed on the stairs. With his big bandage on his right hand, his crumpled suit, dirty shirt and that smell that reminded you of a damp paper bag or a litre of slivovitz spilt on the floorboards of a very old flat, Marić looked the caricature of a Yugoslav. Dara announced to him that she was moving. She had found a small but well heated room in the XVIIth

93

arrondissement, next to the chapelle du Saint-Sacrement. Marić nodded his head several times, his face expressionless, as if he were doing an exercise to soothe a stiff neck. Then he went on his way.

Your mother called on him a fortnight later, when she was already installed in the narrow and friendly rue d'Armaillé that turns off avenue Carnot in the shape of a ponytail.

She checked with the hotel owner to find out whether Tarković was in. She wanted to see Marić alone because she had important things to tell him. Luck had it that Tarković was away 'on business'. She felt moved as she climbed up the stairs and thought back to all the times when she and Branko had played about on those stairs. Standing outside his door, she paused. She was out of breath and her thighs were aching. How long ago it was when she had spent her afternoons doing ring exercises or training on the parallel bars! She told herself she was getting out of form, that she had spent too much time making dresses for cash and smoked too many Disque Bleu since she had left Yugoslavia. She knocked on the door. 'Come in, it's open!' said Branko. She went in. The room was icy cold and swathed in a cloud of cigarette smoke. Branko was wearing two sweaters, one on top of the other. He was sitting in bed reading a racing paper. He made a small sign at Dara with his wounded hand. She went closer. 'You should change your bandage from time to time,' she said. It was greyish and had spots of fat and tomato sauce on it. 'I'll be able to take it off soon,' Branko said. He pointed to the chair he had placed near the bed, but before she sat on it, she had to clear away an ashtray, a kitchen-size box of matches, a packet of Philip Morris, a bottle of slivovitz and a number of newspapers including a copy of a rag published by royalist émigrés. When she made to take off her coat, Marić said: 'I don't recommend it.' There followed a conversation on the need to force the owner to turn on the heating, one of those lengthy, hectic and perfectly pointless conversations that are the preserve of my fellow countrymen. But it wasn't to discuss the heating problem in the hotels of the montagne Sainte-Geneviève that Dara had crossed all of Paris that autumn Saturday morning. There was a story she wanted to tell Branko Marić. Before repeating it to you, I think I should enlighten you on what became known in our country, and in yours too in fact, as the 'national liberation', which gave rise to horrific bloodbaths in some regions, notably in Croatia.

A moment ago I mentioned the figure of Ante Pavelić, failed lawyer, writer of pathetic sorts and terrorist leader of so little talent that he had to ask the ORIM (or Revolutionary Organisation for the Independence of Macedonia) to provide him with a killer capable of assassinating Alexander I of Yugoslavia in Marseille in October 1934, since he only had limited faith in his Ustaše. Pavelić governed Croatia or, more correctly, the Independent State of Croatia from April 1941 to May 1945. Having returned to Zagreb as part of the Wehrmacht's and the Italian army's luggage, the Poglavnik and his 'faithful Ustaše' embarked on a reign of absolute terror over the Croats, Serbs, Moslems, Jews and Gypsies living in that lovely, rich and gentle region. Public places and all forms of public transport were out of bounds to 'Serbs, Jews, nomads and dogs'. Concentration camps were set up, such as those of Jasenovac and Sisak. Serbian peasants were rounded up in churches and killed one by one with a knife; their eyes were sometimes kept to be made into necklaces. In order to speed up the conversion of Orthodox Serbs, some Catholic priests armed themselves with revolvers and daggers. To fascism's natural inhumanity, the Ustaše added the traditional brutality of the Balkans, even though at the same time they claimed that they weren't Balkans or even Slavs, since they considered themselves pure Aryans — a belief that one of the first decrees issued by the Independent State of Croatia had in fact just confirmed for them. The climate of horror they created was such that the Nazis who, after all, weren't exactly squeamish, took offence and insisted that Pavelić curb the murderous fervour of his troops. So sickened

95

were they by the behaviour of their Croatian allies, some German soldiers of the occupying forces even asked to be sent to the Russian front.

On 8 May 1945, the day of the German capitulation, the Poglavnik, his ministers and Ustaše and the Croatian army evacuated Zagreb to which, in a symbolic gesture at the beginning of his rule, Pavelić had given back its Austro–Hungarian name of Agram. While the government fell back to Klagenfurt in Austria, Generals Dragojloff, Herencić and Servatzé's army pitched camp at Celje, a small town in Slovenia. For a few days, the generals hoped to hold a line of defence running to Ljubiana which might allow the main body of refugees to get through into Austria; this they accomplished within a week. But the Anglo–Americans, who had signed specific agreements with Tito's general staff, drove the Croats back, having first taken care to disarm them. So here we had our Zagorans standing empty-handed with their backs to the wall, and in front of them, the partisans who were so intoxicated with their victory as to be quite unhinged, and each one of whom had a friend, father or brother to avenge for the atrocities the Ustaše had been committing for four years. They machine-gunned the Croat columns, using knives to finish off their victims and pulling out their gold teeth. As for the girls and the women, these fierce warriors, who might have washed their pricks once a year at best, first raped them and then cut their throats. Well, Miss Laurens, your mother, Dara Sevnica, was one of those girls picked up by the communists along the Austrian border, dragged behind a bush by the hair and raped by anything between three and twelve soldiers. A partisan colonel who came from Zagreb and whom your mother knew because she'd carried messages for him when he'd been going out briefly with her sister Zdenka, saved her life by miraculously appearing just when one of the four men who'd raped her was about to disembowel her with a bayonet. That's all I know, and I believe that's all she told Marić that Saturday morning in

November 1946 when she called on him.

'I see,' said Branko. As if he felt it unseemly to remain in bed after hearing such a tale, he got up. He asked Dara to forgive him. She said: 'But it's you who are hurt, not me!' As he grasped all the macabre irony and fierce pride contained in that comment, he burst into tears and threw himself at your mother's feet. She buried her hand in his hair and rubbed his head vigorously. It wasn't a caress, more one of those rough, straightforward gestures one makes to pat a dog who's come to beg for a little meat. Dara too began to cry. Branko raised his eyes, straightened up and kissed her. Still crying, she did nothing to stop him. He made as if to lead her towards the bed. She moved away from him and said the time hadn't yet come. 'I shall wait,' he said. Then he sat himself at her feet and they remained like that for a good few minutes, Branko chastely kissing your mother's knees while, with her mind on something else, she stroked the nape of his neck. Then Dara said she had to get back to rue d'Armaillé. 'Let me take you to lunch in a restaurant,' said Branko. She didn't have the time. They hugged in front of the door. 'Drop in and see me next week,' she said. Had he known that two days later he'd have to leave Paris over some small matter of stolen goods and that, when he returned in May 1947, his new mistress, a Marseille woman of mature years he'd met in the Vieux-Port, would threaten to cut him off if ever he dared get back in touch with the beautiful Dara Sevnica, he might have pleaded with your mother to stay with him for a few more hours. And, since he couldn't make love to her, he might have rubbed himself up against her like a cat that wants to mark you with its smell and dotted her neck with slow, attentive kisses, and he might, finally, have tried by some means or other to appropriate that big, motionless body. But confident that he would be seeing her again in two or three days' time, he let her go. He only ever saw her again once, in Dara's, the restaurant, two weeks before he was killed. He was having lunch with the woman whom all his Yugoslav friends now called '*la Marseil-*

laise'. Dara walked in alone; she was dressed in a black suit and had a book under her arm. She was hailed from all directions: '*Dara! Dara! Dođi, Dara!*' She smiled all around. He was worried she might come and exchange a few words with him and ask to be introduced to '*la Marseillaise*', but having kissed a number of people at a table not far from the door, among them Nathalie Balouïev and the former minister Djurović, she perched herself on a stool to eat a plate of goulash at the counter. She refused the glass of white wine the *patronne* wanted to give her, for Dara was a favourite customer of hers. 'If I drink that, I won't be able to push my thread through the eye of my needle,' she said. She paid for her meal, got down from her stool and, having politely taken leave of everyone present and been answered by a chorus of friendly farewells, she left. Her departure was followed by a strange silence, one that gave Branko the feeling everyone present was reproaching him for something.

At the beginning of spring, your mother had come back to live in her old hotel in rue Tournefort. She was given back her room, which was larger than the one in rue d'Armaillé, and so more difficult to heat. That was why, when winter came, she again migrated to the Right Bank. Since the hôtel d'Armaillé displayed a sign claiming there were no vacancies, she went on the advice of a fellow Yugoslav to the Hôtel de la Havane on rue de Trévise where she found a room that suited her. And it was here that, towards seven o'clock in the evening on 3 January 1948, she made up her mind to put an end to her solitude. She put down her needle and thread, slipped on her coat and went out. She walked to the Monte-Carle but the man with whom she'd decided to spend the night wasn't there. She took the *métro* and got off at Saint-Michel. This time round, she didn't turn down the glass of white wine offered to her by the *patronne* in the restaurant where, six months ago, she'd nearly fainted when she'd seen Branko having lunch *en tête-à-tête* with a platinum blonde. She waited for a whole hour. When she walked out of Dara's, she thought she was on her way back to rue de Trévise. She had already wasted enough time! But reaching the boulevard Saint-Germain, she turned in the opposite direction to the one she'd intended going in. It was the first time since she'd left Yugoslavia that she found herself acting against her own will.

She looked for Tarković in the hotel on rue Tournefort and in the cafés and restaurants of the place de la Contrescarpe. She walked up and down rue Mouffetard. She passed a few French students she knew and asked them where her Yugoslav friend was. None of them could help. She was beginning to feel very cold. To save money, she chose to sit on a bench rather than settle herself in a café. It seemed to her that the montagne Sainte-Geneviève was at the centre of a concerted offensive mounted by all of that night's icy winds. After half an hour, she went back to the hotel. Still no one. She once again checked all the nearby cafés and restaurants. In vain. She decided to go home. In rue du Cardinal-Lemoine, she was accosted by a fat man who offered her a sum of money in exchange for her favours. She bent forward her big, sturdy, Sava peasant's body and glared at the fellow with such coldness and inner ferocity that he bolted without her having to say a word.

She walked on for a few minutes, and then heard: '*Kako si, Dara?*' She looked up. Tarković was standing in front of her in a fine flannel overcoat. From time to time a 4 C V Citroën or a Simca 6 went hurtling past as if the driver's only wish was to reach the end of the boulevard Saint-Germain as fast as possible and throw himself into the Seine. Tarković asked your mother what she was doing there. She said she was looking for him. He laughed. His hands were dug deep into his overcoat pockets and she restrained herself from pointing out to him that this habit ruined your clothes. Like a lot of people who have lived in difficult material circumstances, she hated wastefulness.

'You had something to tell me?' Tarković asked. She remained silent for a few seconds and then, because she liked

99

to match words with deeds, gave her shoulders a vigorous rub and declared she was frozen. He took her to have a drink in a dance-hall in the VIIIth arrondissement. She normally only went to this sort of place on a Sunday afternoon, keeping her evenings for sewing or very occasionally for get-togethers with her Yugoslav friends. In the taxi, she asked Tarković if she was well enough dressed, if he wouldn't be ashamed of her. She wasn't unaware that he often went out with elegant young Frenchwomen, though she was only to learn many years later that he despatched a good dozen of them to various brothels in the Persian Gulf. He shrugged his shoulders. 'You will be the most beautiful woman present,' he said.

He brought her back to rue de Trévise towards two in the morning. Under the taxi driver's lifeless gaze, he asked her in Serbian if she wanted to sleep with him, adding 'she shouldn't feel she had to agree'. 'Okay,' she murmured in a ghastly English accent. 'You won't regret it,' he said before paying the fare and rushing around the car to open the door for her. She knew perfectly well that once she had given herself to him, he would no longer pay her that sort of attention, and that it might even be down to her to open doors for him!

Three years later, arriving from London, I landed at Le Bourget airport. Your mother, Tarković and most of their Yugoslav friends had already gathered at the town hall at Pantin for the big royalist émigré ball. I got in a taxi and asked the driver to take me to a hotel that another Četnik, Lieutenant Milan Semilović, had given me the address of. He was living there himself. I found him dressed and freshly shaven. He told me he'd forgotten to warn me in his letter that the day I arrived was also the day of this event that each year brought together our mutual friends and enemies, the cowards who'd run away at the first shot, the repented traitors and the regular army officers who'd suffered their final humiliation with the political successes of that terrible strategist, the former locksmith, Josip Broz

Tito. . . . Everyone would be there! So I had little choice but to have a quick wash and change into some fresh clothes.

I don't recall who introduced me to Dara. Quite possibly I introduced myself. My first memory of her is of a tall, smiling young woman whom I am leading through a faltering waltz. The floor of the hall creaks beneath our feet, which are slightly out of step. I've never been a good dancer, and four years spent up in the Serbian mountains hadn't helped much. On Ravna Gora, it had been the Germans, the partisans, the Ustaše and the militias of the traitor Nedić who'd led the dance — and let me tell you, Miss Laurens, that dance had nothing of the Viennese waltz about it! I can feel my partner getting bored, she's smiling at people over my shoulder. I say something. She answers in monosyllables. What's she got against Četniks, apart from the fact they've been killers? She doesn't laugh. I will soon grasp that she may sometimes be cheerful, but she never finds anything funny. She looks at me as if she's thinking: 'What's funny about that?' She says that, as for killers, she doesn't know anybody who isn't one. At the end of the dance, she throws me a resonant 'thanks' full of cheery indifference and, while she moves briskly towards the buffet, I'm left feeling as if I'm wearing the outfit of a clown who's being pelted with rotten tomatoes by a gang of over-excited kids.

I spent the next hour emptying small glasses of slivovitz, eating smoked ham and discussing the imminent downfall of Marshal Tito in the company of a former Serbian Radical deputy, the wife of a famous Montenegrin sculptor, a lawyer from Niš who'd gone over to plumbing, and four or five others, each more optimistic than the next over our forth-coming return to Yugoslavia. Between dances, your mother did occasionally join our group. She carefully avoided my gaze. At one point, she said that it wouldn't be by sitting there debating matters that we would alter anything in Yugoslavia's political situation. What was needed was action! 'What do you want to do?' asked my friend Semilović. 'Assas-

101

sinate Tito?' 'It would be a start!' said Dara proudly, and then gave in to her partner's pressure and returned to the dance floor where we soon heard her burst out laughing. Semilović shook his head and sighed: 'Ah, these Croats . . .' That was how I learnt that your mother belonged to that Croat people whose strange gentleness is the most disquieting mask that Evil has ever adopted.

Towards midnight, the assembled company split into two camps. There were those who were hurrying off to catch the last *métro* and those who were looking at them with smiles on their faces because they'd decided they'd go on dancing until the first one came next morning and were feeling rather proud of themselves. Semilović was going home. I was dithering over whether I should go with him or stay. Then, as if she'd been waiting for that moment all evening, Dara came towards me and asked me whether it was true I knew King Peter. I asked her who had told her that. She pointed rather offhandedly to a young blond man slumped on a chair, empty glass in hand. This was none other than Dušan Tarković, with whom I came to be on excellent terms all during my relationship with Dara, and whom I would meet again thirty years later in a small street in Buenos Aires, as he tried to elude the police forces of several European states, as well as old acquaintances who had failed to get over the chain of his dishonest dealings that they'd been on the receiving end of. I could indeed recall that in the course of the evening I'd mentioned the financial and marital problems of our dear little king, a creature of radiant charm, an innocent who, following his father's death in 1934, had fallen prey to the foolishness of Queen Mary and the obscure whims of Prince Paul, and whose kingdom Tito would steal from him about ten years later with the help of the Soviets and the complicity of the British and Americans. At present he was living in France, Switzerland and the United States, investing in various shady deals the money from his wife Alexandra's last remaining pieces of jewellery. In the company of a few other

102

Četnik officers who'd managed like me to escape from the communist stranglehold in Serbia, I had had tea with the royal couple in their London residence in Upper Grosvenor Street, which had in fact formerly been the Yugoslav Embassy. As the hall was gradually emptying, I recounted to your mother the hour and a half I had spent in the company of Karageorge's heir. He was a slim young man who spoke Serbian with the distinction of a British plenipotentiary. One of us, a captain whose wife, sister and four children had been slaughtered by the Ustaše in the course of one of their raids and who'd behaved with indescribable bravery during the war, dropped his cup of tea on the carpet where it shattered with all the grace and delicacy that befitted fine old china. Captain Gabrilović blushed beneath the sparse hairs of a beard that was slowly growing back since he'd shaved it before crossing the Greek border, an indispensable sacrifice insofar as a beard was one of the distinctive features that signalled a Četnik. 'I beg your pardon, Your Majesty,' he said humbly to the idle king for whom he'd risked his life at least a hundred times and who — we were far from guessing it then — would end up kept like a tart on émigré funds.

Your mother listened to me with impassioned concentration. I even got the impression she was trying not to blink so as not to distract me from my story. She hung anxiously on my every sentence like an entomologist watching a unique specimen of a lepidopterous insect, and she was so intent that drops of sweat were beading her forehead. The king! I had seen *the king*! At that time, it was unusual to come across any Croats who were at all keen on the Karageorgevich dynasty, but Dara's case was special in that, as she soon told me, she had been born on *exactly the same day* as Peter II of Yugoslavia. She said this coincidence had immediately played an important part in her life. In the Sevnica family, she was called 'Peter's fiancée'. She always spared a tender thought for him on each of her birthdays. She would imagine that just at the moment when she was blowing out the candles, he was

103

doing the same. The idea of marrying the future king of Yugoslavia had seemed totally impossible to her until she was fifteen years old when she became aware of how beautiful she was and started to view the matter from a less pessimistic viewpoint. The war had swept away all these young girl's daydreams. But after these ten years punctuated by so many different ordeals, she still retained a special affection for the king, one that she didn't really differentiate in her mind from the feelings she had about her own past.

After the slight dampening caused by the departure of a third of the Yugoslavs, a frenetic mood prevailed amongst those who were left. The party once again went into full swing. I asked your mother to dance. 'That's how one makes progress,' I said as she pulled a bit of a face and hesitated for a moment before making up her mind to precede me on to the dance floor. To hold her against me gave me a thrill I didn't attempt to hide. I moved my face close to hers. She smiled and said: 'The boy I pointed out to you just now, I've been with him for three years.' I asked whether he was jealous. 'I don't know,' she said. 'I am faithful.' I thought she could have told me that sooner: it would have saved me spending a sleepless night for nothing. At the same time, I could see in her eyes that she was calling out for something. I could guess she needed me but I wondered what for. At any rate, when she turned her back on me and joined Tarković at the end of the dance, I understood that she had established a bond between us. For the next five hours, I waited for her to reveal to me what she intended doing with me, but it was only a week later that she would do so, a week I spent enrolling in a dance class and cancelling my sea passage to Buenos Aires.

You are surprised that a man like me should have yielded to the whim of a stranger, a whim moreover that she hadn't even bothered putting into words. That's because you don't have a very clear idea of what your mother was like when she was twenty-seven. I'm sure you've seen photographs of her at that age but, quite apart from the fact they must have been blurred in your mind by the image of an ageing Dara that, whatever you do, you can never rid yourself of, you've also never stood face to face with your mother as she was when I knew her. She was everything any normally constituted Serb dreams of. She had shoulders to chop all the wood needed for an entire winter in the mountains of Bosnia, hips broad enough to bring a dozen children into the world, and the small breasts of a long distance runner, all utilitarian qualities to which were added the gentle, regular features of an Austro–Hungarian aristocrat and the merciless eyes of a heyduck chieftain. You felt she could be at once a solid guardian of the *kuca* — a Serbian word for both the house *and* the family — a mischievous and courageous sister, or a *Vila* even, a creature out of Balkan legends who goes naked under a short, transparent shirt and spends most of her time moving about from one end of the forest to the other on fast horses. Infinitely desirable, capricious and cruel, the unpredictable *Vilas* either seduce men or shoot arrows at them, unless they decide to drown them in a stream. But as the legend points out, 'whereas most people should avoid *Vilas* lest dreadful things should happen, others can fraternise with them; they school them in their twelve arts and, during a final dance, they initiate them into their secrets...' The 'initiated' are then endowed with supernatural powers. They can produce clouds at will and generally influence the weather.

Nobody quite managed to stay awake until the time of the first *métro*. People dozed off in turn. Those who'd drunk too much had already been sick and didn't feel like starting again. The others couldn't face drinking more slivovitz at four o'clock in the morning. So we all threw ourselves on the supplies of mineral water. As for Dara, she went off with another young woman into the streets of Pantin in search of some hot croissants. I had sufficient money on me to get a taxi at least all the way to Budapest, but I didn't want to part from my penniless compatriots: they all looked so touching to me, with their heavy eyelids and their undone shoelaces.

And so your mother granted me a first date a week later. We met in a bar on the Champs-Élysées not far from her new hotel. She ordered a grenadine and talked exclusively about Tarković. I wondered if this was to put me off or because she had nothing else to say to me. Making the most of one of the few moments of silence, I told her I was in love with her. She shook her head. In love with her? But I didn't even know her! I said maybe that was why. She showed some surprise, giving first the impression she was trying to fathom this remark, then that she was giving up, and finally she reached the conclusion that this was 'all a bit flippant'. After which she looked up to consult the clock that was above the bar and said, in a way remarkably lacking in naturalness, that she was late and had to go.

We saw each other regularly for a number of weeks without ever exchanging anything other than unambiguous handshakes and thoughts on the life and *mores* of Dušan Tarković. He was so vain that his clothes filled the entire wardrobe. Dara had had to borrow a trunk to put hers in. He picked his teeth interminably at the end of each meal. He could only get to sleep if his head was to the north, so they'd had to move all the furniture about in their room, which had led to untold complications with the hotel owner. He made frequent journeys to Belgium, Switzerland and Italy to do business of a mysterious kind about which all she could tell me was that it couldn't be all that successful since he never had a bean. He refused to wash his own shirts and, since he wore a fresh one every day, this meant your mother had a lot of laundry to do. He only ever smoked half of a cigarette which absolutely infuriated your mother. His great — and only — quality, as quite manifestly she'd not been able to discover another one, was that if he felt you needed him, he didn't think twice about coming a thousand kilometres to see you. 'You clap your hands, and there he is!' she said. She also marvelled at the ease with which he could get rid of his friends and countless 'business acquaintances' if she asked him to take care of her for a day or two. Perhaps basically this was what she wanted: to clap her hands and have a man appear beside her, and then clap them again and be alone with her needle and thimble and her dreams.

I had taken a room in a good hotel in the Opéra quarter and it was there that on 2 March 1951, during one of Tarković's numerous 'business trips', I made love to her for the first time. She took a desperately long time undressing in the bathroom and then walked into the room hiding her breasts behind her folded arms. She slipped under the sheets while I stood in front of the bed, naked, quite still, and displaying my prick and my war wounds with a complacency that seems quite deplorable in retrospect. I then got into bed, grasped her around the hips and kissed her. She furtively caressed my armpits. A few weeks later, she confided to me that this was one of the parts of a man's body that she preferred because it was one of the softest and silkiest. I waited for her to show me the rhythm and let myself be rocked. She kept her eyes half-closed and I couldn't guess if this was because she was concentrating on her pleasure or on the contrary because she didn't want to let on that she wasn't hoping for any. Then we started to kiss and I got the feeling I was making contact with her for the first time since I'd known her. I couldn't stop exploring her wide open mouth and I feasted off her body's complete abandon. I told her I loved her. 'Me too,' she said. I don't quite know why, this bilateral declaration, a fairly conventional one after all in this type of situation, sent us into a frenzy. We rubbed our bodies one against the other, we served each other and worked up a good sweat in the process, and when I felt I was coming, it was as if I was clearing the last straight lap in a medium-distance race. Dara came first, or at least that's the impression she gave, and pushed me away firmly, although she kept one hand on my penis and shook it about to bring forth what would very easily have come out of its own accord. After that she rushed into the bathroom where she turned on a tap and started to laugh. I asked her what was funny. She reappeared, rubbing her abdomen with a towel. Bending her head to one side as if she were trying to turn on the charm, she told me it was the first time in her life that she'd come. I shrugged my shoulders and declared I didn't believe a word of it. Something very unexpected happened then. She glared at me with a kind of sudden hatred and tossed the towel in my face. She threw herself on me. I thought she wanted us to make love once again, but when I placed a hand on her shoulder she bit it and then she pummelled me in the stomach. Luckily there were no scissors nearby or I would have ended up with a lot of stitches like Branko Marić! Finally she calmed down and said in a hard little voice, 'I order you to believe me!' I said I believed her and asked her, perfectly logically, if she wanted us to start again. She shook her head. She didn't have the time. Already she'd encroached a lot on her working day! I pointed out to her it was Sunday. 'Precisely!' she exclaimed. 'Sunday is the day when I can work for myself!' I asked her when it was that she got any rest. She retorted that she'd get some when she was old, which might explain why she began to sleep from twelve to fourteen hours a day shortly after she was married to your father and had stopped going out to work. I also got the feeling she couldn't wait to be alone with that pleasure she'd just experienced, like a little girl in a school playground who goes away on her own to savour her afternoon snack or a good mark she's been given in the previous class.

She came back to see me the following evening after work. We stayed in bed for slightly less than an hour. I asked her why she wasn't laughing today. She said it was because she was getting used to it. Then she buried her head in my neck and, muffled by the pillow, I heard a joyful howl.

We went to have supper in a local *bistrot* where everyone ate shoulder to shoulder. The owner, a hard, authoritarian little woman, held tyrannic sway over a clientele that, in the evenings, consisted largely of bachelors resigned to their fate and illicit couples. She sized up your mother and then installed her on the bench seat because it was, she said, 'the fiancés' place'. Also sitting down, I said, 'So we are fiancés now.' Dara smiled, said no with a shake of her head and became engrossed in the menu. She ordered some *céleri rémoulade* and, after I'd explained to her it was a kind of stew, a *potée auvergnate*. She told me the story of how, when she'd first arrived in Paris, she'd been to a Greek restaurant in the Latin Quarter with the Dalmatian friend whose room she was sharing and who, like her, didn't speak a word of French, and they'd taken pot luck and ordered a dish that had turned out to be snails, something Yugoslavs detest nearly as much as horse meat or seafood. In 1943, it was almost more than Milovan Djilas could do to get what was left of the 3rd and 7th partisan divisions who'd been decimated in the Sutjeska valley to swallow a few snails! During the meal, I revealed to your mother that I'd come to Paris to settle a few matters and that I intended to go to Argentina as soon as possible. I also said that I had delayed my departure because of her. She asked me where Argentina was. 'In Latin America,' I said, which didn't seem to enlighten her very much. I added that it was a warm country and a new one, a country with a lot of space and no communists. 'What's the capital city?' she asked. I told her about Buenos Aires, a European city set on the banks of the Rio de la Plata. At last, having wiped her plate thoroughly clean with some bread, she asked when I was leaving. I was surprised and saddened by the apparent indifference with which she had received the news of my departure. I told her so. She asked me if I wanted her to slap me in the face. Then she said she loved me, she was happy with me, that to see me go to the other end of the world would break her heart, but that for one thing, I was the one who'd decided to go, a decision she'd had no part in and that therefore she refused to take any responsibility for, and that for another, she didn't feel she had the right to alter the course of my life. We weren't married, after all! That's no problem, I said, let's get married! 'What for?' she asked. Slightly off my guard, I said, 'To start a family!' She said she had no intention of starting a family and even less of setting one up on the banks of the Rio de la Plata, and then she ordered a chocolate charlotte and lit a cigarette.

Given the small amount of time we thought we had left to spend together, she agreed to come back to the hotel with me and stay the whole night. She undressed by the bed slowly, languorously, and it gave me a glimpse of the kind of idea a young Yugoslav has of strip-tease when she doesn't experience her first orgasm until the age of twenty-seven and a half. As soon as we were in bed the fury unleashed itself afresh. I think we might even have felt a little guilty about what we were doing and especially about the way we were doing it, whereas it was actually all totally natural. But we weren't 'liberated' young Westerners of the Eighties, we were Balkan people of the type for whom, over the centuries, the system of the *zadruga* or communal life had reduced physical love to its most basic expression. Any refinement in this sphere was the preserve of the Turkish invaders, great lovers, incidentally, of tender Serbian flesh, which is another reason why to this day a number of South Slavs consider eroticism to be a vile practice which relies for its existence on the sacrifice of an innocent victim.

The moment he got back, Tarković heard that Dara and I were lovers. His only reaction was to ask your mother whether that changed anything between them. She said it changed everything, which meant roughly that she would stop putting him up, feeding him, mending his clothes and of course sleeping with him. He didn't try to convince her that she would be wasting her time with me, which of course is what she did do. He only asked if she'd let him stay on in her room for a few days, long enough for him to find himself another one. Altogether it took him two and a half months, during which your mother either lived with me or was put up for a night or two by one of the women she worked with. But since she'd stopped paying the rent for her room and

Tarković hadn't taken over the payments, the hotel owner threw him out and she was able to return to her lodgings, although not before she'd settled her friend's debt which cut by half the meagre savings she'd managed to make by working sixteen hours a day. She could have left the debt as it was and taken a room elsewhere, but apart from the fact she loved the little Hôtel de la Havane, finding pleasant and inexpensive lodgings in Paris was impossible then for anyone who didn't have much time to spare.

So for the time being, because I didn't want to part from your mother, I had given up my plan of going to Argentina. I spent my days in the hotel or in cafés getting some rest after our busy nights and wondering how to set about getting her to change her mind about this country, which is so beautiful when you look at it over a long period of time. I sometimes bumped into Tarković. We greeted one another politely. Had I not been a former Četnik officer and, more especially, had I not been renowned for having killed dozens of Moslem Nazis and a good number of communists during the war, I can imagine he would have been far colder towards me. On one occasion, we had a drink together. After we'd exchanged a few platitudes, he advised me to take good care of Dara. I said I intended to do so. He remained silent, scrutinising my face as if he were already looking for the points of entry of the bullets I wouldn't fail to be hit by if I didn't treat your mother properly. He went on: 'It's not for her sake I'm saying this, but for yours.' This was followed by another silence. Even when they've only got one bit of out-of-date information and three bits of string to rub together, I've often noticed in the small-time crooks and policemen I've known this habit of always wanting to create a sense of suspense. Tarković was expecting me to ask a question, but I was too familiar with that sort of character not to know that that was the best way of delaying the moment when he'd cough up the piece of information he'd been dangling under my nose, assuming of course he had one to dangle. So I avoided showing that I was

111

in any way curious. Unable to restrain himself any longer, friend Dušan virtually pressed his lips to my ear and murmured: 'If you get too close to her, you're in danger, whoever you are.' I smiled. 'And so I am in danger,' I said. 'Because I've got *very close* to her.' He shook his head, and then: 'For my part, Mister Nikšić, I've always been very cautious with her, and have never regretted it.' He was beginning to get on my nerves! 'What do you mean by that?' I asked. He said he knew what he meant. So I grabbed him by his jacket collar and said that, as far as I was concerned, I knew he was taking me for a ride and that the few people who'd played that little game were sadly no longer with us to talk about it. He put up no resistance. With his arms hanging loosely and his head thrown back, he was smiling at me. Of course, at that moment, he was the stronger of the two of us. He'd played on my feelings and he'd won. I let go of him and suggested another drink, which was a subtle way of provisionally submitting to his rule. He ordered a cognac. Yugoslavs adore cognac. He downed his in one go. 'I don't know how, why or by whom,' he said, 'but I am sure Dara is *protected*.' He assured me he could say nothing more because he knew nothing more, and he left soon after. I sat on then, in front of my empty glass, trying to visualise the shadowy protection hovering beside my tall, childlike Dara, whose victim I ran the risk of becoming at any moment, if I was to believe Dušan. Impossible! I came to the conclusion that, using the meagre means at his disposal, Tarković was simply attempting to sour my relationship with your mother. I must say that this pathetic ploy was a failure and also that at no moment of my life with Dara did I feel the oppressive presence of the protector who seemed to have so frightened her ex-lover.

My resources were dwindling. I had to give up my room and instal myself in your mother's on rue de Trévise. Having made up my mind once and for all that I would not make my life in Europe, it was only half-heartedly that I looked for a job.

On the possibility of our leaving for Argentina, Dara remained adamant: she adored Paris and wouldn't budge from there for years. I would point out that she was probably the only woman in the world who preferred a town to a man, and that besides, it wasn't Paris that would start a family with her or guarantee her love and protection for the whole of her life, quite the opposite. She would answer that she hadn't asked me to leave and that what she wanted was Paris *and* me, to which my answer was that I wanted Buenos Aires *and* her. We always ended up calling each other 'pig-headed Croat' and 'blinkered Serb', after which we quickly made it up because making love seemed so much more important to us than making plans.

I remember the July evening when, as we were going for a walk on the Grands Boulevards, I announced to your mother that I had not a single *centime* left. She laughed and said she would keep me, she was used to it. I squeezed her wrist and said, 'The moment we get back to the hotel, you're going to get a hiding.' She asked why. Would I rather she ask me to clear off simply because of my bad financial situation? There was a moment of embarrassment which we chased away by sitting down at a café and ordering two *cafés au lait*, to the waiter's great horror.

In all the time she'd spent in France, Dara hadn't had a holiday, but that summer one of her customers invited her to spend a few weeks in a villa she and her husband owned on Lake Chambon in the Auvergne. Dara accepted, although on condition I go with her. The customer said she'd ask her husband if that would be possible. Informed of these negotiations, I criticised your mother for jeopardising such an opportunity of getting the rest and change of scenery she so badly needed. I who did nothing all day could very easily go without a holiday, and besides, it was becoming pressing that I find a job. 'Do you think,' she answered, 'that I'm stupid enough to leave you in Paris on your own when you can't walk into a

113

café or a restaurant without having ten French women instantly ready to kneel at your feet or even to follow you all the way to your confounded Argentina?' The Bauers' answer was in the affirmative and at the beginning of August, Dara and I found ourselves standing outside a block of flats on rue Lecourbe with the two wretched cardboard suitcases which marked us out as impoverished exiles. Pauline Bauer was alone in the flat, as Alexis Bauer was at his garage seeing to some last-minute checks. I immediately felt that, with my excessive politeness, the woman found me charming. You know, Slavs always double up on the good manners they've picked up in the drawing rooms of Western cities.

The Bauers had been married for about twenty years. They had two children, a son and a daughter. The son, aged sixteen, had been sent to Deal in Kent to perfect his English. It so happened that in the course of my English exile, I had stayed there myself, and the description I gave of the small seaside resort's beach and houses with their bow windows was the only contribution I made to the flagging conversation we had in the car between Paris and Chambon-sur-Lac. The daughter, Sylvie, was twenty. In 1945 she'd married a young Army NCO who'd given her three children. Pauline Bauer turned her well-meaning, pinkish face and big, ultramarine eyes towards us and said: 'In fact, you'll meet them, they'll be joining us in a week's time.' I felt a hint of anxiety in Dara's voice when she asked: 'With the children? . . .' Alexis Bauer gave her an amused look in the rear-view mirror and said: 'Of course with the children! . . . That's precisely the whole point of the operation!'

Alexis was the perfect example of the beaming, overbearing Westerner, a man you could be sure had never shaken, had never fallen, and who would only cry the day he died. He wore square spectacles, had a small, straight moustache, and his grey hair was in a crew-cut. In alphabetical order, his great passions were: Ancient Greece, cars, mountain climbing and Wagner. Next to him, I was to feel more and more Balkan

114

than ever, like one of those fanatical and dull-witted heyducks who sew up their own skin when they're putting a hem in their trousers and burst into tears when they come across a dried flower or the photo of a young Istanbul girl as they're looking through the pockets of a janissary whose throat they've just cut.

We were given a bedroom on the ground floor, next to the garage. In the mornings we got up early and went to lie by the lakeside. Apparently impervious to the water's icy temperature, your mother would swim several times. When she criticised me for staying on the beach, I told her I'd had my share of cold at Ravna Gora and that now all I expected from life was to be *warm*. We'd go back up to the villa towards midday and have a drink with the Bauers, although usually Pauline stayed in the kitchen and only came out on to the terrace every five minutes for a sip of her Saint-Raphaël, to smile at Dara in that warm but slightly pitying way she reserved for anyone who wasn't her husband, to announce 'it would soon be ready' and go back towards the house with the heavy, confident gait of a fifty-year-old woman from Lorraine. When we joined him on the terrace, where all the bottles and glasses were already laid out in anticipation of that typically French ceremony called the *apéritif*, Bauer was often repairing something, a bedside lamp, a radio or a toaster that he carried on tinkering with until lunchtime. He quite liked describing what he was doing, but despite his patient and repeated explanations, your mother never was able to understand the principle of alternating current nor even that of short-wave reception. 'But it *is* . . .' Bauer would say as we had just settled down at the dining room table and were unfolding our napkins, 'it is very simple. . . .' Then, as if it were something she'd been keeping carefully covered up, Dara would admit that she was no '*intellectouelle*', after which she'd pick up her knife and fork and attack what was on her plate with a ferocious appetite that was both pleasing and painful to see.

115

She didn't let a day go by without asking Pauline if she didn't have a tablecloth to mend or a dress to shorten. Kindly Mrs Bauer had a job convincing her she had nothing of the sort, and that even if there were a few items of clothing or some table linen hanging about in the villa's many wardrobes that could have done with the attentions of a seamstress, it was out of the question that Dara should see to them. She was *on holiday* here. How many times did she have to be told? Of course, your mother retorted, but aside from the fact she would have been happy to help out when people offered her such generous hospitality, she was also like those pianists who need to play each day to remain in 'top' form, she would say, using the English word, and she virtually suffered physically if she had to abstain from sewing for a week. One morning, Pauline gave in and handed her two or three of Alexis' shirts that were missing a few buttons. Dara settled down in a corner of the terrace with a small sewing kit she'd brought from Paris just in case and, while I went down towards the lake on my own, she happily set to work.

Her other obsession during our stay in the Auvergne was '*excoursions*', as she called them. Each day, as we were finishing lunch, she asked if anyone felt like 'going out in the *environs*'. The *environs*! She always pronounced the word with a voluptuous pleasure. You could feel that for her, real life was only ever to be had in the *environs*, never at the centre! We'd have our coffee on the terrace and then Bauer got the car out. Pauline gladly relinquished the 'dead man's seat' to your mother and came and sat next to me on the back seat. But she usually stayed at the villa to read or listen to music. And so we drove all over the area, from Saint-Nectaire to La Bourboule and from the Mont-Dore to Issoire. Dara would open her window and rest her elbow on the frame. She asked if she might turn the radio on. I felt that Bauer found her both exasperating and fascinating. There were things about her he would always despise, such as her lack of culture or her intrinsic vulgarity, but at the same time he would have wanted to lose himself in her, to let himself be snapped up like a fly by her zest for life and her joyful, jangling love of humanity.

The day when his daughter Sylvie was due to arrive from Paris, with her three children but without her husband, Bauer dragged me off on a sort of forced march over one of the squat mountains that surrounded the lake. He was wearing a pair of khaki shorts and a cowboy hat. At the start of our hike, he picked up a dead branch which lay on the path and hewed it with his Opinel to make it into a walking stick. I was standing with my hands in the pockets of my terylene trousers looking thoughtfully at my moccasins. 'You won't be comfortable for walking, dressed like that,' he'd said when he'd seen me come out of the house. He didn't know how I'd sometimes fought in clothes that got in my way a lot more than this outfit would, or even in nothing more than underpants, like the morning when the partisans had caught us unawares as we were bathing in the Drina!

The sun was beating down hard on the two of us, bizarre-looking walkers that we were. Bauer was ahead of me. He had slim legs. When he turned towards me, I could tell he was beginning to feel the strain: his face was getting redder and redder and his eyes were misting over behind his glasses. He'd ask, 'You all right?' I'd nod my head. With one hand shading his eyes, he admired the verdant banks of the lake, the rocky peak he called 'the virgin's leap', the surrounding hills and villages. Then, leaning on his improvised walking stick, he moved on again.

Shortly before midday, we settled down in the shade of a tree and took out our provisions. There was of course too much butter, too much *saucisson* and too much gherkin in the sandwiches Dara had prepared for me. Bauer ate his corned beef with that fussy daintiness that is peculiar to very practical husbands. There was between us a dense silence, due largely to the fact that we'd known since the beginning of Dara's and my stay that we'd nothing to say to one another.

117

For Bauer to have dragged me this far, he must have had a very specific problem to settle with me, so I patiently waited for him to start talking.

It was as we were coming back down towards Chambon that he broached the subject he had on his mind. It concerned your mother. He liked her. It wouldn't be going too far to say that he liked her a lot. He it was who'd insisted that Pauline invite her little dressmaker to Chambon. When Dara had put the condition I've told you about, it was him again who'd urged his wife to accept, despite all the complications this meant regarding his plan. But there you are, he was quite smitten! He found Dara splendid. Her freshness, her enthusiasm, and lastly, the fact she was such a fine-looking girl had seduced him in a way I couldn't begin to imagine. With an irony that he entirely failed to notice, I asked: 'Does all this concern me in any way?' He looked at me as if he were thinking these Yugoslavs really weren't the cream of humanity, and then explained that he wished to enquire as to the nature of my relationship with your mother. I asked in what way this was any business of his. 'My dear friend, don't take it like that,' he said. 'Believe me, you have everything to gain from this deal . . . .' What deal? He shook his head. A deal, he said, wasn't the appropriate term. Did I prefer arrangement? To my own amazement, he didn't even notice the anger that was welling up inside me, and he started to hold forth like some gentleman farmer debating the price of a calf with a livestock dealer. It was like this: he was well aware of the financial difficulties someone like me would be going through and so long as I left him a free hand where Dara was concerned, he was happy to help me out. I was too busy imagining Bauer's free hand, flitting about your mother's body like a bat, to be able to answer. He sighed. Wasn't he making himself clear enough? He wanted that girl and he would do anything to get her. That was the way he was. And so, rather than involve us in an interminable and tedious conflict, he preferred to come straight to a kind of agreement with me,

118

one that would be mutually beneficial.

The horizon was a hot, hazy blur. I sat down on a large stone. Behind me I could hear Bauer pacing up and down. At one moment, he muttered: 'This mustn't stop us getting back down to Chambon. . . . I am, after all, keen to see my daughter!' I got up and said, 'You'll never see your daughter again, Bauer.' He asked my why not, but by the time he'd uttered the last word of his question, he'd understood. 'Don't be ridiculous,' he said. Do you know, Miss Laurens, it is true that I was very angry with him, but it's also true that it had been a long time since I'd killed anyone, and I do believe I was beginning to miss it. Three or four metres lay between us. That male and craggy face of his, with its self-assured consulting engineer's features, had suddenly turned into the face of a little boy who's up to no good and gets caught red-handed. In a plaintive voice, he said, 'What is it you've got against me, Mister Nikšić? That I brought you on holiday? Provided you with a room? Fed you? Took you out to explore the area? If that's the reward you get for hospitality and generosity in your country. . . .' I didn't answer. You see, the time for words was over. My big problem was how to hurl Bauer into space without giving him a single blow that could be identified as such by the forensic expert who'd be bound to examine the body. I moved closer and grabbed his wrists, leading him into a sort of grotesque tango. I was far younger and far stronger than him. He was yelping, 'Let me go! Will you let me go!' and it didn't for a minute occur to him that if he'd yelled out 'Help!', it would in fact have forced me to release him and carry on with our walk, irrespective of the psychological difficulties that would be bound to arise between us following the little scene we'd just been through together. Right at the end, when he already had one foot dangling in space, he pleaded with me: 'I beg your pardon. . . . I'm sorry. . . .' He was sobbing. As he fell against the rocks with a dull thud, I heard him moaning; then his body did a leap of about a hundred metres before being dashed against the

119

ground. I carefully looked around. There was no one. I set off towards the nearest village to look for help.

Amongst the various studies that have been written about the Serbians, there is one which dwells on the way they so easily fly off the handle and which attributes this short-temperedness to the severe swaddling small babies are subjected to in that part of the world. If I remember rightly, the author underlined how short-lived Balkan people's fits of anger are. As far as I am concerned, the author was perfectly correct because I regretted my action as soon as I realised Bauer was dead. But I had to think of my safety as well as Dara's, and I must say that in that situation, as in many others, I managed to sort things out pretty successfully.

The light was fading when I arrived within sight of the villa. The lights were on in all the rooms and the house glowed like a Christmas tree in the middle of the blue mountains. A damp breeze was blowing off the lake. Pauline was on the terrace. She was sitting in a wicker armchair, knitting by the light of a storm lantern and chatting to a young blonde woman who could only be her daughter Sylvie. Suddenly your mother appeared. She had three children running after her, shouting. Dara pretended to lose her balance and collapsed on the terrace, which inevitably reminded me of the way Bauer had died a few hours earlier. The children showed obvious signs of delight as they smothered her with their three little bodies. She was howling. They'd probably discovered her weakness: she was ticklish! As I was walking resolutely up to the gate, I thought of the great amount of unhappiness I was about to throw over this gentle summer's evening when, in a moment that was now imminent, I would go up to Pauline and tell her that Alexis had had an accident.

4

So, Brigitte, you want to know whether, during the eleven months Dara spent in Italy immediately after the war, she had any dealings with an Aunt Nathalie. I am quite sure I never once heard her utter the name Nathalie, and the only aunt she mentioned within my hearing between June 1945 and May 1946 was Vesna Okrugić, her mother's sister. She had just been taken to hospital in Zagreb with a kidney infection. On the other hand, I do know that in mid-December she met a Yugoslav woman who helped her out over a very specific matter in a way that was quite unhoped-for. She was a royalist Serbian refugee of about fifty. She called herself Christiane. 'A code name,' your mother would underline with a conspiratorial air that seemed as ridiculous to me as the habit she had of always getting up in the middle of the night to check that the heavy front door of our house in Milan had been securely bolted, because she didn't want Tito's 'black trios' — Yugoslav agents who were known by this name because, like the Ustaše 'triads', they operated in groups of three — to catch her asleep, bundle her up and pack her off to a concentration camp in Serbia. When I asked her why this person used a code name, she withdrew into a silence that must really have cost her dear. All she would say was, 'The less you know the better, for your sake.'

When I first got to know her in 1945, I was seventeen, with big blue eyes and plump cheeks which meant that everyone assumed I was the daughter of a former fascist, whereas in fact my father had contented himself with improving the productivity of the farms we owned in Tuscany and stuffing my mother and me with their copious produce for the entire duration of the war — binges that sometimes ended in such terrible dyspepsia that we then had to spend the next day or

121

two in bed. Needless to say, I fell in love with the first American soldier I came across! He was a slightly built officer who arrived at our house laden with army rations. Mama casually set them all down on the hall table. The young man had seen too many of his comrades acquiring the virginity of an Italian schoolgirl in exchange for *one* silk stocking not to be surprised by the cool reception we gave to his tins of bully-beef. Mama showed him to his room. When she came back down to the sitting room, she declared she didn't find him very tall for an American. She added, in a disappointed way, that at the most he was 'two or three centimetres taller than the Duce'.

Over the next few days, I came across him a number of times around Milan. He drove a jeep. He would pull up as soon as he saw me and say a few words in Italian. His accent really made my girlfriends laugh. Quite unruffled, he went into raptures over the fine blue Milan sky, the sweetness of the air or the architecture of the cathedral, but luckily these tedious remarks were drowned by the noise of the engine that he kept running. I was dying for him to invite me to climb in beside him, but he must have felt I was too young to go parading up and down the streets sitting next to a foreign army officer. Then my friends and I would go into Sempione Park, where we would soon be joined on our bench by a few soldiers out on a spree, their pockets overflowing with chew-ing-gum and bars of chocolate. The most uninhibited amongst us would allow themselves to be led off into some distant corner of the park to get up to things that, once evening had come, would plague my imagination — for, sad as it made me feel, I did not belong to that category of more forward girls. Ahead of me loomed the moment when I'd have to set off home along the red and gold streets smelling of warm sweat and fried onions, streets that seemed endlessly to beckon me towards love and adventure with their bare-armed young boys sitting along the pavements, their open-air cinemas, their terraces crowded with soldiers eating alongside girls whose disgusting good luck it was to be a few years older than me, their back-firing jeeps, their little orchestras playing on makeshift platforms. By the time I reached corso Magenta where our house was, I was quite convinced that happiness had forever passed me by.

One June evening, I got back to corso Magenta earlier than usual. I opened the sitting-room door and gave my parents a vague greeting. I was about to race into the kitchen and wolf down my tea when I realised that Papa and Mama were looking rather peculiar. I asked what the matter was. Mama turned her fine, tired face towards me and said, 'John has asked to marry you.' She examined me from head to toe with an air of consternation as if, without the least hope of success, she wanted to find out what it was that this child in white ankle socks and a straight skirt could possibly have to arrest the attention of an American officer. For my part I was so unaware of the interest Lieutenant Berenson showed in me that I asked if this wasn't a joke. 'No, it isn't a joke,' Papa said gloomily. He got up and came towards me with his arms outstretched, but I was too overwhelmed by what I had just heard to be able to stand my father's embrace. All of a sudden I had outgrown this kind of thing! I dodged by him and ran across to sit down next to Mama so we could have a proper woman to woman conversation about all this. She told me John had come to have coffee at home shortly after I'd left for school, as if he'd been waiting for me to be out before talking to them about his plans. He wasn't quite wearing white gloves, but he certainly looked like an English minister officiating at a princely burial as he announced to my dumbfounded parents that he wished to marry me and take me to Concord (New Hampshire). Papa asked him what justified such a decision and Mama added that she would like to know whether I was aware of the step he was taking. He said he loved me. In spite of my tender age, to him I was the very embodiment of the feminine ideal. If he'd chosen to speak to them first, it was to avoid giving rise to any bitterness

123

in me should they answer negatively. 'Perhaps Giuliana would be very annoyed if we said yes,' said Mama, and my father concluded, 'In any case, it is not up to us to say yes or no.'

John got back around eight. I'd had time to look up Concord in the *Encyclopedia Britannica* and find out where it was, to wash my hair, to spend at least an hour hovering in front of my wardrobe before choosing the dress I'd wear when I told Lieutenant John Berenson that I agreed to become his wife, and lastly, to write a letter to my best friend who'd long been a neighbour but was now living in Fregene near Rome. I had then settled myself by my bedroom window and gazed out at corso Magenta, reflecting on how I would soon be free of Milan and of that awful fate confronting me as a young Italian girl. The moment I heard the doorbell go, I was on the alert. Following the example of those American movie heroines who filled the imagination of every young European girl of the time, I rushed out of my room and threw myself down the stairs as if into a void. John was there. Standing. Looking extremely pale. The emotion of it all, I thought. He gave me a sad little smile as if he wanted to comfort me. He said: 'The 92nd division is re-deploying towards Trieste.' — 'When?' I asked. He took my hands in his and said, 'Tomorrow morning.' I asked him when he'd be coming back. He didn't know. Istria was then at the centre of a closely fought struggle between the governments of Italy and Yugoslavia, and it's an amusing coincidence, although one which I don't suppose will have carried much weight in History's great march forward, that this struggle was to be finally resolved in Paris in December 1946, in other words a few months after Dara Sevnica's arrival in the French capital. I said it didn't matter, it would simply delay our engagement for a few weeks, or at worst a few months. He asked, 'Do you wish to be my wife?' Drawing a breath, I said yes by simply closing my eyes, but that wasn't enough for him. 'Do you agree we should marry?' he asked. I should make clear that this conversation took place in English, a language everyone at home could speak fluently. Yes, I said. I agreed. I totally agreed. He then leant towards me and kissed me on the cheek. I had the feeling he was congratulating his young cousin for having won a school prize. 'Wait,' he said. I was standing alone in the middle of the passage, dazed and with my eyes glued to the front door which had just shut. He came back a few minutes later with two huge bunches of flowers. One he handed to Mama, the other to me. 'And what about me?' asked my father. There was much laughter that evening around the family dinner table adorned by my fiancé's flowers and on which the maid set several delicious dishes. John, whom we had gradually weaned off corned beef, did great justice to these.

At midnight I made my way up to bed. My head was spinning from the champagne Papa had given us to drink at the end of the meal. Once in my room, without putting on the light, I opened the window and lay down fully dressed on my bed. Jeeps drove past in the street. I heard footsteps coming towards the door. Could it be . . . John? No, no! It was impossible! John Berenson was the kind of man who would respect me for six months following our marriage to give me time to get used to the idea I was no longer really a young girl. So the idea of consummating the marriage before our engagement was officially made public. . . . The door opened. A uniform. There was no doubt: it was him. He came to a standstill a little way from the bed while, with my heart thumping, I carried on pretending to be asleep. He whispered, 'Giuliana. . . .' I couldn't control the trembling that, bit by bit, was affecting my entire body. The only way to hide it was to move. I opened my eyes, sat up, asked, 'What are you doing here?' John sat on the edge of the bed. I moved away. He took my hand. Furious at my own silliness, I said, 'What are you doing?' — 'Try to understand, Giuliana . . .' John began. This insistence of his, calling me 'Giuliana' since our official engagement! I felt like a cat standing on a vet's surgery table whose owner keeps repeating its name to get it to draw back its claws. 'Tomorrow, Giuliana, I'll be far away. . . .' Me: 'Trieste isn't the other end of the world!' Him: 'You must try and understand, Giuliana, I'm mad about you, it's been two months and if it goes on any longer, they'll soon have to lock me up in a madhouse!' I was so astonished to hear this that I let him put his arms around my waist without reacting. So he was mad about me? But he didn't even used to look at me! 'It hurt too much to look at you,' he said. I was about to retort that I didn't believe a word of it when he covered my mouth with his. A minute or two later, amazing though it may seem, he'd got all my clothes off. I had done nothing to stop him: I was enthralled by the speed and dexterity with which he operated, it was like a conjuring trick. While he was undoing his shirt buttons, he rubbed his face against my stomach, placed his cheek on my breasts, moved his mouth across my neck and shoulders, emitting a very loud, slightly worrying sound, a mixture of a wail, a grunt and a sort of spasm. Occasionally he moved away from me and, shaking his head, gazed down at me. It was as if he couldn't believe his eyes.

So that was the day I lost my virginity. But I'll spare you the details. Exhausted by this string of extraordinary events, I fell asleep. I woke up the first time shortly before dawn and saw that John had already gone back to his room. Voluptuously, I dived back into sleep. When I next opened my eyes, it was daylight, but from the sharp coolness of the air and the excited singing of the blackbirds in the garden, I could tell it was no later than six. I heard noises coming from the ground floor. John's leaving! I thought. Why hadn't anyone come up to let me know? I simply had to kiss my fiancé before he left! I hurriedly pulled on a nightdress, rushed out of my room and started down the stairs, but I soon came to a standstill half-way down, stopped in my tracks by an unexpected sight. In his pyjamas and dressing-gown, Papa was standing opposite a tall young woman dressed in black. She had on a hat with a feather and her brown hair escaped from under it in every

126

direction. She was waving about a rectangular piece of paper and jabbering in an incomprehensible jumble of Serbo–Croat, Italian and English. I was struck by the intensity of her gaze and even more so by her colour: she wasn't tanned so much as blackened by long walks in the sun and endless time spent waiting by the roadside. There was about her the acrid smell of those who are constantly on the move and only ever wash in station toilets. She had set her cardboard suitcase down between her legs as if afraid someone might steal it from her even in this upright bourgeois home.

Papa read the piece of paper she was holding out to him. And then, speaking very slowly, he told her in Italian that he would be happy to help her out, and he bent down to pick up the suitcase. But she was quicker off the mark. Evidently, she had possessions in there that she wished no one but her to carry. 'As you like,' he said. He turned towards the stairs and saw me. I explained I'd thought it was John leaving to join his regiment and had wanted to kiss him one last time. 'He left the house at five o'clock,' said Papa. And, pointing to the young woman in black: 'I'd like to introduce Dara Sevnica. She's a Yugoslav political refugee. She's going to be staying here for a few days.' Realising that Papa was talking about her, your mother turned her small dark eyes towards me and, with an engaging smile, bowed her head slightly, I think as much in greeting as to assure me there and then of her friendship and perhaps even of her obedience.

Early the following year, she told me in great detail what had happened to her between the moment she'd clandestinely crossed the Italian–Yugoslav border at Divača and her sudden arrival at our house. Her first night in the West had been spent in the waiting room at Trieste station. She had danced, sung and played the harmonica along with other Yugoslavs. The next day, she made her way to the address of the aunt of one of her Zagreb girlfriends, a friendly widow who offered to put her up in her kitchen. She accepted. Once evening had come and she stretched out on the inflatable mattress her

127

hostess had organised for her, she felt she had scored a victory over fate. Above her she could see the four legs of the table, shelves, a post-office calendar and a clock that chimed the hours, half-hours, and even the quarter-hours! The following day, she made her way to piazza Goldoni, meeting place of all the Yugoslavs who'd fled the communist régime. There were hugs and cigarettes changed hands. By way of lunch, they went down to the harbour and ate bread and *saucisson* sitting around a mooring post they used as a table. Dara threw a little bread to the birds. They told her off: it was no doubt due to this habit that she was so thin. The huge midday sun dominated the sky. 'I feel very happy and at the same time very frightened,' she said. They answered that she had every reason to feel frightened, and this was when she heard first time about the notorious 'black trios', which bolstered her determination to leave Trieste as fast as she could. The large industrial port was far too close to Yugoslavia to give any sense of security to the sister of a former Domobrani officer. But where should she go? She would have had a job buying a train ticket for any Italian city whatsoever since she barely had the funds for the next day's food. They advised her to go to the Red Cross. She went there the following day. With the dozen or so Italian words she'd already managed to learn, she told them she'd crossed the border illegally because she wanted to be reunited with her Italian fiancé who lived in Milan. It so happened that a convoy of refugees was leaving for Milan three days later. They would make space for her. Your mother often described to me the euphoric happiness that reigned for the entire length of the journey in the cattle wagon she shared with about thirty fellow Yugoslavs. One of them had wanted to brew some coffee. They lit a fire. It soon acquired alarming proportions. So all the men present stood in a circle around it and put out the blaze by peeing on it. Dara recounted this anecdote to me several times during the eleven months she spent in Milan. It was as if what had most affected her in her journey was this circle of improvised firemen with their unusual means of putting out a fire in a cattle wagon.

The train had stopped in Verona. The refugees spent the night in a school. They slept in sleeping bags on the floor. The following morning they were given some broth and a piece of bread. Dara struck up a conversation with a young primary school teacher who was a relative of Papa's. He was very taken up by your mother, so beautiful, impulsive and friendly was she, and he was also moved by her obvious ill-health and poverty. He gave her our address and a short letter of recommendation.

The young woman reached Milan shortly after midnight. The Red Cross had fixed up a dormitory in the second-class waiting room. Dara fell into a camp-bed and slept until dawn. She was woken up by the sunlight, had a hasty wash in the toilet and, full of the delight of having an address to go to, she immediately set off towards our house without for one moment thinking it might be a little early to knock on someone's door and ask for their hospitality.

It had amused me that the town of Trieste should send us this young Yugoslav just when the American army high command had despatched my fiancé there, but in the light of subsequent events, that is, John Berenson's betrayal coupled with the ever increasing part your mother was to play in my life, this coincidence takes on a rather disquieting character. It seems as if the moment Dara turned up anywhere, something else turned up alongside her, a sort of obscure power which, perfectly concealed by the young woman's gentleness and good nature, altered the balance of things.

She had lunch and supper with us. At the beginning, she barely said anything and clearly had to make an effort not to knock over her glass or drop food all around her plate. We all felt slightly embarrassed when she quite conspicuously crooked her little finger to have a drink of water. She forced herself not to eat too fast. After each course, she couldn't help patting her stomach in a satisfied way to make clear to us how good it had been, a gesture that in her private code of etiquette was probably the equivalent of the Chinese belch or the brief note of thanks that French people send to their hostess the day after a dinner-party. She would ask what the Italian was for fork, knife, jug, bread etc. . . . She was always the first to leave the dinner table after having supplied us with an impressive list of excuses: she was off to via Meravigli or, if it were evening, to a customer who was due to try on a dress she was making for her on the quiet or, on Sundays, to her room. There she would sit by the open window mending Mama's blouses, the household sheets or some other trifle: it was her way of paying a kind of tribute to my parents, as she couldn't pay them any rent.

Quite soon she was speaking Italian. A month and a half after her arrival in Milan, it was possible to hold a coherent conversation with her. I'm pointing this out because in the early days of her stay in Paris, she would write to me that she was finding it difficult to learn French. Perhaps this was because our lifestyle suited her better than yours. It even seems to me that despite the thirty-five years she spent there, France always remained a mystery to her, whereas in Italy her spirited approach to things and her generosity opened all doors to her. I am sure she would have led a far happier life here, but she wished more than anything to go to France and especially Paris: for her, it was the capital of the world and of fashion, a magical city brimming over with princes, film actresses and 'bohemian' artists.

Mama was rather taciturn by nature — we all knew this in my family and in the neighbourhood — and we soon noticed how she cheered up in the company of our lodger from Zagreb. She who normally showed so little patience, to the point that she'd walk out of a restaurant if she wasn't immediately asked what she'd like to have or wasn't instantly served what she'd ordered, she now never tired of correcting your mother when she made grammatical errors or mispronounced something, and each day she taught her a set

130

number of new words.

One day she saw Dara on her way out wearing an English Red Cross uniform. Dara explained she'd made it herself out of a military jacket and trousers she'd picked up at the flea market. Dressed in this way, she could go for a drink, lunch or supper at the Hotel Gallia which was then reserved to British officers and NCOs. You ate well for a modest sum, and in the evenings there was an orchestra with a singer and you could dance. Mama had found the idea rather jolly and had expressed a wish to go with her if only just once: the very next day, Dara made her a uniform which she tried on in the sitting room with Papa looking on, horrified. As for me, I felt it was the first time in Mama's life that she was having fun! I can picture them now, walking arm in arm along corso Magenta in their brand new outfits, stopping at regular intervals to have a good laugh. 'They're a pair of schoolgirls,' Papa said as he closed the window. The schoolgirls got back towards five o'clock. It was a Saturday so Dara wasn't working at via Meravigli, but she'd just hired a sewing-machine to satisfy the demand from new customers who, as it happened, had been put on to her by the cashier at the Hotel Gallia, and she was determined to make the investment pay, so she quickly slipped off to her room. Mama walked into the sitting room. It was Papa who told me what happened. He looked up from his game of chess. He often played chess on his own, and would swear like a trooper each time he managed to take his queen from himself. Mama sat on his knees. 'So, was it nice?' he asked. She shook her head and kissed him with a quite unusual ardour. He never was able to find out any more. She put away the uniform in a wardrobe. It wasn't until about thirty years later that it was taken out again when, after Mama had died, Papa decided to sell the house on corso Magenta and settle down in Tuscany where he still lives now. He told me that he often caught Mama standing quite still in front of that wardrobe, gazing at the uniform she'd only worn once and that perhaps stood for her as a symbol of her last

131

moment of youth.

The friendship she bestowed on Dara was returned to her a hundred-fold, and it got on my nerves. I felt jealous of both your mother and mine. I decided to set about winning over the Yugoslav woman, with all the more reason since Lieutenant John Berenson's first letter was taking a painfully long time to reach me and I was beginning to suffer from a kind of damming-up of feelings. But I didn't choose my day very well. When I got to Dara's bedroom, her door was open and I saw the young woman filling a suitcase that was placed on the bed. My immediate thought was: something terrible has happened. Noticing I was there, your mother gave me a broad, cheerful smile. I asked her what she was doing. 'Packing,' she simply said. She was off to live in a room one of her compatriots had rented. They would share the cost of it as well as any upkeep and food bills. 'Everything's cheaper when there's two of you,' she said. I asked her why she wasn't staying on here. She shrugged her shoulders. But because that had never been the intention! My father had offered to help her out, that was all, and now that she could stand on her own two feet, it was out of the question that she should continue getting in our way. So I asked who had told her she was 'getting in our way'. Where had she got that fanciful piece of information from? 'Certainly not from Mama, I shouldn't think,' I said with a touch of dismay that made her smile. She assured me that the gratitude she felt for my parents was unbounded. It was simply that she had to ensure she didn't become a 'fixture' in our house. It was quite true that she'd been living in clover here and that she might regret her decision to leave but, even though she was hardly the type to have principles, there was at least one that meant a lot to her: not to encroach on anyone's independence and never to endanger her own. I said, 'I was hoping we'd become friends.' And so, she said, in what way would this alter anything? She would give me her new address and I would drop in and visit her whenever I felt like it. I said it wasn't the same thing. She wouldn't be alone, she'd have other things to do. I noticed she was staring at me with a look of surprise. She must have been wondering why I was creating a scene over her leaving when I'd barely talked to her more than a dozen times during the three weeks she'd just spent in the house. I myself was finding my determination to keep her from going difficult to understand. As I was talking, using simple words that I carefully separated from each other and hammered out until they sounded almost like German, I felt like a bobsleigh launched down an icy track. Impossible to stop or reverse. I told her I was terribly lonely, especially since John had left for Trieste. She asked who John was. 'My fiancé,' I said. She exclaimed. 'At seventeen, you already have a fiancé!' I looked up at her with a pitiful expression: 'I've even got a lover.' She said, 'Well then, you're not as lonely as all that!' But she didn't understand! My fiancé was also my lover, he had left the house three weeks before to follow his regiment to Trieste, since when he'd not shown any sign of life. 'Perhaps he's dead!' was her comment. Seeing how crestfallen I looked, she hurriedly added, 'Of course, I hope not. . . .' And then, 'But you know, men. . . .' She explained to me one should not count on men too much. The only thing that interested them was getting their end away. 'And then, *ciao*,' she said. As she was delivering this pessimistic lecture on the opposite sex, she carried on filling her suitcase. We sat on it to close it. 'How are you getting there?' I asked. A Yugoslav was coming to fetch her in a car. Leaning on the ledge of the bedroom window, we waited for him. Rather at random, I asked, 'Are you in love with him?' thinking she'd cluck disdainfully and declare that no man was worthy of our feeling anything for him, or alternatively that she hadn't the time to devote to love. Far from it, for she gravely nodded her head. Yes, she was in love with him. She thought about him non-stop. And in fact she was sure I too would fall in love with him as soon as I saw him, which wouldn't be long. Sure enough, five minutes later a white car appeared on corso Magenta and your mother said, 'That's him.' I was surprised to see there was a woman in the car. 'That's my *camarade*,' said Dara. So her boyfriend hadn't come to pick her up on his own? 'He's not my boyfriend,' she said. 'He wants us simply to be *camarades*.' It was funny, all these anti-communists who made such a cult of comradeship!

The following morning, my parents received a letter from Lieutenant John Berenson. He asked them to impart to me the sad news of the breaking-off of our engagement. He recognised that he'd got rather carried away over this idea. On reflection, he felt I was too young to make a suitable wife. In addition he hesitated to take on the responsibility for transplanting a young Milanese girl to New Hampshire. He feared such a pretty Italian bloom might soon wilt under the pale, cold Concord sky.

I heard about the broken-off engagement in more or less the same circumstances as those in which I'd got to know I'd been asked to become someone's wife. I was just back from school. My parents were in the sitting room. They looked at me and, because of the contrast with the last time, I immediately understood what had happened.

Reading John's letter, I realised that neither Papa nor Mama had been in a position to gauge how shabby his behaviour had been and that it was probably for this reason the American had written to them rather than to me. Behind each of his measured, dignified sentences that he'd occasionally embellished with an Italian word in order, I suppose, to let us know there remained a *sentimental* bond between him and our country, I could see once again that night of love-making during which he'd had me, used me up with an enthusiasm that was now perfectly understandable. I could picture the little smile, at once mocking and slightly bitter, that probably hadn't left his face the whole time he was writing that letter. Because he couldn't have not thought about that famous night, just as I couldn't! The sheet of paper shook in my hands. While my parents were advising me not to be sad 'over such a little thing', I was crying with rage. I thought to myself that the morning John had asked to marry me, he'd known that twenty-four hours later he'd be leaving for Trieste. And perhaps it was even because he'd known that that he'd asked me to marry him!

I'd really been *had* by Berenson, in every sense of the word, and, even though I was really far less of an innocent victim and less of a badly bruised one than the American probably thought, there was only one person who might comfort me for having been taken for a ride like this, and that was your mother. 'I must go and see Dara,' I said. Papa nodded. I got the feeling he was delighted at having got off so lightly: my being upset over this was the sort of thing he didn't begin to know how to deal with. As for Mama, she showed no interest in the matter; she told me in a lifeless voice, almost as if she regretted having to say it: 'Don't come back too late.'

After she'd opened the door of her new abode for me, your mother drew me to her and kissed me on both cheeks for the first time since we'd known each other. She was on her own, as Dinka had gone to have an English lesson with a teacher who lived on the outskirts of the town. She said it was nice of me to have come to see her the very day after she'd moved in.

Visiting the flat was limited to wandering around one large room with bluish walls and quite high ceilings. There was only one bed. Two armchairs that didn't match faced each other in one corner; the sink and coal-burning stove stood in the opposite corner. 'The sitting room,' said your mother. 'Make yourself comfortable, I'm going to make some cocoa. . . .' The window panes rattled each time a tram went past. 'It reminds me of Maksimirska,' she said. Maksimirska is the street in Zagreb where she spent most of her youth. The Singer sewing-machine sat proudly in front of the open window. Dara told me there were mice. I lifted my feet off the floor the tiniest bit. She added, 'They only come out of their hole at night. But Dinka doesn't like them because they leave little droppings on the sink.' She handed me my cocoa. I said

135

I'd had news from John and it wasn't good: he'd broken everything off with me. As you can imagine, your mother cried out that, on the contrary, that was good news indeed! To marry was idiotic, but to marry at seventeen was sheer lunacy! Oh, how pleased she was for me, so pleased that she was going to kiss me this instant, there! Freedom, she said as she sat down again and lent over to pick up the cup she'd put on the floor for herself, freedom was the only real thing. In fact, it was partly due to the lot that befell women in Yugoslavia that she'd left the country. She'd seen her mother washing your grandfather Josip's feet a few times too often. In a world that reduced a woman to slavery the minute she wore a ring on her finger, or treated her as if she were less than nothing if she tried to stay single or dared to get a divorce, in such a world a young woman with a thirst for freedom, independence and why not say it, adventures, could neither live nor blossom!

Branko Marić turned up around eight o'clock, followed a few minutes later by the man your mother was in love with: Stefan Miljus. He was very tall, like all the Yugoslavs I was to meet that year. He began telling some story in Serbo-Croat. I of course couldn't understand a thing and was having the greatest difficulty in putting up any kind of show, with Dara who seemed highly amused on one side, and Branko Marić on the other who kept eyeing me knowingly as if to say: 'He's really hilarious, isn't he?' As he reached the punch line, Stefan turned towards me; this gave your mother the idea of warning him I didn't speak their language. I gathered she was also filling him in on what had happened to me, which quite ruined poor Stefan's story. He never did tell the end. He said a few basic things to me in Italian such as, 'Americans good for war not love' or, 'You too pretty to be sad' and then Dinka Mirovats got back from her lesson and I was once again submerged in a tumultuous torrent of Serbo-Croat. From time to time, one of these boisterous exiles would stare at me, smiling and nodding as if to agree to a sentence I might have uttered in some miraculous way. All four of them were getting a distinctly sensual pleasure from smoking Chesterfields that they helped themselves to from a packet Branko Marić had put on the table when he arrived. At one point, at the end of a sort of fever-pitch debate which I thought I'd correctly identified as a political discussion, whereas in fact they were simply deciding where we were going to spend the evening, Stefan stood up and the others followed suit. I told Dara I was going to make my way home. 'Why?' she asked. 'We've been organising the evening with you very much in mind!' Branko smiled at me. He said, 'We're going to celebrate to make you forget how unhappy you are.' His Italian sounded even more melodious than the real thing. He took me by the shoulder and led me down the stairs.

It surprised me to see Dara and Dinka automatically sit on the back seat of Stefan's car and encourage me to do the same while Branko installed himself comfortably next to the driver. However fanatically macho Italian men may have been at the time, they would still let their wives or girlfriends sit on the front seat when they were out together in the car, and I failed to understand why your mother and Dinka — hardly what you'd call submissive females — would happily hand over this privilege to Branko Marić. But this was such a well-established part of the group's ways that each time I got in a car with them, things happened in the same fashion. In fact this did nothing to impair the friendly, jolly atmosphere that existed among them. The men sat in the front and the women in the back and that was all there was to it.

All the way to that restaurant in Monza where I was going to 'get plastered' for the first time in my life, I sat closely wedged against Dinka who didn't speak a word of Italian. She wasn't much interested in Italy, and communism so terrified and disgusted her that she would never have agreed to set up home within an hour's flight of Belgrade. Which was why, as she waited for her visa to the United States, she was learning English, and it was in that language which she already spoke well that, over dinner, we exchanged views on the world, life and especially Dara Sevnica. Halfway through the evening, when I was still more or less clear-headed, or at least sufficiently so to notice your mother and Branko dancing a kind of *kolo* crossed with the charleston in between the tables, she said to me, 'When you know about her past, you wonder how she manages to be so buoyant.' I made some rather silly comment like: 'You have to turn your back on the past, especially when it's been unhappy.' Then I added, 'And anyway, you've all lived through pretty much the same things, haven't you?' She gave me a sad smile and said, 'Perhaps you don't know *everything*.' Offended, I retorted in a voice that sounded as whiny as if I'd been holding my nose: 'I'd go so far as to say that I know just about *nothing*.' And her: 'Dara has lived through far tougher things than most of us.' Of course I asked what. She said it wasn't for her to tell me. All I had to do was question your mother. But would I be kind enough to avoid mentioning that she had put me on that track?

I wonder what Dinka and your mother found to talk about during all those evenings they spent alone together in their lodgings on via della Moscova that summer, because as far as their cultural backgrounds were concerned they were as different as day from night! At twenty-six, Dinka Mirovats was a highly qualified legal expert, whereas Dara's only qualification was the *Poslovna Knizitsa*, a certificate she'd been given in August 1941 at the end of three years studying at a vocational school. Nevertheless, there wasn't a hint that they were kept apart by anything they couldn't share. This was perhaps due to Dinka's view that no great culture can exist which isn't in some way self-mocking and doesn't occasionally link arms with the most straightforward manifestations of uncultured life. As for your mother, you know how she had a quite unshakeable ability to adapt, and she even derived a certain pleasure from mixing with people who spoke about things she didn't understand. It gave her a thrill.

At one in the morning, without having bothered to ask for

a bill, Stefan handed the waiter half a dozen notes the size of handkerchiefs. We got to our feet. There were several empty bottles on the table. White wine and mineral water that had served to initiate me to what Dara, as a Croat, called *gemicht* and Dinka, a Serb, called *špricer*. It's a drink that seems so harmless you can't help overdoing it, which makes it far more fearsome than your cognac or our grappa. Four measures of white wine to one of fizzy water. It's the champagne of the East European countries.

I remember that your mother and Dinka helped me to the car. Branko and Stefan were just outside the restaurant talking to a fat, bearded fellow. We waited for them, leaning on the bonnet of the Panhard. Dara told me the restaurant belonged to the bearded fellow. 'He's a Montenegrin who emigrated before the war,' she went on. He was also Stefan's *pobratim*. She explained what a *pobratim* was. 'But in that case why did he make us pay?' I asked. Then in my drunken state, I imagined with a weird clarity that I saw Dara casting a most worried look at Dinka Mirovats. I wondered what on earth I'd said that could be so worrying to the two young women.

The restaurant owner embraced Stefan and shook Branko's hand. Our two friends walked back toward the car, which was soon racing along the bumpy road; I dozed with my head resting alternately on Dara's and her friend's shoulder. All of a sudden, everything went very quiet, and I realised we'd stopped. We got out of the car. I wondered why the grass was so damp as there hadn't been a drop of rain for a week. Could it be so late in the night that the dew had already settled on it? Branko's white shirt made a dazzling mark on the blue of the grass as he crouched to spread out a blanket. 'We're sleeping here?' I asked innocently. I understood straight away what his smile meant, but for a reason that was very similar to the one that had made me pretend I was asleep when John had walked into my room after our engagement supper, I carried on playing the innocent and exclaimed, 'That's lucky: I'm

139

tired!' Then I lay down with my two hands tucked under my cheek like a pillow and closed my eyes. Branko took a few steps around the blanket and finally sat down on it. He lit a cigarette. To this day I find it impossible to smell the smoke of a Chesterfield without immediately having all the events of that evening in July 1945 passing through my mind. Branko put one hand on my thigh. I opened my arms and soon had a huge teddy bear lying on my chest speaking words I didn't understand as he busily stripped the clothes away from the lower half of my body and his. Thinking I was still a virgin, he penetrated me gently. When he realised there was no more than the usual resistance, he looked at me with surprise. I guessed he was saying to himself, 'That American's been this way.' This seemed to sadden him, but for my sake more than anything, so that as I reached my climax I felt wrapped as much in compassion as in a lover's tenderness. After many quiet, warm minutes had passed during which I fought off as best I could the temptation to fall asleep, I asked Branko where Dara, Dinka and Stefan were. He said he'd no idea. I asked if there was another blanket in the boot of the Panhard. He laughed. 'No,' he said. 'I don't think so.' So, I asked, how had they managed? 'Perhaps they haven't had to manage anything,' Branko said with slight embarrassment. I said I didn't believe a word of it; that he and Stefan had premeditated what seemed more and more clearly to me to be a gang rape. I got up: 'Let's go and join our companions in debauchery!' He laughed and told me I was crazy. He folded the blanket. I could guess I'd disappointed him, but then I had done so on purpose.

We came across Dara first of all, about twenty metres from the car. She was leaning against a tree smoking a cigarette. 'What are the others doing?' I asked and, seeing the livid look Branko gave me, I got the feeling I should have kept quiet. I noticed that your mother was crying. There followed a great out-pouring of Serbo-Croat. Dara was railing against I don't know who while Branko, who'd put his arms around her neck, was trying to calm her down, talking to her gently, agreeing with all her incensed talk in a way clearly intended to soothe her, and kissing her cheeks two or three times. Standing a little way from them, I was quietly reflecting that Dinka was a 'bitch', since I wasn't yet aware that it was only because your mother had refused to give herself to him that Stefan had had recourse to the lawyer's services. Contrary to what I'd imagined, at first Dinka had taken no notice of his advances. She'd only yielded to Stefan after she'd been pressured by your mother who felt it was unfair that her two friends should deny themselves a pleasure because of her. That was absolutely typical of Dara! Because at the same time she was incredibly hurt by Dinka and Stefan's twofold betrayal, a betrayal she herself had engineered! But there you are, her spirit of *camaraderie* had won the day. Of course you're wondering what had led her to reject a man she found so attractive. It's not so difficult: she didn't want to be merely one more woman in Stefan's life. And he'd explained to her that it wasn't by sleeping together once, or even several times, that they would become anything more than they already were for each other. For your mother, making love was more than physical exercise. No, it meant many things — a deep commitment of one's being, a complete gift of oneself. And so she preferred to leave Stefan to her best friend rather than be no more than an instrument of pleasure who would rejoin the well populated ranks of Stefan Miljus' '*camarades*' once the business was over.

The sky was beginning to lighten. Stefan and Dinka emerged from the screen of trees behind which they'd disappeared an hour earlier. They were holding hands and were both smoking cigarettes. Despite the anger I felt at the offhand way they'd behaved towards your mother, I couldn't help feeling close to them. I had an urge to put my arms around them and ask: 'So, was it nice?' Dinka, out of provocativeness, an oversight, or simply because she was hot, had neglected to button up the top of her blouse so that we could see the best part of her ample breasts, glistening with sweat in the darkness. Without seeming in the least ashamed, embarrassed or anything of the sort, she was avoiding looking at us; rather she looked as if she wanted to carry on thinking about what had occurred between Stefan and her, to keep safely locked away inside her the pleasure she had just had. As for Stefan, he slid into the driver's seat and started the engine. But before driving off, he turned around and, without paying any attention to his two Yugoslav friends, he gave me a look full of gentleness and said, 'Now we'll get Giuliana back to her mama.' Then he asked: 'Giuliana won't get told off?' As if it could have mattered to him in any way! I shook my head to say no. '*Perfetto*,' said he, after which he drove us into Milan at top speed.

At around three-thirty the same day, Dara and Branko rang the doorbell of the corso Magenta house. I was just coming out of the shower and while I dried myself and got dressed, Papa made them welcome in the sitting room and offered them a drink. Mama was out shopping. Coming down the stairs wearing a lightweight belted dress, I heard them laughing loudly, then your mother began to talk and in her flowing Italian once again told the story of how her fellow refugees had extinguished the fire in the cattle wagon between Trieste and Milan.

I was grateful to Dara and the others for having come for me after our escapade of the previous night. Their attitude showed both that they hadn't given up trying to distract me from my grief and that they wanted to tell me they'd had no intention of taking advantage of me in the course of that night; their friendship could survive a session of that sort without any problem. Branko got to his feet as soon as he caught sight of me. I held out my hand to him in a rather weary way, then I kissed Dara who'd also got up, and finally sat down next to my father. He explained to me that my friends were planning to go on an excursion to Venice and that they'd called by to ask his permission to take me with them. Your mother said we'd stay there overnight and would get back the following evening. 'I can't decide on this alone,' said Papa. 'I must talk it over with my wife.' The problem was, we didn't know at what time Mama would get back from her shopping. And, as Branko put it, we had to 'leave immediately to get to Venice before dusk'. I told Papa he knew very well that Mama would have no objections. Yes, he replied, but you only had to take a decision without her that you were sure she'd not object to for her to start having countless objections! Finally, he let me go.

I had been to Venice with my parents before and after the war, so I knew it well enough. We stayed on the Lido, in a suite in the Hôtel des Bains. I made sandcastles on the beach and played yo-yo with the children of Russian princesses in exile, and in the evenings, washed and shampooed, we'd meet again, this time sitting at opposite ends of the huge dining room from where we exchanged discreet signs of complicity.

Needless to say, Stefan Miljus and Branko Marić did not take us to stay at the Hôtel des Bains. Nevertheless, the *pensione* where we installed ourselves for the night was a good category one. It was not far from St Mark's Square. We took two rooms: one for the boys and one for the girls. Dara protested that this was unfair since the girls had to share between three of them a room that was in every way identical to the one the boys had between only two of them. Stefan shrugged his shoulders and smiled, as if to say unfairness between men and women was one of the basic components of society's workings, and neither he nor she would ever be able to do anything about it.

We had supper in one of the open-air restaurants that line the Grand Canal near the Rialto Bridge. The country was still short of electricity and a single candle lit the white tablecloth and our five beaming faces. We ordered a large dish of scampi, a large dish of spaghetti and some Tokay, an Italian white wine that is somewhat similar to the Hungarian wine of the same name. During the meal, Branko kept glancing at the bottle as if he'd been keeping watch over it. He filled the glasses the moment they were half-empty, ate voraciously and kept looking at us, Dinka, your mother and me, hungrily. He looked as if it was the entire evening he wanted to gobble down. Along with Stefan he dominated the conversation and answered his friend as briskly as if they'd been playing some kind of match. I was provided with the occasional Italian version of their jousts, but mostly it was all too rapid for your mother to have time to translate, so I just gave the odd chuckle of polite incomprehension.

Stefan settled the bill with one of those huge 10,000 lira notes he appeared to have inexhaustible supplies of. A great silence weighed down the table while we waited for the change. I put it down to the emotion poor people always feel when they see someone spending on one single meal a sum they could live on for a fortnight, but in fact it was something quite different. Stefan slipped the notes into his wallet. Then while Dara had already moved away from the terrace and lit a cigarette, Stefan asked Branko a question, and Branko nodded. They asked for two plum brandies which they sat calmly sipping without saying anything. At that point it seemed to me that rather like those cyclists who hang back for several minutes in order to be the last to go and then have someone ahead of them to focus on, they were playing a game to see who would be the last to empty his glass. After a short time, Dinka let out an irritated sigh and went and joined your mother who'd sat down on the first steps of the bridge. I stayed on the terrace, sitting on my own opposite the two Yugoslavs. They finally got up and I trotted along behind them as far as the bridge. We all set off towards St Mark's Square. The two women walked ahead of us, arm in arm. Stefan and Branko had their arms around each other's necks. Slightly excluded from this little *zadruga*, I brought up the rear.

When we reached the basilica, Branko asked me: 'Is this where you'll make wedding?' We could hear all the waiters in

Florian's shouting out their customers' orders from the end of the terrace. Dinka had taken your mother under the gallery where they were both looking at the expensive jewellery on display. Dara glanced in the windows: she said people were mad to pay such vast sums for such small stones, and given the choice, she preferred costume jewellery. The stones were bigger and prettier. And then at least when you lost them you didn't have to make a scene! Stefan had walked up to her: 'Is there anything you'd like?' She answered sharply that he knew very well what she would like; she took Dinka's arm and went off towards the other end of the gallery. As for Branko, he'd made the most of the darkness in the arcades to take hold of me and kiss me. It didn't displease me to find that Stefan was being left out by the four of us.

We wandered about rather aimlessly for a while. Dinka and your mother were definitely keeping apart. Irritated by this dilly-dallying, Branko took me towards the riva degli Schiavoni; I suppose because he didn't know what to do, Stefan followed us, and while he was looking at the façade of the Gritti Palace Hotel, examining it with a mildly disdainful expression on his face, we got onto Paglia Bridge where we kissed with a passion that soon aroused the gondoliers' enthusiasm. Then we came back towards St Mark's and all five of us settled down at a table at Florian's. Stefan ordered a bottle of champagne. The waiter said he only had sparkling wine. 'Sparkling will do fine!' Stefan said. He'd decided to liven up the atmosphere and nothing was going to stop him! He bought three bunches of jasmine from a little street pedlar and handed one to each of us. Your mother tucked hers behind her ear. It stood out beautifully against her mass of brown hair. After this, Stefan turned towards me and told me in his dreadful Italian how, to escape from the communists, he'd crossed the whole of Yugoslavia on a bicycle disguised as a priest. He travelled at night and spent the days in monasteries. Whereupon the sparkling wine arrived which Stefan poured out for us in generous glassfuls. Then I asked

him why he'd been running away from the communists. He
didn't answer straight away. He looked at his Yugoslav
friends, raised his glass to their health and drained it. Then he
turned his face towards me and said, with that air of
unimpeachable intellectual superiority you always see on the
faces of refugees from the East when they talk about communism, whether they're world famous scientists or former café
waiters: 'Communists are tyrants. Like fascists. Like Mus-
solini.' I said that in Italy the communists had fought Mus-
solini. He shook his head: 'Impossible you understand.' I
replied: 'I can't see why you should understand Italy any
better than I understand Yugoslavia.' So then Stefan pointed
at me; he pretended to look scandalised and, calling the
others to witness, shouted out: 'She's a Red! Giuliana's a little
Red!' Branko burst out laughing. Dinka was giving me a cold,
scornful look. As for your mother, she kept glancing about,
trying to detect the presence of any of Tito's agents who
might be around. She said in a whisper that it wasn't wise to
touch on such subjects in public. Branko protested: 'This is
Italy! A free country! We can talk.' Dara cast him an
indulgent, almost motherly look. You could tell it really was
only because she liked him such a lot that she could forgive
him his absurd naïvety. 'The communists are everywhere,' she
said. 'They spy on people and report everything back to their
bosses.' Stefan gave me a gentle tap on the knee: 'Like
Giuliana!' Branko laughed. Stefan only had to open his
mouth and say something jokey — anything — for Branko to
start laughing. This was beginning to get on my nerves. So
then I asked them: during the war, when they'd captured
communists, what had they done to them? 'Lots of things,'
said Stefan. 'Cut ears. Pull out eyes. Hang by feet and dance
kolo all around.' He sniggered, drank a mouthful of wine and
said, tapping me on the knee once again: 'Jokes. We Serbs
joke much. Like to laugh.' Silence, then: 'Branko and I didn't
fight war. Don't like war.' He called the waiter, paid, got up
and, passing behind Dinka's chair, deposited a kiss on the

lawyer's bare shoulder. He said something to everyone in Serbo-Croat and he and Dinka went off hand in hand. They were going back to the hotel, and Stefan had just asked his friends to allow them half or three-quarters of an hour's grace — something Branko passed on to me in a confidential tone while your mother puffed nervously on a cigarette and took to the wine with unaccustomed gusto.

I've lived through some unpleasant half-hours in my time, but that was one of the worst. Your mother didn't unclench her teeth except to drink or smoke. Branko had grown gloomy. I could feel he was wondering how to devise a way for us to make love too. When the agreed period had elapsed and we reached the *pensione*, Dara told us she felt like having a stroll around Venice on her own. Branko said it wasn't wise. 'What can happen to me?' she replied. She asked him if he would just leave her his packet of Chesterfields and a box of matches. Before turning away, she said — and it was one of the rare occasions when I detected a certain sense of humour in her — 'I'll be back in . . . half or . . . three-quarters of an hour . . . .' Then without giving us time to come up with an answer, she set off down the narrow street, stopping a few paces later to light a cigarette.

I followed Branko into the room. He undressed me hurriedly. I was thinking about your mother. I was picturing her, a solitary figure standing near a *vaporetto* landing stage, her mind full of this secret I so wanted to penetrate. She would be pacing up and down small brick bridges and empty quaysides. There was a knock on the door. 'So soon!' Branko exclaimed. I pushed him away, pulled the sheets up over my shoulders and said, '*Avanti!*' It was Dinka in a silk dressing gown — a recent gift from Stefan — who'd come to suggest we join them. '*Stefana ideja*,' she said, and then chuckled. She was utterly obscene: too big and soft-fleshed for that loose-necked dressing gown that revealed her breasts, her intelligent features looked distorted as she tried — unsuccessfully — to hide her embarrassment beneath a feigned off-handedness.

147

'Do you want to?' Branko asked me. It wasn't that I exactly wanted to, but deep down I knew very well it would come to this. I nodded, aware that yet again I was disappointing him. We got up. He'd kept his trousers on. I was naked. 'I'll take you under my dressing gown,' said Dinka. There were about ten metres to go to reach the other room. Dinka put me down delicately in Stefan's bed and then set about pulling down Branko's trousers. 'Nice surprise,' said Stefan while I rested my cheek on his chest with the delicious sensation that I was committing an unforgivable act of sacrilege. Then he made me take his penis in my mouth, thinking perhaps that he'd be teaching me something new.

While we were in full swing, I thought I noticed the door being hurriedly opened and closed by someone who could in any case only be Dara. But when, during a lull that found me resting my head on Dinka's stomach, I mentioned this to the others, they assured me they'd neither seen nor heard anything of the sort, and then when I questioned your mother about it some weeks later, she swore it hadn't even occurred to her to go and see what we were up to. 'I had a shrewd idea you weren't playing cards!' she said.

Dinka once again took me under her dressing gown to get me back to our room. The window was open and the shutters hadn't been closed. Lying on her front with her head buried in the pillows, Dara was fast asleep. I shut the window because the chilly breeze that heralds dawn even in the hottest countries was blowing into the room. I hadn't been in bed five minutes before your mother got up and, as if she'd been sleep-walking, made her way towards the window and re-opened it! She then went and drank a glass of water from the tap, setting the pipes rattling on at least three storeys, and finally got back into the double bed next to Dinka.

She woke me at around ten o'clock. She was already dressed and had a towel tucked under her arm. 'We're going to the beach!' she said. Her excitement and cheerful mood showed on her face and made a pleasant change from her loftiness of

148

the previous evening. I thought better of confessing how tired I felt and got up. 'What about Dinka?' I asked. She shrugged her shoulders and said breezily, 'Dinka can do whatever she pleases.' Whereupon Dinka woke up and asked what we were doing. 'We're off to the beach,' said your mother. 'I'll come with you,' said Dinka and emerged from the bed, naked. By the bathtub she pushed me aside. 'Give me some space!' Dara left the room. She was going to find out from the boys whether they wanted to join us. When she came back, she said, 'They can't come along because they've got some business to settle, but they want you both to give them a kiss before we go.' She would wait for us down at reception.

The two boys were lying on their beds in the nude, their hands clasped behind their heads, but Dinka and I had tacitly agreed that there was a time for everything and that in this instance it was time to go to the beach, so we didn't let them get their way. I must tell you, even so, that Stefan insisted on kissing what he himself called my 'little hole'. To save trouble, I turned around, lifted my skirt and pulled down my pants, while for her part Dinka was forced to give Branko's penis a suck. We finally managed an orderly retreat towards the door.

We found your mother engaged in conversation with the receptionist who greeted us by bowing all the way down to the floor. We left the hotel. For a number of reasons, that splendid July morning has stayed unforgettably in my mind. We took the *vaporetto* from St Mark's. The three of us stood at the prow of the boat like emblematic figures of Antiquity. The air was slightly sticky. 'It's better than the *motoscafi*,' Dara finally commented. 'More jolly. And anyway, it's less pricey.' We went past the Doges' Palace which was surrounded by the usual swarms of tourists. A few educated young Venetians set about telling us when and how Venice had been built and who by, a story laced with furtive caresses of our arms and shoulders and plenty of their devastating winks, but your mother soon put them in their place with the self-assurance she always showed in public and which I found so wonderful. They turned away sheepishly, and the rest of the way to the Lido we were surrounded by a respectful silence.

As soon as we'd spread our towels out in a neat line on the sand, Dara suggested we have a swim. Then, even before Dinka had had time to undress, she told her: 'You'll swim after us, you keep an eye on the bags.' Without so much as a glance, the lawyer nodded her agreement and lay down on her back. I don't know whether she was already dozing by the time your mother and I dipped our feet in the water, but when we came back, she was sound asleep.

I had imagined that, following my night-time tribulations, it would have been up to me to win back Dara's friendship, so I was both surprised and relieved to find that it was she who was trying to win back mine. Later I was to realise that when someone betrayed your mother, she didn't start hating that person but wondered instead what had led them to start hating her to the point of betraying her, and her feeling of insecurity was so pronounced that she would do anything to plaster over this crack in the ever precarious structure of her life.

You know how at the Lido you have to wade for fifty or a hundred metres to get the water up to your waist. As we made our way, rubbing our arms and shoulders vigorously, Dara told me she didn't in the least hold it against me that I'd 'been' with Stefan. She assured me she no longer felt anything for him, but that on the other hand she still very much valued our friendship.

She did that sideways breast-stroke she referred to as 'Indian' that no one ever does nowadays. Not wishing to wet her hair, she held her head very erect. I played about, swimming under water and catching hold of her legs. She occasionally swam on her back, kicking her feet up and down, keeping her arms along her body and her neck as stiff as before. I swam about, coming and going around her and beneath her

150

and springing out of the water. 'How well you swim!' she said. We came back towards the shore after we'd begun to feel rather too closely encircled by three or four young men who were making an awful fuss with their Europeanised crawl, the kind the Italians favoured at the time. They'd take a minute to swim five metres, kicked up a fantastic spray and breathed really hard as if they weren't getting enough air when in fact they hadn't even put their chins under water.

We stretched out on the sand. Your mother kept glancing around, really only looking for something to talk about; and each time I was about to fall asleep, she gave my arm a tug and told me to look at those peculiar so-and-sos who came to the beach wearing dark suits, that woman bathing whose body looked as though it had been sculpted by Michelangelo, or that little boy and girl walking hand in hand along the water's edge 'like a pair of lovers'.

Around one o'clock, we folded our towels and walked across the island to get back to the *vaporetto* landing stage. We were meeting up with the boys at the hotel to have lunch with them before setting off for home. As we were going along the main street with its shady terraces, I noticed that Dinka had got her shoulders badly sunburnt. I remember that we treated this as some sort of catastrophe, and all reeled off the whole range of remedies we knew about.

A man drew level with us. It was Branko. He'd loosened his tie and undone the top button of his shirt. His features, always so lively, were now in a complete state of uproar. I asked him what he was doing here and what the matter was with him. Dara and Dinka, on the other hand, had immediately understood what had happened and were bombarding him with questions. He poured out his words at a speed that was record-breaking, even for a Yugoslav. After several minutes, as I was making desperate attempts to capture the attention of the shouting trio, they deigned to inform me that Stefan had been arrested. Stefan arrested! But why? 'We'll explain later,' said Dinka, and she pushed me into the *vaporetto* which got under way.

Venice slowly moved closer. I thought to myself that this marvel of grace and beauty must have become a nightmare for Stefan Miljus, and that to find oneself in prison in Venice must be worse than in any other city in the world. I pictured Stefan locked up in a police station and sweating so profusely that drops of sweat fell on the lapels of his lovely white jacket. I also wondered why he'd been arrested. Ridiculous though it was, since there was no sense in which the Italian and Yugoslav governments were hand in glove, my first thought was that it was something political. But politics had absolutely nothing to do with it. Before breakfast, Stefan had gone to buy one of the pieces of jewellery that your mother and Dinka had been looking at the previous evening. Branko stayed on the terrace at Florian's chatting to a third Yugoslav, an old acquaintance they'd bumped into. That was what saved his life. Because a few minutes later, two police inspectors in civilian clothes walked into the jewellery shop and arrested Stefan. Branko saw his friend come out of the shop in handcuffs and understood that the counterfeit 10,000 lira notes Stefan had been handing out left, right and centre over the past few weeks had finally caught up with him. In a letter he wrote to me from Paris that December, Branko told me his friend had been extradited to Yugoslavia where he'd been tried for war crimes, condemned to death and executed within hours of the verdict being returned. What comprised Stefan Miljus' war crimes, that I never found out, in the same way as we never found out for whom he'd intended the piece of jewellery that was to prove fatal to him. Maybe for Dara, maybe for Dinka . . . . Or maybe even for me!

We took the train back to Milan, because when Stefan had been arrested he'd had the keys to the Panhard on him and, more importantly, he'd also been carrying the papers for it. We only just managed to cram ourselves into a stopping train that took the whole afternoon and part of the night to reach Milan. In different circumstances, I suppose your mother would have sufficiently livened things up in our bit of the carriage to make the return journey to Milan into something of a party, but she kept absolutely quiet.

I felt terribly sad as I reflected how that evening, in his cell, Stefan was probably thinking of us speeding along the road towards Milan, free and still glowing with the warmth of the sun we'd caught during the day, but equally I felt frightened at having spent three days in the company of a counterfeiter and appalled that neither Branko, Dinka nor Dara had warned me about it, especially when my father had requested that they take care of me.

I spent August in Tuscany, mulling over this grievance against your mother. I realise now that it was positively criminal of me to attach more importance to the unhappiness I felt at having been misled than to the grief Dara must have felt at being separated from Stefan and especially at knowing he was in jail. Anyhow, my resentment didn't hold out against the longing I soon felt for that atmosphere of mischievous fun and affection she and her Yugoslav friends had shared with me, and even though, during my month in the country, I'd resolved never to speak to Dara again in my entire lifetime, I rushed over to via della Moscova on one of the first days of September.

Your mother welcomed me as spontaneously and effusively as if we'd parted the day before, but there now hovered about her a subtle, just perceptible fear and trembling which, together with her unaccustomed pallor, made me think that this lonely month of August had been hard for her to bear, following as it had done on the arrest of the man she loved. She settled me down in an armchair and looked for something she could offer me to eat, but failed. Try as I might to assure her I wasn't in the least hungry, she seemed very upset at being unable to observe the rules of hospitality like this. Finally she sat down opposite me and, taking my hand, said I was looking wonderfully well. I heard that Dinka had got her visa for the United States and had immediately left for Trieste

153

to find a ship bound for New York. Hadn't she wanted to go with her? She shook her head: 'America is too far away.' She underlined several times the fact that her friend's departure had doubled the cost of her rent. Now, to make ends meet, she had to 'pull the needle night and day'.

Next, without any preamble, with the almost comic dismay of a child spilling its glass in a smart restaurant, she revealed to me that she was pregnant. She shook her head vigorously and added, 'And I don't know what to do!' She gazed past me at the damp marks on the blue walls which vibrated with each passing tram. It seemed as if this news was suddenly taking on proportions she'd never suspected it had until she'd broken it to me. She got up and said in a cross and doleful tone: 'I have no luck, you know . . . I simply have no luck!' To think how she'd believed she had left unhappiness behind her when she'd crossed the Italian border. She'd thought she was starting a new life here. In her efforts to secure every possible chance for herself, she'd balked at nothing. And now, the Yugoslavia she had fled from, the Yugoslavia with its retrograde family structures and its communist terror which had put her off ever living there, far from having rid herself of it, she had in some peculiar way brought it with her! *Inside* her! She wondered what she'd done to God to find herself landed in such a situation. Indeed she even wondered if there was a God! As a matter of fact it wasn't the first time 'someone' seemed to be making fun of her in this cruel way: she had been born during the worst economic crisis the then very new Kingdom of the Serbs, Croats and Slovenes had ever known, so that when her father, a modest carpenter who already had a wife and two children to feed, had peered into her cot on 6 September 1923, he had felt a deep consternation. As she was pacing up and down the room listing all the adversities she'd been the victim of since her birth, the last but one of which was of course Stefan Miljus' arrest, I was asking myself a few questions. If the child had been conceived in Yugoslavia, that meant Dara was at least three and a half months pregnant and therefore that at the time of our Venice excursion, she'd been aware of her state. So that was her secret! I asked whether Dinka Mirovats had also known about this at that time. She shook her head. 'You're the first person I've let into the secret.' Both the windows were wide open, so that our conversation was taking place amid a deafening noise, a fact Dara seemed quite unaware of. 'And,' she said, 'you don't know everything. . . .' She stopped talking and looked at her shoes dejectedly. I asked: 'And the father . . . who is he?' She shrugged her shoulders. For a moment, I thought this was because she had really no idea who the father might be. 'That's the problem,' she said. 'The father. . . .' Rather at random, I asked whether he'd stayed behind in Yugoslavia. She said, 'Yes, and for a good reason. . . .' He was somebody 'very, very high up' in the communist hierarchy. The *communist* hierarchy? Yes, I had heard correctly, the *communist* hierarchy. She was going to tell me the whole story so that I'd really understand what the 'Reds' were capable of. . . . But first, I suggested, couldn't we shut the windows? Were Tito's agents not everywhere? Your mother had the windows shut in a flash; she then spent at least a minute watching the to-ings and fro-ings out in the street before taking me by the arm and drawing me right to the end of the room where we could be safe from prying ears and, who knows? maybe from bullets too. . . .

The partisans liberated Zagreb on 8 May 1945, a task made all the easier by the soldiers of the regular army of the Independent State of Croatia and the Ustaše units who had abandoned the city to rush to the Austrian border, like watchdogs desperately racing after masters who no longer wanted them. When Tito's men reached Maksimirska, like most of their neighbours Dara, her sister and her parents stood at their windows and noted with some alarm the state of physical and sartorial dilapidation this army was in: it couldn't even walk in step and, as Josip Sevnica remarked, its ability to keep its line was deeply suspect. What a contrast after the

Germans! Your grandmother was very shocked to see there were women in the ranks. Women in uniform! Now they really had seen everything! The partisans had neither tanks nor motorised vehicles. All their equipment was transported on ramshackle carts pulled by emaciated donkeys. The look of mistrust, contempt and even anger that was written on some of these faces, faces burnt by the sun and sunken with hunger and tiredness, had made a big impression on Dara. There were some very young fighters among them, youths who stared straight ahead or young girls who'd gathered their hair under the famous beret with its red star — a fashion Tito himself had started. All of a sudden, leading a column, Dara recognised Nikola Dunak, one of their former neighbours who, following a brief and somewhat ill-considered period with the Ustaše at the time of Pavelić's return to Zagreb in April 1941, had, as early as September of that year, joined up with Tito's partisans who were then occupying the town of Užice in Serbia. He was walking next to the standard-bearer. He wore black gloves and had a revolver tucked in his belt. Unlike most of his comrades, before entering Zagreb he'd taken care to polish his boots or have them polished for him. 'He's surely an officer,' your mother reflected, and despite the distinct feeling of repulsion Dunak had always provoked in her, she had not found this displeasing. Your aunt Zdenka called out: 'Look, that's Nikola!' The entire Sevnica family, with the exception of your mother, gave the communist hero a few friendly waves which he didn't bother to return even though he looked up towards their windows and was staring at them. From under his black moustache, he merely gave a hint of a small, cold smile. The column moved on past the building.

To have among the country's new rulers a former neighbour presented an unquestionable advantage for a family whose elder son was retreating towards Klagenfurt in Austria at that very moment and whose father had kept his job as head clerk in Zagreb town hall for the duration of

Pavelić's rule. And yet your mother was wondering whether it wouldn't have been better for them all had Nikola met his death in an ambush laid by Četniks or Ustaše up in the Bosnian mountains. Her instinct told her pretty clearly that rather than let his neighbours benefit from his power, he'd abuse it, and she could guess that he'd never entirely forgiven her for having turned him down in horror when he'd asked her to marry him in 1939, and this without so much as mentioning it to her parents. She may well have been dreading the moment when she'd pass him on the stairs in their block of flats and be forced to enquire politely 'how things had been up in the mountains', but she was very far from imagining that it wasn't simply a case of his not having forgotten the affront he'd suffered from her, he'd also been pondering his revenge throughout the war years and had decided a long time since to carry it out as soon as possible — which meant the very day following his return to Zagreb.

Josip Sevnica knew very well that sooner or later he was in for a brush with the new rulers, but he was surprised by the haste they showed in coming to arrest him. He hadn't thought of himself as such an important figure. In her nightdress, her eyes all puffed up with sleep, Dara saw him on his knees tying up his shoelaces in front of two men in uniform who were hurrying him up in strong Montenegrin accents. They pushed him out of the door, impervious to the plaintive sounds coming from your grandmother and your aunt Zdenka who'd sought refuge in each other's arms. It was six in the morning. A pink, warmish day was rising over the city. Through the window, Dara's eyes followed the militiamen as they led your grandfather away to the police station on Kvaternik Square. She had a thoughtful look on her face which contrasted with her mother's and sister's weeping and imprecations. She'd realised that Nikola Dunka had just made the opening move in a sort of chess game in which he would only allow her the pawns she needed to defend herself with. She went back to bed and of course shocked her sister and mother with this

apparent lack of concern over the dreadful event which had
befallen the family. It is true that Dara was not too fond of her
father, and that Nikola Dunak would have dealt her a much
more serious blow if for example he'd had the young
woman's mother arrested. But the fact that Josip rather than
Milena Sevnica had been arrested was no doubt part of a
strategy which your mother would come to understand in the
course of the battle she and Dunak would be waging against
one another in the coming days.

Collaborators or suspected collaborators were taken to a
field on the outskirts of the town where militiamen watched
over them as they slept, ate and relieved themselves. Lucky
that the spring of 1945 was particularly mild, for no form of
shelter had been organized! There were lawyers and doctors,
shopkeepers and journalists, as well as many civil servants.

It was a woman neighbour who, two days after your grandfather's arrest, let Milena Sevnica know his whereabouts.
Milena and her two daughters made their way there that
evening. They took the tram from Dubrava to the terminal
and then walked for half an hour. The sun was already low in
the sky when they reached the entrance to the camp; it echoed
with the voices of all the prisoners and their families who, like
the Sevnicas, had come for news and to bring food and
clothing. Unfortunately that second operation proved
impossible because of the wall of militiamen keeping the
detainees and visitors apart. Two flocks bleating in the
twilight — that was how your mother remembered the sight
that greeted her eyes that evening at Dubrava.

Straight away she picked her father out in the crowd of
prisoners. He was among the shortest and the fattest. When
he recognised your mother, he gestured to her with his hand
and then waddled across to a militiaman. She thought that,
quick as he'd always been to get on to any fiddle, he was
trying to arrange to see his family in private. This undertaking
was most certainly doomed to failure, but she admired her
father for not losing his customary sense of initiative nor any

of that nerve he had in such abundance, in a situation that was so unfavourable to him. Meanwhile, the militiaman was showing every sign of assenting quite happily to your grandfather's rather over-zealous explanations and was at the same time trying to identify Dara in the crowd; finally he warned the other guards he was breaking rank and walked purposefully towards her. 'Follow me, comrade,' he said when he drew close to her. What's Papa cooked up this time? thought Dara, while her mother called out rather desperately, 'Don't go! Don't go!' Dara reflected that firstly she didn't have much choice, and also that if the partisans wanted to arrest her, they could do so at any time of day or night in Maksimirska. She followed the militiaman.

A silence as if the world had ended suddenly surrounded her like a glass cage. She felt upon her all the astonished, envious and even hateful eyes of mothers who'd been unable to get anywhere near their sons and wives who'd have sold their souls in exchange for one last embrace with their husbands before they were sent God knows where. She was unable to understand what lay behind this privilege, but once she was within a mere ten or so metres of Josip Sevnica and able to see the look of deep unease on his face, it all became clear: this was Nikola Dunak's second move of the game. She was filled with an icy anger and her mind was made up within a fraction of a second: she would yield to *all* the demands of their former neighbour, and she would also hate him until the day she died.

Her father took her by the arm. Behind his round spectacles, his large blue eyes blinked incessantly. He kept scratching his chest at regular intervals because of his embarrassment and also because, like most of the other detainees, he'd fallen victim to a flea offensive, fleas which had abandoned the partisans' lean flesh to throw themselves on to all these better-fed citizens of Zagreb. He smelt of sweat and digestive problems, and his three-day beard made him look like a lunatic sauntering about in an asylum. While on either side of the militiamen, the prisoners' and their families' voices were gradually resuming their hopeless chant, this is what he said to your mother: 'Nikola came by this morning. . . . He's in fine shape. . . . Gave me a few cigarettes. . . . English ones! Parachuted by the RAF! . . . And he also gave me this.' Out of his trouser pocket he took a piece of paper folded in four: 'His address. . . . He's found a place on Zrinsky Square. . . . Luxurious apparently. . . . Collaborators on the run. . . . He's installed himself. . . . He's quite right, don't you think! He's the master now, he's making the most of it . . . . Who knows whether I might not behave in the same way if I were in his shoes! Here, this is for you.' Dara took the piece of paper but didn't unfold it. 'You do whatever you like, hmm!' Josip went on. 'You don't have to go. . . . He told me himself: your daughter doesn't have to, Mr Sevnica. . . . He's polite, for a communist. . . . He didn't once call me "comrade" . . . .' With her eyes downcast, Dara asked what would happen if she didn't go. Josip sniggered: 'A bullet in the neck and bye-bye. . . . By the way, not a word of all this to your mother. . . . Now that would be worse than anything!' Dara said she couldn't see why Nikola Dunak hadn't asked *her* to come and see him. 'He wanted to humiliate both of us,' said Josip. 'A strange boy. . . . When I think that I knew him when he was no taller than that. . . . The war hasn't done him much good.' He kissed Dara's cheeks. 'Run along now. . . . I know I shouldn't have passed the message on to you, but I'm afraid of dying. . . . Ridiculous, at my age, isn't it?' Your mother said that, on the contrary, she was very pleased that he had done so, since she was now in a position to save him. She ran back across the field to her mother and sister and simply said that Josip had asked her to let them know that, thanks to Nikola Dunak who'd interceded on his behalf, he would soon be free and soon be home again.

5

In 626, the Croatian prince Klukas was *invited* by Emperor Heraclius to come and settle with his people along the Adriatic's Eastern shore. So far, the Croats had lived in Central Europe, around what has now become the city of Krakow. In 681, they gave the pope an undertaking never to take over land which didn't belong to them. So it was in an atmosphere of both pacifism and hospitableness that the Croats came to inhabit the region stretching from Riyeka to the inlets of Kotor. Following the death of Zvonimir, the last Croatian king, and that of his son Stanislav, the queen obtained the near unanimous support of the nobility for her brother Ladislas of Hungary's candidature to the vacant throne. So in 1091, Ladislas crossed the Drava to come and take possession of Pannonian Croatia and Bosnia. This is one of the reasons why nowadays there are so many Hungarian restaurants in Zagreb.

Thus, while the Serbs, Bulgars, Moldavs and most of the other Balkan peoples were gradually coming within the dominion of the Sublime Porte, the Croats were carving out a relatively comfortable place for themselves in the kingdom of Hungary and then, after 1526, in the Austrian Empire. They ensconced themselves in the rather fervent and sentimental Catholicism the Habsburgs were the arch-defenders of. Zagreb, or Agram as the Austrians called it, became a little Vienna, and it was partly with the help of Ban Jelačić's Croat soldiers that Franz-Joseph quelled Kossuth's Hungarian revolution in July 1849. Once again, the heroic Hungarians were flat on their faces. That's the Hungarians for you: ever heroic, and ever flat on their faces.

This loyalty was ill rewarded by the Habsburgs, especially considering they had so far always treated the Croat people as a bit of a favourite. Had they not tolerated from them a Sabor that was sometimes sharply critical of Vienna, the use of Croatian in the administration and in schools, and lastly, an intelligentsia which under the leadership of Bishop Josip Juraj Strossmayer and his Yugoslav Academy was busy devising and perfecting Yugoslavism? Under the influence of his wife Elizabeth, a neurotic Bavarian who had developed such a passion for Hungary that she had learnt the language and would on occasion array herself in its traditional dress, about twenty years after the events in Budapest, Franz-Joseph gave back their lost sovereignty to the Magyars and even went so far as having himself crowned King of Hungary on the spot. So Croatia then fell into the clutches of Budapest which started enforcing a programme of Magyarisation of the area against which our peasantry put up a sardonic resistance, peaceful but dogged. Archduke Franz-Ferdinand was the first of the Habsburgs to show any concern over the brutal and economically catastrophic hold the Magyars had over the fertile regions of Croatia and Voyvodina. In order to offset the increasingly powerful influence of Hungary within the Dual Monarchy, he had even devised a plan to create a sort of confederation of Balkan states rather like the one Tito would be dreaming about half a century later. But as you know, the fanatic Serb Princip and his accomplices didn't give him the time to reach this goal, nor indeed any other.

In a general way, the twentieth century didn't prove very successful for the Croats. These jovial, naïve and disinterested creatures, who painted as if the rules of perspective hadn't yet been invented and who'd have happily done without cows to plough their fields in order to simplify matters, just did not connect with the modern world of machinery, profit and ideologies. After they'd had their only friend among the Habsburgs killed — the only Habsburg ever to have lent them a sympathetic ear — they lost the war alongside the Hungarians while the Serbs were winning it alongside the French. They grasped fairly quickly that the Serb, Croat and

Slovene State being set up by the fantasy-prone minds then at work in the world of Western diplomacy spelt out roughly, for them, that they'd also lost the peace. There are two famous photographs which illustrate the Croats' joy at being freed from the Hungarians and their despair at falling into the clutches of Serbia. The first shows the citizens of Zagreb asssembled on 29 October 1918 to hear the official proclamation of the Serb, Croat and Slovene State. It's a cold, grey autumn day to which the crowd's enthusiasm lends its warmth. The second photo was taken a few days later. A Serbian officer mounted on a white horse is marching past, leading his troops across Jelačić Square. What the citizens of Zagreb, tightly packed along the pavement, are witnessing without quite being able to believe it, is the handing over of their destinies to Serbian soldiers renowned for their brutality and some of whom have faced Croats of the regular army or the Domobrani divisions in hand-to-hand combat along the banks of the Drina. On the photograph, the equestrian statue of Ban Jelačić turns its back on them nobly. One guesses that the trams which normally converge on this square have been brought to a standstill on Illica or Jurišićeva Martićeva Ulica to allow the Serbs the space they need to show off their military might. The buildings in the background look wan. Zagreb, city of mirth and mischief, Zagreb the sparkling, Zagreb the proud has hidden her face behind a mask of shame and sadness she'll never really shed again.

There is, without a doubt, nothing more dangerous than pacifists once they decide to resort to violence, if not in a good cause, then at least for a good reason. The Croats, one of the few peoples in history never to have picked a quarrel with their neighbours, will alter dramatically in the wake of the creation of Yugoslavia, and particularly after the assassination of the Croat peasant leader, Stefan Radić, in June 1928. With the founding of the Ustaše in Austria, the assassination of King Alexander I in Marseille in October 1934 and the nightmare that was the Independent State of Croatia, their legendary mildness and joviality will be translated into an unbelievable barbarity which they themselves are terrified by and which to this day leaves them perplexed and trembling.

To my mind, the two figures who best embody the Croatian people in the twentieth century are still Archbishop Stepinac and Marshal Tito, one as much a believer and a puritan as the other was an atheist and a sensualist. And yet, with all their most glaring dissimilarities and despite the fact that they were mortal enemies, these two exceptional men coincided in many a way. They both spent the first years of their mature lives doing nothing, or very little. Tito went from town to town, took various factory jobs, watched women go by, bought himself expensive clothes the moment he'd got a bit of money set aside and dreamt of emigrating to the United States and becoming a Rockefeller. As for Stepinac, after attending a seminary and fighting the war as a lieutenant — a war during which he didn't hesitate to sacrifice a Croatian stretcher-bearer's life in order to bring back a wounded young Pole who himself died during the journey — he returned to the family farm where he attended Mass more frequently than he needed, while awaiting a sign from heaven. In his life, Rome would play the same role as Moscow would play in Tito's. Notice how both these Croats went abroad to seek out their truths and to start living out their destinies. As a prisoner in Russia at the time of the October Revolution, Tito decided to devote his life to communism, or rather to use communism to seduce and possess Yugoslavia and then stand her out on the streets alongside the other non-aligned countries. Stepinac spent seven years at the Vatican. He was appointed Arch-bishop-Coadjutor of Zagreb in 1934, three years prior to Tito's accession to the post of secretary-general of the Yugoslav Communist Party central committee. As you can see, it was the same spectacular success following a lengthy period of waiting and perhaps also of laziness.

As a child, Aloïs Stepinac would spend hours standing enthralled in front of the Virgin's effigy. His other passion was for order. As early as nine years old, he was telling off his brothers and sisters for not obeying their parents more promptly and more frequently. But it was in the army that Aloïs confronted his greatest test when, each Sunday, he clambered up the five hundred and sixty-one steps to the Sanctuary of Our Lady of Trsat under a hail of gibes from his barrack-room mates who, for their part, were making their merry way to the nearest brothel. The post-war years proved an equally difficult period for the future archbishop of Zagreb. The capital city of Croatia disappointed him. It had become a crossroads teeming, as he later put it with disgust, with 'people imbued by a new spirit'. Can you imagine, a *new* spirit in *Zagreb* in *1918*! Stepinac had much rather not witness this and hurried back to Krasić at top speed. There he wandered about, singing to himself, trailing his boredom here and there and praying. At the wedding of one of his sisters, so deep in thought was he as he led her to the altar that the priest had to nudge him back to reality before he'd hand her over to the groom. Was he tempted to incest perhaps? A few months later he became engaged to Maria Horvat, a modest, pious girl whose father was Aloïs' former schoolmaster. Following the exchange of engagement rings, Stepinac withheld the traditional kiss and declared haughtily: 'This is not as yet a sacrament.'

Aloïs was never to kiss Maria Horvat. He broke off the engagement shortly before leaving for Rome, whence he did not return until the early Thirties. From 1936 he was Archbishop of Zagreb, the man who would have the mission of guiding Croatian Catholics through the dreadful events of the Second World War. He never gave his consent to Pavelić's methods, indeed he even condemned them from his pulpit without ever naming the tyrant and his accomplices, but nevertheless he carefully avoided ever calling into question the legitimacy of the Ustaše government. The truth is that throughout those four years, he did no more than stand very upright outside Zagreb cathedral and proclaim to a world he probably thought mesmerised by his courage: 'Evil shall not enter here.' Elsewhere Evil was free to roam around and tie its innocent victims to burning bushes, but that was no longer his business. No Jew, no Serb would be killed in *his* cathedral, and that was all there was to it! My dear little Brigitte, there you have the model Croat, Stepinac: Catholic to the tips of his chewed fingernails, so concerned with legitimacy as to be no longer able to distinguish between Good and Evil, kind, but of the most self-regarding kindness, and finally politically inept in the most unfailing way.

After the end of the war, Stepinac retained his freedom for all of sixteen months, remaining at the head of the Croatian Catholic hierarchy and working at the reorganisation of the country alongside the communists. But during this period of violent anti-clericalism, which Tito's partisans could hardly not encourage, Aloïs finally decided that living conditions for himself and his clergy had become intolerable and, convinced that he possessed a kind of immunity and that the only person he would ever cross swords with was God, he complained about them from his pulpit.

Arrested on 18 September 1946, he was condemned a month later to sixteen years' hard labour, a sentence immediately commuted to five years in gaol which he served at the presbytery in Krasić, his native village. 'I do not accept this sentence, which is the most shameful thing in the twentieth century,' he said. *The most shameful thing in the twentieth century*! For Aloïs, compared to this, Auschwitz was perhaps nothing more than a regrettable incident in the Catholics' triumphant march towards a gradual moral and physical purification of the Christian West.

As you can guess, the interest little Josip Broz took in the Virgin Mary was always rather limited. The son of a peasant, he occasionally had to slip out through the back door to escape from the farm work and get to school. Not tempted by the supposed wisdom of the Croat peasantry — founded more often than not on their ignorance and naïvety, but much vaunted by Vlado Macěk, leader, after the death of Stefan Radić, of the Croatian Peasant Party — young Josip favoured the hard and fast knowledge that the schoolmaster handed out. At the age of twenty-one, he was the youngest NCO in the 25th Domobrani regiment. And he certainly wouldn't have sacrificed the life of a Croat to bring back a wounded Polish enemy to his lines! Russia, where he'd been deported as a prisoner of war, sprang on him the surprise of the Revolution. He promptly enlisted in a unit of the International Red Guard and spent the winter months of 1917–1918 keeping watch on the railway line near Omsk for the Bolsheviks.

Tito was among the oldest in the CPY just as Stepinac was among the oldest in Rome's *Germanicum* seminary; and, just as Aloïs had known how to win Mgr Bauer's confidence, so Tito would know how to win Stalin's. In 1937, the Kremlin's master was busy liquidating the CPY. Already he'd had its entire leadership executed as well as most of its former secretaries-general and any of its other members who happened to be in the USSR. Thanks to this bloodthirsty purge and even more to his native prudence that would save his life on a number of occasions during the war, Josip Broz could now take over the leadership of the party.

During the war, while the solitary Stepinac gazed out over Zagreb from his Kaptol, a spot as icy and deserted as a schoolyard in the Christmas holidays, Tito, surrounded by the most valorous of Yugoslavia's youth, was fighting in the Bosnian mountains. This was the time when the Yugoslav communists stood as united as can be around their leader. They paid thoughtful attention to his every need. For example, Tito had his own cook. The partisans also kept a cow with them so that he could have fresh milk every day. He had a terrible fit of temper the day the quartermaster had the animal slain because it was supposedly no longer producing milk. This cow had survived all the most ferocious offensives without ever balking and we had all grown fond of her. Tito ordered that the quartermaster be reduced to the ranks, although in fact Ranković simply removed him from our 'Old Man's' immediate entourage.

It was a dirty, cruel war, one where the fighters sometimes changed sides according to their mood or the situation and gaily massacred the previous day's friends before being massacred in turn by friends of the day before that. We were always lice-ridden, dressed in rags, starving and exhausted, but this wretchedness and the threats that constantly hung over our heads swathed us in something like a layer of cotton wool inside which we somehow felt protected. Many of us were bad shots, and we were happier fighting the Italians than the Germans, as they were even worse shots than us and, on top of that, they were wondering what they were doing there in the first place whereas that was a question not one of us felt the need to ask. We always chose to die rather than surrender and the only prisoners the Nazis took were partisans they'd caught sleeping. The doctors from Berlin and professors from Heidelberg who were murdering without respite the peasants and students of the Balkans in the steep valleys of Bosnia were astounded by the rage that possessed us. Similarly we failed to understand why this élite among peoples was so determined to immerse itself deeper each day into sheer horror, as if it believed that in the deepest depths of horror there lay something very precious, with which it wished, at all costs, to enrich its national heritage.

All this might explain to you why we so loved Russia and what a real wrench it was for us when, after the war, we had to part from her and we even had to be prepared for an attack from her. As we ran like rabbits along the mountain paths with the Luftwaffe pounding us and the best SS divisions on our heels, what kept us going was the thought that our Russian brothers — the peasants of Siberia who'd never seen a tank before in their lives and who rushed at them as if they were mammoths whose eyes you simply had to gouge out to make them fall, the Cossacks, the Estonian sharp-shooters, the Muscovite doctors who dressed the wounds of Uzbek shepherds under a hail of machine-gun fire — the thought that all of these men were, like us, fighting the world's most efficient and most merciless soldiers. And somewhere deep within our terror, our exhaustion and our despair, we knew that in the final event we would win through with the Russians, even though all of Europe was falling over itself to say we wouldn't.

And so it was a great day for the Yugoslav resistance when in February 1944 we welcomed the first Soviet mission. Rather than jump with parachutes as the British had done, the Russians chose to land with their planes, which meant they had to wait several days while weather conditions improved. The partisans showed some surprise at this as most of them were perfectly capable of jumping out of a plane *without a parachute* if given the order to do so. It was later explained to us that General Korneïev who was leading the mission had been 'wounded in the foot'. On 23 February, he came tottering off the plane, but no one noticed him limping. Some of us made the comparison with Randolph Churchill, the British Prime Minister's son who was also in command of a military mission, and who would always be found at the bottom of a cave surrounded by empty bottles once the bombing was over. Tito even told us that one evening when he'd been left alone with Korneïev, the latter, who was drunk, had kissed him on the mouth, calling him, 'Oska, Oska . . .', the Russian diminutive for Joseph. This was not at all how we imagined Soviet heroes. But once the initial shock was over we grew to like the Russians just as they were: sentimental in what concerned them and brutal towards others.

In 1946, Tito is in power and Stepinac in gaol. At his trial, the Archbishop refuses to defend himself, which is tantamount to refusing to acknowledge your adversary's political authority. And there, Brigitte, you have another typically Croatian attitude: that denial of what is a blatant fact, which leads them straight down the path to disaster. In 1568, rather than surrender to the Turks, Nikola Zrinsky, one of the

169

richest lords of the Sziget region and general of Transdanubia had, without any fire-power, made a sortie against their artillery — then the most powerful in the world; his end came as he was massacred alongside the last of his men. When Tito says no to Stalin, he knows he has the backing of all of Yugoslavia and that he could turn to the West for help or possibly even to the United States; but when Stepinac says no to Tito, he is forgetting that he only has the backing of a Catholic clergy in a state of disarray and a mass of believers who are utterly terrified by Yugoslavia's new masters, while in the West, Tito's glory is at its height and the Archbishop of Zagreb is seen as a war criminal, which he isn't. The no he shouts will find its only echo within the four walls of his Lepoglava prison cell.

When I marched into Zagreb at the head of my men on 8 May 1945, I felt a little as if I'd stepped into the shoes of one of those Serbian officers who, on the day of unification, took up position at all the strategic points in our capital, like poor relations turning up without warning and making the masters of the house eat at the far end of the dinner table. Frightened young girls handed us a few rare bunches of flowers. As we made our way up Maksimirska towards Jelačić Square, I was filled with a feeling of anguish — just at the moment when I was walking in triumph into the city where I was born and should have been feeling a joy to match the fullness of our twofold victory over Nazism and the Yugoslav bourgeoisie. The May sun dancing on the slate roofs dazzled me. As the citizens of Zagreb looked down from their sash windows, there was consternation on their faces. An armada of small clouds straggled across the sky which, despite the heat, was a chilly, distant blue. My house, with its narrow entrance, its single storey and drab windows was slowly drawing closer. Looking up, I caught sight of Dara Sevnica's face and understood immediately why that feeling of failure and waste linked to her memory was once again laying hold of me after having left me pretty much in peace during the four previous

170

years: the gymnast with permanently grazed knees, the American film enthusiast who never missed the Saturday evening shows in the big cinema with wooden benches on Kvaternik Square, the beautiful, romantic young girl you had to take to the Strossmayer Promenade if you wanted a chance of kissing her on the mouth: I still loved her! She was leaning on the window ledge in that sitting room where I'd spent countless afternoons before the war playing chess with Josip Sevnica and stuffing myself with walnut biscuits that his wife Milena brought us from the kitchen; as she made her way back, she'd mutter that I really didn't eat a thing and that if this wasn't supposed to demonstrate a lack of good will, then it surely meant I was coming down with something serious. Your mother had lost weight, but not as much as me. She had cut her hair. Tidily parted to fall on either side of her broad forehead and high cheekbones, it reached down to her collar. Just as before, I was struck by the extraordinary gentleness of her face. Unlike all the people gaping at us from the pavements or those watching us pass from their windows, she showed no fear. Rather, she seemed to be eyeing us with a mixture of amazement and pity. I really wonder whether she didn't despise us a little too! We were so shabbily dressed, you know! When our eyes met, I had to make a real effort to produce the merest hint of a smile to which, I may say, she gave no reaction. Then I turned away, feeling unable to understand why the slight glimpse of dissatisfaction on your mother's face had been enough to sweep aside four years of great struggle, sacrifice and exaltation. I thought my pockets were brimming over with my victory and all of a sudden, faced with Dara, I found myself stripped of everything. The mere thought of what your mother — elegant Zagreb woman that she was — might be thinking about all those Montenegrins dressed any old how or the thick-set Serbs I had hanging about me was almost enough to bring me to loathe them. I continued on my way, with each step rediscovering the familiar pain that had kept me company throughout my

171

adolescence. I was of course aware that now things would be very different between your mother and me, but without suspecting that five days after my arrival in Zagreb Dara would call on me, in the lodgings I had requisitioned, and offer herself to me!

The flat on Zrinsky Square had five rooms. Even for that time its ceilings were of a considerable height. Its owner, an industrialist who'd been closely allied to the Ustaše and who, like most of them, was no doubt following the so-called 'rats'-route' to safety in South America, never again set foot in Yugoslavia. He had left all his furniture behind. Among his books, I came across a copy of *Ljepa Plavka*, Pavelić's first and only novel. I'd already read it, but nevertheless I experienced a certain pleasure in spending — me, Nikola Dunak, a partisan officer — my first evening in Zagreb in the flat of a fugitive collaborator whose plum brandy I sipped as I re-read the colourless prose of my former mentor. It was the first time since September 1941 that I found myself alone for a night in an enclosed space. My companions hadn't been able to understand why I'd chosen to retire into my tent like a brooding emperor when they were sauntering about town yelling communist slogans and singing patriotic songs, one hand on the butts of their sub-machine guns and the other convulsively clasping the neck of a slivovitz bottle. A few years later I recounted this solitary evening to Tito, though I skirted around the sort of book it was I'd been reading while my companions were lighting bonfires all over Zagreb to celebrate the liberation of our nation. It was at the time of an official visit to Slovenia. Tito was wearing his famous white cap and a long army mac that flapped about below his knees. We were gazing out from Triglav at the snowy peaks of the Alps. The Marshal suddenly turned towards me and said, with that innocent smile of his on which all of Churchill and Stalin's most sophisticated diplomatic weapons had shattered: 'A very difficult moment to have to live through, the one when you finally hit your target.' He added, 'Some never get over it. The target, for instance.' His face became round and mischievous, and a moment later we both burst out laughing, to the great surprise of the local communist officials who were no doubt wondering what there was in this majestic landscape to set off such mirth in the head of state and one of his collaborators. Not wishing to seem to be straying from the Party line, they also began to chuckle, discreetly at first and then, seeing Tito react to their enterprising move with a kindly amusement, they began to laugh in earnest — some of them were even doubled up and splitting their sides with laughter.

Around three o'clock in the morning, I was dead drunk and my tunic was dotted with bits of tobacco and splashes of slivovitz; I closed *Ljepa Plavka* and began wandering about the flat. Later I stretched out on the sitting-room carpet. I began a rather disenchanted debate with myself, and followed this up with a declaration of love to your mother. I had switched out all the lights and was looking out through the window at the chestnut trees on Zrinsky Square. The sky was sapphire blue, a blue at once deep and luminous; and, all of a sudden, I burst into tears. Amongst the various factors that brought on these tears, there was of course the fact that I'd drunk far too much, the lovely mild night, the pleasure of being alone for the first time in four years, the fantastic relief of no longer having to live in constant fear of violent death, but above all, there was my love for Dara, a love so fiercely resistant to time and events, a small flame that the great storm of the war hadn't managed to blow out and with which I'd just understood I would live to my dying day. Full of the pain of my enthusiastic heartache, I huddled up and fell asleep.

I was woken up by a milky white dawn just in time to have a shower and shave before presenting myself at headquarters. I spent the following days trying to lay hands on the very few collaborators of Pavelić's régime who'd had the lack of fore-sight to stay on in Zagreb. While we were about it, we eliminated a few notorious anti-communists. These punitive expeditions gave me a chance to see once again the various places in Zagreb where I'd spent time with your mother in the past. When, in the Dolac marketplace once, we only just managed to catch a former Croatian Peasant Party official who we'd turfed out of bed and who was trying to escape through Bakačeva Ulica, I recalled with some emotion the Sunday morning when I'd come out of the cathedral with Mama and had bumped into Dara in front of a vegetable stall. The greengrocer, a young Zagoran with unruly hair and half-rotten teeth, was making all sorts of crude remarks to her that were making her laugh. When she saw me with my mother and my missal, she put on that friendly and slightly annoyed little look she always had when we passed on the stairs in Maksimirska. Another day in the old town, after I'd used my bayonet to chase an eighteen-year-old Ustaša out from the cellar where his parents had hidden him, I couldn't resist the temptation of going back to the exact spot where I had first kissed your mother. It was in the narrow street that joins Stefan-Radić Square to the Strossmayer Promenade. I remembered how we'd both kept our eyes open and also how Dara had linked her hands behind my neck. In the distance Zagreb, baking in the sun, unfurled its church spires, tramways and quaint old buildings. Finally there was that sexton; we knew he had tortured to death a number of our comrades in Pavelić's gaols, and we found him at the far end of Maksimir Park where he'd survived on a diet of nothing but roots since the day of the liberation. After they'd beaten him black and blue, my men locked him in the lions' cage at the municipal zoo and settled down comfortably to watch the show, although it didn't take long before they tired of it. But I couldn't take my eyes off the bear pit opposite which, a few days after our first kiss, Dara had announced with a sad little smile that that was where our story ended. 'What story?' I asked. She shrugged her shoulders. I said I didn't understand. I wanted her at least to give me her reasons. 'I don't love you,' she said. Then she turned away and ran off. That was the twenty-sixth of July 1939.

In the evening I'd get back to Zrinsky Square feeling exhausted and also slightly disgusted. I'd peel an onion or two in my large kitchen, pour salt over them and bite into them. I'd then move into the sitting room and settle down with a bottle of slivovitz in one of those period armchairs that I hadn't quite got around to taking the dustcovers off.

The most important scene of my life was something I lived through with just one idea on my mind, which was: Don't I smell too strongly of onion? It's true, because when your mother presented herself at my flat on the evening of 13 May 1945, I'd been back from HQ since the middle of the afternoon and I'd already assuaged the passion I have for this condiment, so loved in the Balkans that it is thought of as a vegetable and eaten as such, and I spent a good part of those three hours — which was how long my final encounter with Dara Sevnica lasted — turning my head away, rinsing out my palate with slivovitz and breathing hard through my mouth. When I heard the first, timid ring on the doorbell, I didn't move from my armchair, and I even belched loudly to indicate that I was indeed in but didn't want to open the door to anyone. The person insisted. I told myself it was probably a gang of recalcitrant Ustaše who were planning to make rope out of my intestine, tongue and a few other organs that come in handy in such cases. Do you know that the Ustaše's favourite joke during the war was to shake the hand of any young woman of their acquaintance and leave behind in her palm an ear or nose they'd cut off that very morning from the body of a Serb, Jew or communist? I got up and went to fetch my revolver. I'd taken my shoes off for once, so that when I opened the door for Dara with an abrupt, angry shove, I was wearing nothing on my feet, I was drunk, I stank of onion and I was armed. Faced with Dara, I stood stock-still for a second, barely able to take in what was happening. She had her eyes riveted on my revolver and didn't dare say a word or move an inch. 'I was cleaning it,' I said, slightly embarrassed, and then

175

stepped aside to let her in — a woman now, so different to the young girl I'd had the privilege of hugging on the Strossmayer Promenade six years previously. She took her coat off and looked about as she walked a little way into the sitting room. She was wearing a printed chiffon dress cut low at the back, and around her neck she had a string of small pearls of a nasty grey colour. On her wrist I noticed the cheap watch her parents had given her at least ten years earlier. It was the same watch that she used to consult rather absent-mindedly in July 1939 when she got fed up with our kissing and wanted to get back to Maksimirska. There was something tender, proud and tremulous about her bare back and arms. She stopped for a moment beneath the painting of a country scene that hung impressively above the fireplace, as if she wanted to find out who the artist was. Then she turned towards me. 'This all belongs to you now?' I corrected her: 'To the Party.' And then I pulled a face, meaning to look very mocking and confirm her opinion that for a partisan officer, there was little difference between requisitioning something for one's own personal benefit and confiscating it in the name of the Party. She did not react in the way I'd expected. Instead of the complicity I'd hoped for, I got the sort of icy glare she usually saved for people who claimed in her presence that Gene Tierney was a bad actress, Prince Peter Karageorgević had one shoulder lower than the other or that a woman's sole duty in life was to obey the man who had married her. She prowled about in the corridor, quickly peered into the kitchen and then came and planted her large athletic body in the middle of the sitting room, rather as you might plant a flag at the top of a mountain; she put on a pert expression and said: 'So in the end, you haven't done too badly for yourself.' I felt that despite the sarcastic and even hostile tone in which she'd said those words, it didn't displease her that 'I hadn't done too badly for myself'. I shrugged my shoulders modestly and sat down to put my shoes back on, declaring that, all the same, the first four years had been tough enough. She sat down opposite me.

176

'Do you know that my father's in prison?' I nodded, having seen Josip Sevnica's name on the list of suspects to be arrested immediately, and again on the list of people being sent to the Dubrava camp. I said I was very fond of Josip, but there was nothing I could do for him. We had to get one thing clear: had he or hadn't he been working in Zagreb town hall when it was nothing more than an Ustaše stamping-ground? 'So? You were with the Ustaše too!' exclaimed your mother. 'For twenty-one days,' I said drily. She was beginning to get on my nerves! Her behaviour towards me gave no sign that the tables had turned since that time in July 1939 when I'd thought happiness lay just around the corner, whereas in fact my sorrows were only just beginning. 'I am very sorry,' I said. 'I can be of no use to you.' I got up and asked her if she wanted anything to eat or drink, reflecting that had I been calling on her, that would have been the first thing she'd have said to me. 'If I give you what you want, can you fix things to have my father released?' she asked. Without answering, I looked at her long crossed legs, her small bosom quivering beneath the chiffon of her dress, her hands gripping the arms of her seat. She begged softly: 'Nikola. . . . If I give you what you want. . . .' I drank a mouthful of slivovitz and said, 'I'd rather not make any promises.' At that moment she gave me a look I'll never forget, a violent, misty look that tried hard to convey the impression that she wasn't merely offering herself to me, but that her whole body was aflame at the prospect. The irony of it was that, contrary to what I imagined and probably to what she herself imagined, she would end up crying out in my arms, taking a strange pleasure in giving herself to a man she didn't love in order to save a man she hated. I sat down at her feet and rested my head on my knees. I began caressing her legs meticulously, lingering over the softness of her calves and moving down to her ankles, so sturdy and yet graceful, and then I parted her thighs one from the other and met with no resistance. 'Are we going to stay here?' your mother asked in a strangled voice. I lifted the dress and pressed my face against her stomach. Above me I heard: 'We'll be more comfortable in the bedroom, Nikola.' I didn't answer; I was too busy nuzzling the little bump of her pubic hair under the lace underpants. Very nearly in tears, Dara kept imploring: 'Not here, Nikola. . . . Take me to the bedroom. . . .' That request seemed to be the last thing she was hanging on to that might restore to her a semblance of dignity. I took her at random into one of the flat's four bedrooms.

At first, she kept her lips firmly sealed and her eyes closed, and when I asked if I wasn't hurting her too much, she merely shook her head to say I wasn't; then gradually she relaxed. Her first gesture towards me was when she linked her hands around my neck as she had when we'd kissed at Gornji Grad. As the minutes passed, I could feel her yielding. This woman who had clambered on to the bed as stiffly as a lesbian queen forced to sleep with her husband at least once to provide the kingdom with an heir, was now spilling out over the sheets like a large pool of oil. And soon that large body that I'd had to disarm became a molten mass: I found myself assaulted by powerful arms, lips as hard as stones and supple gymnast's legs, and straight away I understood there was no point in my wrestling against all these youthful weapons; which is how on 13 May 1945, around ten p.m., your mother took me in the way you take a woman when she doesn't want it: lying on me with all her weight, holding me by the wrists and making herself come endlessly by delicately rubbing the sides of her vagina against my erect penis.

So you see, contrary to what she told Giuliana Altieri, Dara came to see me on her own initiative and quite without my needing to speak to Josip Sevnica or to get word to him through a militiaman on duty at the camp. Why did she lie to her Italian friend? No doubt she was ashamed to admit that she'd come and offered herself to a communist, and very probably this sense of shame haunted her throughout her life, especially when she thought back to the pleasure she had experienced that evening.

What I felt for her had oscillated between admiration, pity, passion and lastly, a few seconds before we reached the orgasm we'd postponed for six years for reasons that, to this day, I still don't know, love — pure and simple. Now, as I lay sprawled on the bed with one hand still on her out of the fear I always had that she would leave without warning as she was apt to, I allowed this feeling to sweep through me and almost to choke me with happiness. I was forgetting to what end your mother had slept with me; in my muddled mind, what had just happened symbolised a genuine union between us; I didn't doubt for a minute that Dara would agree to marry me as soon as I asked her and that we'd soon have the empty rooms of the Zrinsky Square flat filled with bawling, chubby-cheeked babies.

We had one of those conversations peppered with 'ohs' and 'ahs' and 'oh reallys' that former college or regimental friends have. Your mother told me the news that, just before retreating to Austria, her brother Vladimir had married a certain Ana Crnjević, a hairdresser's assistant in a salon on Illica. As for Zora Popović, the only daughter of the couple who lived on the lower ground floor of the house, what the English call the basement, she had died the previous winter, a victim of tuberculosis. Poor Zora! We went on through the list of all our mutual friends, then Dara got up, slipped into the bathroom where she spent a minute or two, came back into the room and got dressed. When she had zipped up her dress, she rested a knee on the bed and kissed me on the cheeks, saying, 'I'm relying on you for my father.' Taking her arm to hold her back, I asked, 'Do we only do it once?' She smiled coldly. 'That's the one that counts, isn't it?' The cynicism amazed me, coming from her: an hour before she'd still been a virgin! I told her I loved her and that she loved me too. She shook her head. 'You loved me just now,' I said. She said, 'Just now, yes. But now, no.' Why not? She didn't know. That was the way it was. I was actually beginning to see that she was both fascin-

179

ated and disgusted by me, and more particularly by what I was able to do to her: I could deprive her of that sacrosanct freedom of hers because I could push her into a realm where she would lose control over herself, the shadowy realm she fled from throughout her life, the realm of unbridled sensual pleasure for which nature had made her.

I caught hold of her by the waist and tipped her on to the bed. 'Not that,' she said softly. When I tried to kiss her she bit me. Then, while I was pulling her pants down for the second time that evening, she became lifeless, as heavy as a stone at the bottom of a pool of water. I wanted her to cry out again, so that I would know I existed for her, but she remained stiff and mute. I'm convinced that it was at exactly that moment that we conceived our son Ladislav. In fact, when I withdrew from her, your mother didn't bother to slip into the bathroom. She simply wiped herself with the sheet, which incidentally struck me as being in extremely bad taste, and then with her hair all over the place and her dress rumpled, she went towards the door. Something dejected about the stooped back; the neck suddenly seemed over-long and the arms gangly: through all this I sensed the forlornness of an innocence derided. I wanted to throw myself at her feet, but instead, with all my juvenile stupidity, I didn't move from the bed and whined instead, 'You're forgetting the curfew.' She turned towards me. 'What am I risking?' I said she might be arrested and shot. She asked if that was all. I felt it was already rather a lot. She shrugged her shoulders and left. I said, 'Wait, I'll come with you!' Then I heard her racing down the stairs as if she'd had Marshal Tito and all his officers on her heels. I rushed after her, although not without having first taken the precaution of equipping myself with my revolver. I caught up with her on the pavement of what is today 8 May 1945 Street; but all the way to Maksimirska, she let me get no closer than about thirty metres. She was an athlete, you know, she could run much faster and for much longer than me. Each time I quickened my pace or shouted to her to wait for me, she broke into a sprint that made a mockery of my pathetic attempts to catch up with her. I can see us now, following each other from afar through the deserted Zagreb streets. It was such a funny situation that despite all that had happened between us that evening, Dara burst out laughing when, up by Kvaternik Square, she turned around and saw me hobbling after her, waving my revolver about over my head as if it were a white flag. It was a mild night. Our steps echoed along the empty street. Your mother pushed open the door of number 38, Maksimirska and disappeared into the small grey building where I'd spent twenty years of my life.

The following day, in the late afternoon, I rang the doorbell at my mother's. Since I'd arrived in Zagreb, I'd only called on her once. She looked at me distrustfully, as if I'd come to carry out a search or even to arrest her. For her, all communists were devils, including her son. It wouldn't even have occurred to her that I might have done something other than from murdering priests during my years in the *maquis*. Even so, she gave me a glass of tea and a slice of cake. Keeping her distance, she sat down in a corner of the room and got on with her embroidery. She was a small woman with a broken nose and grey hair that she wore pulled back. I had long since given up trying to chat with her about anything. We couldn't even agree on the weather any longer.

The flat had not changed since I was old enough to remember it, and it would not change until my mother's death, except that, following Stepinac's arrest, she hung the archbishop's portrait in her bedroom. We were sitting in the kitchen, in Central Europe the most important room in a house. It's here that you entertain your friends, that children do their homework, that you listen to the radio. We could hear the patter of the rain on the corrugated roofs of the woodsheds that ran the length of the yard. This was the first bad weather we'd had since Zagreb had been liberated. The ceramic stove that also heated the water for baths and for tea gleamed in the half-light. I got up and switched on our old wireless. On the yellow dial, you could read the names of all the main cities in the world. As a child, I would sometimes spend hours in front of this set that I was strictly forbidden to use when I was on my own. The idea that one could move from Moscow to Paris by turning a knob for half a second had me positively paralysed with pleasure, and each day I would impatiently await the moment when my father would get back from work and switch on the radio to listen to the news. If I made enough of a fuss and if he had nothing else to do, we would roam on the air waves from Madrid to Istanbul via Milan, Amsterdam, Hamburg. . . .

Just as I had anticipated, the Sevnicas arrived at Maksimirska around five o'clock. I had installed myself in my old bedroom because it looked out over the street. Looking lofty and triumphant, Dara was the first to step off the tram, followed by her mother Milena whom I recalled being a very beautiful woman, though your mother had told me the previous evening that she'd lost all her teeth during the war. Finally, helped by his oldest daughter Zdenka on whom he was leaning, Josip Sevnica made his ungainly and unsteady appearance. They hurried across the road because the rain was coming down more and more heavily. Dara came hopping up the steps to the front door. It was the last time in my life I saw her run towards me.

It obviously wasn't right for me to instal myself like this in the best seat to witness the family reunion, for I could hardly consider myself its benefactor, my services having been duly rewarded by the prettier of its two daughters, but I simply hadn't been able to resist the temptation. If only I'd remained safely tucked away at my mother's and then discreetly slipped off! But no! As soon as I saw Dara, I couldn't wait to be close to her, talk to her, kiss her; I rushed down the staircase to meet the Sevnicas. Josip immediately threw himself into my arms. He smelt dreadfully bad. I stepped aside and, forcing a smile, I said, 'You're lucky to have been released the day it starts raining.' From behind his round spectacles, his eyes were shining with a mixture of mischief, gratitude and also a kind of distrust in the face of what he must have considered to be my incurable folly. He said: 'I am indeed lucky, very lucky.' He patted my shoulder and then led me up towards the flat. Milena, who'd taken to hiding her mouth behind her hand whenever she said something, which in any case happened only very rarely, hurried into the kitchen to organise refreshments worthy of the occasion. Arm in arm, Josip and I followed her, while your mother's eyes went straight through us like two laser beams. She brought up the rear, holding herself very erect in a black dress buttoned right up to her neck. She wasn't wearing any jewellery. When I turned towards her to hold the door open, she eyed me coldly, but also very anxiously. She must have been wondering what dirty trick I had up my sleeve. But the fact is that, at that point in the afternoon, I had absolutely no idea of what was going to happen an hour later, something that was to determine Dara's future to a certain extent, and therefore your own. I gave myself over to the simple pleasure of feeling once again part of that family I was so fond of, and that both my break-up with your mother and the war had kept me away from for six years. I was an only son and had lost my father at the age of twelve, so it was a delight to re-immerse myself in the genial atmosphere Josip Sevnica was good at creating around him, despite his authoritarian temperament. The chess set, the piles of newspapers and bottles of white wine were all in their customary places. We sat down and began eating and drinking.

We started a game of chess. I recognised Josip's favourite opening move and also that way he had of revealing his strategy while at the same time keeping its most threatening element well hidden away. As his pieces gradually advanced towards me as if to make me atone for my behaviour that some might have described as vile, I felt I was being projected back into the past and transformed into that pimply, obstinate youth who'd sat with his cheeks resting between clenched fists, fighting tooth and nail to save his king from certain death while the fifteen-year-old Dara went swirling about the flat, wearing her age as if it were a priceless gem and whipping up the air for some ever uncertain purpose. All of a sudden, Josip's knights, queen and black bishop leapt out from all over the place and in two moves I found myself checkmated. Laughing, I said I'd let Tito do so much winning that I'd lost the knack. Josip slapped his thighs and poured us some *gemicht*. Your mother was sitting right at the end of the table, silently mending a nightdress. I was surprised she'd stayed with us, having expected her to find any excuse to go out and join one of her many girlfriends. As for Zdenka, a chubby mischievous-looking blonde, she couldn't keep her eyes off me. It was quite plain she was prepared to do anything to have an affair with a communist officer. No sooner were the cakes out of your grandmother's hands than she'd be bringing them to me; I got a clean napkin every quarter of an hour, and enthusiastically she suggested that I take the last salted gherkin in the larder. During the second game I played with Josip, she kept her eyes glued to the chessboard. Her long hair kept brushing against my cheek and I was quite expecting her simply to get up and lie on top of me at any moment. Every now and then, Josip would ask the odd cautious question about what I had done 'in the forest'. I said I hadn't done anything much, that I'd mostly been cold, tired, hungry, frightened and had sore feet. He slapped his thighs again and poured us some more *gemicht*. 'You'll be drunk,' Milena said. His answer was: 'That's precisely my intention!' and then he plunged his head back into the forest of the chessboard where nothing could yet be made out but everything was already settled.

When I saw the sky turning dark outside the window, I realised how painful I was going to find it to part from these people and this flat and go back to Zrinsky Square on my own, so that it was partly to gain time that I decided to ask Dara if she would marry me. I had a pretty good idea that she would turn me down, but I was a thousand miles from thinking that the proposal would so frighten her that the very next morning she'd be on the road to exile. Josip raised his eyes to heaven and said in a facetious tone: 'At last a man who's interested in one of my daughters! I was beginning to give up hope! Because the fact is, Dara's twenty-two now!' Those were the days when, at the age of twenty-two, a Croat woman would have been married for five or six years and had several children — that is, if she hadn't already died in child-birth. Milena was looking alternately at her daughter and her husband, uncertain whether she should fly into their arms or stay near the stove and wait to see what happened next. She wiped her hands on her apron. Your mother eyed me harshly and said, 'I shall never marry you.' I smiled. I badly wanted to give her the impression that I'd anticipated her answer and that I'd only ventured to make this hopeless request because I had some mysterious aim in mind, one that would be to my advantage and that she'd never be able to fathom. In the smoothest voice I could muster, I asked, 'Why not?' She said she didn't know. She didn't love me. She'd already told me, hadn't she? She got up, fetched a jumper and went out. 'Don't worry,' Josip said to me, 'she doesn't love me too much either.' Making my own way down the stairs, I had as yet no idea that I wouldn't see your mother again before that day in December 1967 when I bumped into her quite by chance on the Strossmayer Promenade with you and your father.

The Sevnicas entrusted Milena with the task of telling me that Dara had left. They knew I was prone to violence, and no doubt felt that I would contain my anger in the presence of a worthy, toothless housewife. And that's precisely how it went. Without a word, I turned on my heels and rushed back to headquarters to put out a notice for your mother to be found — a step that unfortunately proved of no use. Dara slipped through the net. That was an art at which she excelled.

Here is a letter from your mother. It was posted in Milan on

6 September 1945. I shall read it to you: 'How are you, Nikola? I hope you are taking care of your mother and also of mine! They say life is not easy in Yugoslavia, but I expect that for you it is a little easier than for other people. Here everything is working out as I wanted it to: I have a job and modest lodgings that I was sharing until recently with a Yugoslav girlfriend who has just left for the United States. I've especially got freedom and, as you know, that is my great love!

'Nikola, this is why I am writing: I'm pregnant by you. I haven't wanted to have an abortion because it's such a crime and a sin and also because I was very scared that it might be the end for me too, but nor can I keep the child because I wouldn't have the money to feed and clothe him properly. And on top of that it would remind me of something I'd sooner forget.

'What am I to do with this little child who is going to be born? I can't help thinking that later on he would never forgive me if I didn't try to convince you it would be a good thing for him to benefit from all the advantages a man like you is in a position to bring him in Tito's Yugoslavia. And so I am asking Nikola Dunak, the "great communist", to take him under his protective wing. You should think of it as if, through him, it would be a bit of me that you'd have near you. I wonder in fact if that hasn't always been my dream: to be near you and at the same time very far away.

'You frightened me terribly with your idea of marrying me, but I'm over that now. Sometimes I stroll through Milan in the evening and think of that night in May when I went back to Maksimirska with you walking a hundred metres behind me. Everything else is horrible but, God knows why, that is a good memory. I'll wait to hear from you. Greetings. Dara.'

She didn't give an address. So I wrote to her poste restante to let her know that I was absolutely wild with joy that our brief affair had borne fruit. I added that through our legation there, I'd already ordered from London everything that would be needed for the baby to whom I already referred as

Ladislav. I underlined the fact that the high office I held might well allow me to take care of a baby in great style, but I could also look after a young woman in a quite passable manner, and that my advice was that she should get back to Zagreb double-quick and marry me to become one of the most envied people in Croatia. She didn't answer this letter and, as you may know, poor Ladislav died two days after his birth, the victim of a heart malformation. The baby's burial was paid for by the Italian branch of a Serbian royalist organisation run by a certain Christiane whose real name was Mira Radoman and who was secretly working for the CPY, as I learnt from Ranković, the head of the UDBA. She died in a car crash in Austria in 1966, a detail that was also supplied to me by Ranković just as he was about to be fired.

Now it is time to tell you about this Aunt Nathalie you were asking about at the beginning of our conversation. She too was secretly working for us. You know, the great strength of the socialist bloc countries was the way they managed to infiltrate the émigré organisations immediately, at the highest levels. Before the war, Nathalie Mikhaïlovna Balouïev was a communist mole in King Alexander's secret police; she joined Peter II and his staff officers in exile in England, and between 1941 and 1945 she was our major source of information in London. So successful was she at winning her masters' confidence that at the end of the war, they entrusted her with important tasks like vetting the security of all anti-communist émigrés in France, and this was how she came to be so promptly brought into contact with Dara in May 1946. At my request, Ranković instructed her to take care of your mother, and that was why, when we received a report from the Russian woman stating that some wheeler-dealer by the name of Branko Marić had used violence against Dara, I asked that he be eliminated, a measure Ranković very happily agreed to. Never seen a more accommodating fellow when it came to liquidating someone. 'The fewer the merrier,' he would say with that obtuse expression that virtually never left

187

his face.

1948 will always be remembered as the year of Gandhi's death and of the Yugoslav schism. Nathalie could no longer serve Tito without betraying Stalin. She chose to get out of the game. But, Brigitte, this is a game one can never completely get out of. The Russians were prepared to do anything to destabilise Yugoslavia, so when, in the Sixties, the KGB asked Nathalie to become the secret link between the Soviet Union and the various Ustaše groups in Berlin, Munich and Madrid, she had no choice but to agree. That's the reason why, on 17 December 1966, the UDBA had her killed.

The last time I saw Dara, I had no idea she was in Zagreb with her husband and daughter as I'd lost all contact with the Sevnicas after my mother's death three years before. I was coming out of the Sabor. It was about five in the afternoon. It had been an exhausting session and I decided to stretch my legs on the Strossmayer Promenade before getting into my car. Tucking my Russian leather briefcase under my arm, I walked along Matoševa Ulica as far as the Ban's Palace, and then, with my senator's gait so well known among all the dignitaries of the League of Communists of Yugoslavia, I headed towards Lotrščack Tower.

The snow gleamed under the blue sky. I saw a tall blonde woman in a red anorak. She was speaking a language that sounded like French but wasn't really. I recognised your mother. The colour of her hair was different but her face still had the same freshness, the same sweetness. I moved closer and, all of a sudden, she rested her eyes on me, eyes that were intrigued, bright, sparkling. The eyes of a young girl. She raised her arms in surprise. 'Nikola! How are you?' I complained that she might have let me know she was in Zagreb. Let me know? But she didn't even know where I lived! I smiled calmly beneath the broad brim of my round hat and said, 'In Zrinsky Square.'

6

In winter it would snow virtually every night, and so heavily that in the morning each family would send at least one person out to clear the pavement and the roadway, which was something you had to do according to an old law dating back to the Austro–Hungarian Empire. Alerted by the factory workers who were always first up, civil servants, students, shopkeepers and *rentiers* would go down into the street and wield their shovels with varying degrees of efficiency, stopping occasionally to drink a mouthful of plum brandy or bite into a piece of sausage. Occasionally little Dara Sevnica would kneel on her bed and stick her nose against the window-pane. That day she noticed that her father was taking it easy as usual. Leaning on his shovel looking very relaxed, he was holding forth, giving people a drink, filling his pipe. He even got an impromptu snowball fight organised which was an instant success. For a while, your mother went on gazing at the surrealist spectacle of all the neighbourhood men playing at being navvies in the dark small hours, then she snuggled under her eiderdown and went back to sleep.

Josip brought Boris Ciliga home with him. He was a colleague from work who lived in the next door building and every morning your father used to get the tram with him. They installed themselves in the kitchen. Milena served them milky coffee. When Dara appeared in the passage, Boris Ciliga gave her a friendly greeting and said to your grandfather that now she was no longer a child, but a lovely young girl. Josip looked at your mother and smiled, no doubt recalling that he'd hit her the evening before because he'd caught her reading a book under the bedsheets with the help of a torch — a French novel that was considered pornographic in Yugoslavia in 1937: Émile Zola's *Nana*. 'I'd sooner she were

189

obedient,' he said. Dara had a mouthful of her coffee and left.

The tram stop was opposite the house, on the other side of the street. The snow had been collected into the centre of the roadway to make a sort of brownish hedge; and when, about twenty-five years later, pictures of the Berlin wall being erected were shown on French television, your mother was moved by the memory of the winter mornings in Zagreb when Maksimirska was divided in two every time it snowed.

You could see the tram coming a long way off. It had a single carriage. Having paid her fare, Dara sat down directly behind the driver. She took off the multi-coloured mittens her mother had knitted for her that always caused a stir at the dressmaking school where most of the pupils wore kid or leather gloves. She fingered the coins she had in her pocket. She'd taken them from her sister's coat during the night. Zdenka worked in one of the largest hairdressing salons on Illica and was given generous tips from which once or twice a month Dara collected a nocturnal tax that contributed to improving her life-style. It was also a way of taking revenge on her elder sister, who always agreed with Josip when it came to punishing her for something. Yesterday evening, for example, your aunt hadn't lifted a finger nor said a word to shield her from the rage your grandfather had flown into; instead she had made sure she was sitting comfortably in her bed in order to enjoy all the more the spectacle of the thrashing her little sister was getting.

Jelačić Square — now Republic Square — was simply glittering. The lighted windows in the buildings made you think of candles balancing unsteadily on a Christmas tree. Schoolchildren with satchels strapped to their backs skidded and jostled about around the statue of the Ban as they waited for their tram. The passengers getting off there scattered like ants to the four corners of the square: some disappeared towards the Upper Town, others hurried towards Zrinsky Square or rushed into the shops on Illica, and the last few raced towards the Kaptol, Archbishop Stepinac's realm that

190

he shared with the icon merchants and the city's best restaurants.

The dressmaking school was situated three tram stops further along, on Klajčeva Ulica. Dara walked into the yard and made for her best friend, Lela Bokić, whose father managed a factory just outside Zagreb. Lela often invited your mother to tea at her house. The Bokić family lived on the west side of the city in a flat where all the reception rooms looked out over the Botanical Gardens. The station was close by and you could watch the trains leaving for Riyeka, Vienna or Paris. The two friends often stayed at the window until long after nightfall, drinking cups of hot cocoa and imagining the journeys they would go on when they were older. Lela was dreamy and fanciful by nature and even at this early stage left it to her friend to take care of all the practical side of the adventure — a task your mother was not the least bit daunted by, as I probably don't need to tell you.

Dara was tall for her fourteen years. Her face was open and cheerful, and she had white, solidly set teeth. She wore her hair pulled back, showing off her well rounded, innocent forehead and her mischievous little hazel-brown eyes. She was emotional by nature, and it took little to make her blush or scream or cry. She walked fast and tended to sway her shoulders and swing her schoolbag back and forth. Overall she gave the impression of being lively and impulsive, but also slightly ill-at-ease, although this was perhaps due to her devastating clumsiness. Your mother always dropped *everything*, and at Maksimirska Milena preferred to do without her help, even though the child offered it most enthusiastically, rather than have to keep an eye on her daughter's every gesture without the least hope of saving the situation in time when she did whatever silly things she was bound to do sooner or later.

Most of the pupils at the school came from better-off backgrounds than Dara. They spent their summers in Slovenia, never wore shoes with holes in them and didn't have

191

to share their bedrooms with their brother *and* sister. They were also given a little pocket money, a custom quite unknown in the Sevnica family. During the ten-thirty break, they bought little chocolate-filled pastries. Meanwhile your mother would hide under her smock the bread and dripping that her mother prepared for each morning, and look for a quiet spot where she might eat away from prying eyes. When, as today, she had managed to steal some money from her sister or to scrape some up here and there, mostly by carrying out a few small chores for Josip — anything that didn't call for a deft hand — she would blithely join her schoolfriends, squealing as they did around the concierge and proudly holding out her small coins. But as she actually preferred dripping to chocolate, she would quite happily give her pastry away to any of the girls who were even worse off then herself: a pastry that on other days she'd have suffered agonies at not having the money to treat herself to.

She always sat in the middle of the classroom, and her results were always above the pass-mark in every subject except Cyrillic. She could copy out a hundred times over the letters Ж and Ф (two that she rightly felt were among the hardest to remember), get herself endlessly quizzed by Vladimir who was barely more gifted than her, and spend entire evenings poring over her books, the Cyrillic alphabet just wouldn't go in! I wonder incidentally whether the antagonism that exists between Croats and Serbs isn't largely due to the fact that little Croats are forced to learn an alphabet that's so different from the one they've already had such trouble learning!

Dara went back to Maksimirska for lunch. Classes started again at two. Afternoons were given over to sewing, for which your mother showed a certain talent. Her teacher, Mrs Vukelić, even told her half-jokingly one day that she'd end up a millionairess if she went to work in Paris. It was an insignificant remark but one that would nevertheless work its way firmly into the young girl's mind.

The week came to an end on the Saturday evening after an hour and a half of gymnastics in a small hall nearby to which the pupils walked in double file supervised by their PE teacher. Dara was the best in the class. In fact she trained with such keenness that in April 1941 she was selected for the Balkan Olympic games that were to take place in Belgrade. Unfortunately, the bombing of the city by the Luftwaffe meant that the competition was adjourned *sine die*. That's why, to your mother, the destruction of Yugoslavia's capital city was always synonymous with misfortune, like a roof tile falling quite unfairly on an innocent head.

Dara was always first into the changing room; she'd slip into her gym clothes and leap into the hall like some little imp. That evening she started training before anyone else: she did a few forward and backward rolls and then, with her teacher's permission, while the other pupils were still only just emerging in twos from the changing room, all rather timorously holding each other by the hand, she hung herself from the bars and worked through a few routines before elegantly falling back to the floor. After about ten minutes, the teacher, Renata Janković, put her in charge of the class and went and shut herself up in the storeroom with a good-looking young man in uniform whose gangly silhouette had appeared in the changing-room doorway. She claimed he was her fiancé, but if Dara asked her when they were getting married, she promptly changed the subject. What the girl understood by this was that the soldier was simply Renata's lover. This didn't shock her. After all, wasn't she surreptitiously reading *Nana* herself? Each time she was fascinated by the misty eyes, scarlet cheeks and secret air of delight Renata couldn't help displaying to her pupils when, followed by the soldier, she emerged from the storeroom; he would then give all the girls a friendly wave and move off towards the changing room in his ostrich-like way.

To go home, Lela and Dara got the tram together. 'Tomorrow we're going to have some new neighbours in Mak-

simirska,' said your mother. 'Who?' asked Lela. Dara didn't
know their names but knew they were a mother and son.
She'd passed them on the stairs when they'd come to see the
flat. Lela asked what the son was like. 'Not bad, but too short
for me,' said your mother. 'Perhaps he's not too short *for me*,'
Lela pointed out. Dara asked her if she was on the look-out
for a husband. 'Well, you know, I'm afraid at my age you
have to start thinking about settling down,' this pretty little
red-head said pensively — she was fast coming up to fourteen
and a half. They burst out laughing, and Lela buried her
grinning face in Dara's neck. She got off at the stop on Jelačić
Square. From the pavement she shouted to your mother: 'You
must tell me all about it on Monday!' Dara nodded. She'd
already planned to do just that. And in fact it wasn't so much
the prospect of having new neighbours moving in that
delighted her as the thought of the heated and funny account
of it that she'd be giving her best friend on the Monday
morning.

As in most middle-class Yugoslav families, supper at the
Sevnicas consisted simply and solely of a bowl of hot milky
coffee, into which you dunked pieces of bread that you then
fished out with a spoon. Josip would look for an interesting
programme on the wireless, and if he couldn't find one, he'd
ask his children to sing some Croat folksongs with him, or tell
them stories of things that had happened to him when he was
in the army, in the days when he was one of Emperor Franz-
Joseph's subjects. Afterwards Zdenka read fashion magazines
from Vienna or Belgrade, Vladimir played chess with his
father and Dara did her homework, until the time came for
the electricity to be switched off to save money, leaving the
red glow of the embers in the coal-burning stove as the sole
source of light. In the darkness only Vladimir and Josip
carried on, doggedly, with their game. Zdenka closed her
magazines, Dara her exercise book, and before going to bed,
they would put their arms around each other's shoulders and
hum one or two old songs with Milena.

That evening, just before bedtime, your mother asked Josip if he knew their new neighbours' name. 'Dunak,' he said, without looking up from the long drawn-out checkmate Vladimir had taken nearly an hour to trap him in. Then, furious, he gave the chessboard a kick, picked up his coat and went out. Milena looked at Vlado with gentle reproach. Vlado gave a nervous laugh and with his mother's help picked up all the pieces that had fallen on the floor; he then went into the bedroom where he undressed and got into bed. His two sisters soon joined him. Milena stayed in the kitchen. Josip came back in the middle of the night reeking of alcohol and tobacco. Dara heard him insult his wife, hit her, and then make love to her on the far too noisy bed they'd had for nearly fifteen years. The young girl didn't fall asleep before it was nearly morning, not long after the first tram had gone past.

The Dunaks' removal cart pulled by two horses drew up outside number 38, Maksimirska at the very moment when Milena Sevnica appeared on the front door step. Just as on every Sunday morning, she was on her way to the seven o'clock Mass; afterwards she'd do a bit of shopping at the cathedral market and hurry home to Maksimirska to prepare lunch. She gave a warm welcome to Tereza Dunak and her son Nikola, a pale-faced youth who looked thoroughly put off by everything going on around him. The only things he looked at without too patent a displeasure were the horses, a pair of phlegmatic old animals who bared their yellowing teeth to him the moment he brought his hand too close to their nostrils.

What struck your mother, glancing through the window and taking stock of the furniture the Dunaks owned, was their wireless set: far more impressive than Josip's. She was also touched by Nikola's affectionate attitude towards the horses. She decided this meant he was kind-hearted and told herself she might let him join the little crowd of teenagers she sometimes went skiing or sledging with in Maksimir Park on

195

Sunday afternoons in the winter.

The day was one of those bitterly cold ones that the Medvenica occasionally brings to Zagreb. The sky was quite blue and still, as if frozen on the spot. The trams moved along without a sound, making their contribution to the general silence. When Milena got back from her shopping, the tip of her nose was bright red. Dara spent a number of minutes rubbing her feet for her to warm them up. After lunch, Zdenka decided to go to the tea dance, which meant your mother had to go with her, for Josip would never have allowed one of his daughters to go out alone without the other to act as her chaperone. Dara loved dancing, but that day she'd rather have gone to the cinema with her brother, made friends with Nikola Dunak or slipped away to Maksimir Park for a wild afternoon. She was wavering at first, but then, because her sister insisted, she refused outright, and this led to one of those hysterical arguments that were quite usual between Dara and Zdenka. For peace to be re-established, it was enough for Josip, settled by the wireless with the bottle of slivovitz which he'd bought that morning and started on without bothering to wait for his friends to arrive, to threaten the two monkeys with a good hiding. In the end, they found themselves walking arm in arm along Maksimirska, quite ready, with all the elation of the bright December afternoon, to lay down their lives for each other!

Dara was three or four years younger than most of the girls and boys who danced at Biščović's, and so hers was a slightly special place among the regular clientele. Zdenka, who introduced her offhandedly as her chaperone, was surprised to find her dancing so frequently and even more surprised to find her attracting a steady stream of good-looking young men to their table. My mother could find no logical explanation for this phenomenon, as to her eyes her young sister was nothing more than an overgrown kid and as attractive as a rake. As she swirled about in her partner's arms, she couldn't take her eyes off Dara who, with her elbows on the table, eyes sparkling and jaw moving aggressively, was managing to hold her companions' attention by telling them anything that came into her head or by getting up and imitating the way her father staggered about the passage when he came home from one of his sprees around the city's bars. If one of the boys at the table showed any sign of shyness or kept to himself, she'd drag him forcibly onto the dance floor. She wanted everyone, absolutely everyone, to have fun. She really was very kind-hearted, and maybe that was what people liked about her. The Slavs have a sort of passion for innocence. Hence the frenetic love they show towards children and animals and their mothers. The boys at Biščović's found Dara attractive because they felt quite safe with her, and also because she wasn't frightened of them. She was the dream little sister, the ideal playmate, and these young men, all about to get married or go off and do their military service, could rediscover in her company the forgotten flavour of childhood pleasures.

Josip always asked his daughters to be back at seven-thirty sharp. To be a minute rather than an hour late made no difference to what they could then expect. That was why, when the two sisters felt they might not get back punctually, they took all their time. They danced the last waltzes, got someone to treat them to a last ice cream, made their way back from the dance-hall on foot and wasted a good minute before drawing lots to decide which of the two would ring the door bell. More often than not, it was Vlado who came and opened the door for them. He would look at them with ironic consternation and then make way for them very respectfully, as if he were the page in a very smart restaurant where a sumptuous feast awaited them. Dara would walk proudly ahead of the others until the moment when Josip's heavy hand caught her full in the face so she nearly turned on herself. Without crying out or shedding a tear, she put a furious determination into not rubbing her sore cheek and stood facing our grandfather, looking at him with a glimmer of contempt in her eyes that brought her a second slap which

197

Josip followed up with a request for an affectionate kiss. She obeyed with deliberate indifference. Then Josip would go off in search of Zdenka who had tried to find a hiding place while her little sister faced the first wave of the paternal offensive. Once she'd been chased out into the open, she would start yelling in the hope of attracting the attention of the neighbours below or even of passers-by, a ploy that did nothing to halt Josip's punitive expedition. She too would get a couple of those slaps that could have your head off. Soon after, the whole family would sit down around the table as if nothing had happened. The wireless would be switched on, out came the chess set and, half an hour later, father and daughter would be singing merrily together or trying out a few dance steps in the kitchen to music relayed live from Vienna.

The Dunaks came to supper on the Monday evening. A few slices of smoked ham and some sweet and sour gherkins were added to the ritual coffee. Mrs Dunak related the story of her husband's death; he'd been a building site foreman and had fallen off some scaffolding. Dara asked Nikola if he wasn't too sad at having lost his father. He answered, 'No, not too sad. Just enough.' Your mother was extremely shocked by this response, and maybe this is where one should pinpoint the start of the deterioration in her relations with Nikola — that is, before they'd even begun to exist!

No doubt Dara told you the fabled story of the cat and the little turtledove. She had been feeding two turtledoves, a male and a female who spent the nights in the huge loft at the top of the building. Their noisy lovemaking resulted in the birth of a little male who, one day as he was making his hedge-hopping way across the courtyard, got snapped up by a marauding cat. This took place in mid-December, about a week after the Dunaks had moved into Maksimirska. Your mother had witnessed the scene from the kitchen window and went racing down the stairs. She soon found herself face to face with Nikola who'd just come back from the shops. They hadn't

seen each other since the evening at the Sevnicas. 'Follow me!'
she ordered. Your mother barely gave Nikola a chance to put
down his shopping basket before dragging him out in pursuit
of the cat who, by now, was leaping from one vegetable
garden to the next, clutching its young prey in its mouth. As
she climbed over fences and clambered over any obstacle she
came across, Dara put Nikola in the picture as best she could.
The sight of the young turtledove struggling between the cat's
jaws very nearly had her in tears. Then, all of a sudden,
because it felt tired or bored or because, paradoxically, it was
entirely unaware of having done anything bad, the cat set the
bird down delicately on the snow and sat next to it without
paying the least bit of attention to the two mad Croats
advancing upon him. It was a silver tabby with oyster-like
green eyes, the flattened nose of a boxer and ears that showed
every sign of having come through a good few street brawls.
So confident did it feel that it was just beginning to clean one
of its paws when Nikola grabbed it by the scruff of the neck.
Dara rushed over to the young turtledove and, realising that it
was dead, burst into tears. Then, distracted from her grief by
the furious mewing coming from the cat that Nikola was
holding prisoner, she sat up and slapped the beast incredibly
hard and followed this by pulling out a number of its
whiskers; then, slightly disgusted at what she'd just done, she
told Nikola to release it. He shook his head and refused. He
had a better idea.

Towards the end of her life, Dara regularly came to spend a
few days in Zagreb; she would arrive with ground coffee and
perfume and set off again with a smoked ham weighing six or
seven kilos, *saucissons* the size of truncheons and most
important of all, numerous bottles of slivovitz which she
assured us you were mad keen on; and not a day passed when
she didn't mention the cat you'd given her and that you'd
called Moses because, thanks to her, it had been saved from
the water in your toilet. As she lovingly detailed the adventures of this little creature, there would always come a point

199

when the memory of that cat she'd let Nikola Dunak torture forty-five years earlier would encroach on her story. The thought that her Moses might one day have to undergo the same treatment made her wild with remorse. And yet things hadn't been all that nasty. Dunak had stuck a walnut shell to each of the criminal cat's paws and attached a saucepan to the end of its tail; after this, he had opened the door of the flat and said with a smile, 'Now go and play.' The poor cat probably found some kind soul to help him out of his sorry state within five minutes. But that didn't stop your mother still having deep in her ears half a century later the pitiful sound of those walnut shells tapping on the stairs and the sad and puzzled cacophony of the saucepan. I sometimes wonder whether that nameless cat, whose only mistake had been to behave according to the way nature had made it, was not some sort of secret divinity who, encountering on his way down the stairs the problems we can all too easily imagine, had put a curse on Nikola and your mother, a curse that would strike her at all the decisive moments of her life and in whose grip she would still be desperately struggling until the day she died.

At the time, Dara hadn't felt any resentment against Nikola. She even felt that without his help she would have been unable to give the cat the punishment it deserved. She could appreciate the true worth of the imagination and initiative Nikola had shown on that occasion. That was why the following Sunday she suggested he go with her to Maksimir Park, and there they met up with a dozen or so other boys and girls. Among these was Lela Bokić.

To reach the small pavilion where the 'gang' congregated, you had to weave between the sledges and the people on skis and come under fire from several salvoes of snowballs. The sky was as white as the ground. Your mother introduced Nikola to her friends and got someone to lend her a pair of skis; on these she went down the short slope that she'd just walked up with her neighbour. When she reached the bottom,

200

she nimbly took off her skis and started walking up the hill on which the pavilion stands. Nikola was standing quite still watching the skaters gliding past on the frozen lake; there was a smile on his face, and he didn't really look prepared to join in any of the sporting activity. Lela Bokić asked him what the matter was. He said he was in love with Dara. She promised she would sort it out, and as soon as your mother got back from her expedition, she took her aside and explained the situation. Dara listened attentively while blowing her warm breath through her mittens to revive her freezing cold fingers. She had that pert look that girls have when they've just come off a ski slope, the look of someone at once famished and sated, extraordinarily healthy and also slightly lustful. She repeated to Lela what she had told her on the tram two weeks earlier, which was that she found Dunak too short. 'I can't tell him that!' said Lela. Your mother tied her skis together, slung them over her shoulder and, just before leaving the pavilion, said firmly, 'You can tell him whatever you like, I couldn't care less!' Lela went and joined Nikola, who had been standing ten metres away throughout this conversation, turning his back on the girls ostentatiously. 'As we both fancied you,' she began, 'we had to toss a coin, and I won.' Seeing the boy look rather taken aback, she added, 'But of course, if you don't agree, there's nothing that says you have to. . . .' Nikola thought for a moment, then glanced towards Dara who was climbing to the top of the hill. Rather than any sadness at having gambled away a boyfriend, her back expressed determination. Nikola took Lela into the pavilion. There, leaning against a wall with her eyes closed, she received her first kiss. The two youngsters spent several weeks together, kissing whenever they had an opportunity, but then Lela had to break it off as her family didn't want her to be going around with a non Jew. She was to die in the summer of 1941 in the camp at Jasenovac, as did all her family in fact.

Tereza Dunak had asked her son to get back early as she wanted him to chop enough wood to last the week, so Nikola

201

left Lela and Dara to end the day together. Your mother gave the skis back to the boy who'd lent them to her and took her friend with her for a walk around the park. Night was just falling. The snow was blue. The sky was the same sallow colour as a secret drinker's face. As they walked, Dara said that later on she was going to go and live in Paris. She wouldn't get married. She would become a famous *couturière*, be very rich, surround herself with good-looking men and travel the world.